The Italian Stiletto

Ralph Riffenburgh

PublishAmerica
Baltimore

Hardcover 978-1-4512-9388-3
Softcover 978-1-4489-4759-1
PUBLISHED BY PUBLISHAMERICA, LLLP
www.publishamerica.com
Baltimore

Printed in the United States of America

Chapter 1

She entered the crowded bar at the Hilton Hotel in Pasadena. There were many looks as she walked the length of the room in her short skirt, emphasizing her long legs. Her carefully coiffed jet black hair called attention to an attractive face with wide eyes and a well rounded mouth. She appeared not to notice the looks and finally found a small vacant table near one wall. She sat and ordered a Martini. The small black tote bag she carried fit easily under her chair. The printing on it had become indecipherable from repeated washing.

She glanced casually around the room as she sipped her drink but her eyes didn't fix on anyone. After a few minutes, a large, florid faced man approached the table, carrying two drinks.

"May I offer you another Martini?" he asked.

"Thank you very much." She replied with a smile.

"May I join you?"

"Please do."

"I'm Mike Tilson."

"I'm Rachael Compton."

He sat and sipped his scotch. "I think your eyes are pretty. The grayish color is unusual with the black hair.

"Thank you, sir. Are you attending the chiropractic convention?" she asked.

"Yes, I am. I practice in Modesto."

"Did you go to school here?"

"At the LA College of Chiropractic. I practiced for a time in San Francisco and took a residency in X-ray one day a week at the school there. That is my particular specialty, though I see all sorts of cases." He placed his hand on her knee as he was talking. She put her hand on his and he thought she was going to remove his hand but she just gave it a couple of pats. He slid his hand up and down her thigh, going a little higher each time, as they talked.

"Do you live in Pasadena?"

"Just across the border in Altadena. But I teach in Pasadena."

"What do you teach?"

"High school biology. I also do a little consulting on teaching techniques."

"Does the school mind that?"

"I consult out of my sister's address in Northern California so they never know. But yes, they wouldn't be happy if they knew I used the local schools as bad examples."

His hand slid a little higher and found a tuft of pubic hair, not covered by underwear.

"Surprise," she said. "It saves a lot of trouble when you have to pee."

"Being a doctor, I understand all that. The knowledge of anatomy also helps me do a good job with sex. I might say in all modesty that I'm pretty good at satisfying women."

She looked at him a moment. "It must be wonderful to have all that training."

Then she asked, "Are you staying at this hotel?"

"Yes, I am." He paused, then said, "The noise in here makes it difficult to talk. Why don't we take our drinks to my room?"

"That's a plan." And she pushed back her chair. He jumped to help her and they walked to the elevator. He put his arm around her and she leaned against him in the elevator. A short walk up the hall and he ushered her into his room. They placed their drinks on a small table with two chairs. Before they sat, he pulled her to him and kissed her. He felt her tongue in his mouth and held the kiss a long time. He reached for her blouse buttons. She pushed him away. "Let's finish our drinks. We don't have to be in a big rush."

He sat in one of the chairs and took a big gulp of his drink. "I'm not usually in such a rush but you really have me turned on."

"That's flattering. We'll let it build for a few minutes." She sipped her drink.

"Are you married?" she asked.

4

"I was but not any more. She got so carried away by being a society matron that she forgot about keeping house and taking care of me. We've been split for about three years. And you?"

"Been too busy. I've had some nice friendships though."

She got him talking about his work. "I'm trying to orient my practice toward people that can afford good care, not just the working guy who strains his back. That way people keep coming back and I have a long term relationship. It makes for a more steady income."

"What do you do with the person who doesn't have a back strain?"

"I adjust the spine to give them maximum efficiency and I work with them on nutrition. You can't believe how bad the average American's diet is."

"Does the time spent on nutrition get reimbursed properly?"

"I stock nutritional supplements and make a profit on helping them get the right ones."

"And you find that the normal person does better after adjustment?"

"So many people are a little out of line. Afterwards, their muscles don't work against each other and they don't tire as badly."

"I didn't know you could do those things. I thought just about backs out of line."

"So many people do. We can provide help to even the most normal person."

"That's very interesting."

Rachael sipped the last of her drink, got up and walked around to his chair. She leaned over him and kissed him again. He pulled her to him and held the kiss for some time. "Wow, that was a good one," she said.

Another quicker kiss and then he started unbuttoning her blouse. She didn't have a bra on and he gently cupped her breasts. She turned and unbuttoned his shirt and then took his nipple between her lips. He was breathing heavily as he sat on the bed to take off his shoes.

When he took off his pants, she saw he had bright red-checked boxer shorts. She turned off the room light, leaving only a little light from the bath. "Those are dazzling." she laughed. Then she just dropped her skirt and stepped out of it. "It is so much easier for me."

He laughed and started to pull her to the bed.

"Let me make sure it's ready." She kneeled down in front of him. She looked with distaste at the semi-erect penis arising from its nest of kinky hair. It looked like a huge, sallow white caterpillar—no, a worm—with its pink head. She took it in her hand and it firmed. She leaned forward and took his erect penis in her mouth. He moaned as she caressed it with her tongue. Then she clamped her teeth into it hard. "What—" and then screamed as the pain hit him. He jerked forward, bending with the pain and his chest ran into the stiletto that she had pulled from where it was taped to her thigh. As his chest ran onto it, just below the breastbone, she shoved it forward to the hilt, so that the tip entered the heart muscle. Then she pushed the handle upward, rotating the blade down and cutting a long slit in the heart. She pulled the knife free as he fell to the floor.

Going into the bathroom, she washed the blood from her face and mouth. Then she cleaned the knife. Taking a damp towel, she went out and wiped any fingerprints from the chair she had touched. She emptied her drink in the sink and dropped the glass into her tote bag. After she slipped back into her few clothes, she pulled a maid's outfit out of her bag. She put this on over her clothes and put a scarf around her head.

She paused a moment, mentally checking the things she might have touched. Opening the door with the towel, she found no one in the hall. She walked quickly to the service stairs and slipped through the door. After descending, she found the stairs opened on a small hall which had an external door. She went out here, dropped the towel in a trash bin, and crossed the parking lot to the street. Her car was in the next block and soon she was on the freeway away from the area.

At her motel she sat quietly in front of the muted TV. She re-enacted the scene in her mind. "How do I feel about this? The arrogant prick deserved his punishment. I feel relaxed and relieved. This is what I came for and it seems to be right for me." Then she realized that it was the same feeling she had in college when she was beating up men, though now it was stronger.

She went to bed and slept soundly through the night.

She woke refreshed and feeling better than she had for weeks. Then she remembered the previous evening. She played it over in her mind. She felt cleansed.

She had felt a terrible need and this had satisfied it for the moment. Why had she come back to Pasadena where she grew up to do this? She didn't understand the need but it had taken control of her life.

Then another thought came to her. What had he said? "I like your gray eyes with the dark hair. It makes a striking combination." That meant it was memorable and she didn't want that. It was better that they weren't so identifying.

She fixed a cup of coffee and read the paper that the motel had left at her door. After showering and dressing conservatively, she went to Linden Optometry on Colorado Boulevard. The place was huge and there was little personal attention. It specialized in welfare patients and had many young optometrists, just out of school. She wouldn't have gone to such a place for care but it was just what she needed. No one would remember her.

"Can I help, dearie?"

"I want some colored contact lenses."

"One of the doctors will see you in just a few minutes."

"I only need plain ones, no prescription."

"Well, you need a check to make sure you can wear them."

The young doctor checked her vision and said, "You don't need any glasses."

"I know but I want some colored contacts."

"Why do you want those?"

"My gray eyes don't seem to have much personality. I'd like them a little brighter when I'm out socially."

"OK. Here is a plano prescription. Take it to the contact lens department on the left."

"Thank you."

At the contact lens department, she presented the prescription to the contact lens technician. "I would like a pair of colored contacts."

"Would you wear them all the time?"

"No. Just in the evening, socially."

"It makes a difference in the type you get, whether you wear them three hours or sixteen. What color do you have in mind?"

"Bright blue, I think. How do you think that would look?"

"I think that would be striking. It depends on the personality you want to present. Is your hair natural? I don't mean to be insulting but the hair color makes a difference when one is picking contacts."

"Yes, it is. But I often wear a black wig for social events."

"Let's try on a pair of these." He pulled out a set of contacts and put one in her eye. It felt odd but wasn't painful and didn't seem to change her vision. Then he put in the other one. She looked in the mirror. Her eyes were now a bright blue. She didn't really like the striking color but it was just what she wanted. People would note it, rather than her other features.

"That's going to be fine."

"Let me check them for motion." He looked with a magnifier and then said, "That's a good fit. Let me show you how to take them in and out."

After a few minutes she was able to handle the contacts. The optician asked, "Do you want extra pairs? You only should wear a pair for two weeks."

"No. This is just a temporary change. Thank you very much."

"You're welcome. Here is the bill. Pay at counter C."

At counter C she paid in cash for the exam and the contacts. She took her receipt and walked out.

Chapter 2

Porter Carson savored the last of his cassoulet with the fine wine. Well, the cassoulet didn't have all the nuances of fine French food—really it was a simple bean casserole with chunks of pork and some slices of turkey sausage. It was left over from his cooking day, three days before. And the fine wine was "two buck chuck", the two dollar a bottle specialty of Trader Joe stores chain. Well the meal was a hell of a lot better than the take-out slop that most of the single men in the department washed down with beer. He did take the time once a week to make a casserole of some kind that he could warm up for dinner several times during the week.

He looked at his watch: nine-fifteen. Late for dinner but he had stayed on at the office to finally catch up all his back paper work. Nobody cared when he got home since his wife left two years ago for an investment counselor who was home to take her golfing at three thirty. In a way he missed her but the last couple years of the marriage had been a constant conflict over his hours. He had just made lieutenant in the Pasadena Police Department and been given a lot more responsibility and this led to more irregular hours.

She was constantly nagging him about his time working. "Now that you're a lieutenant you should be able to have your workers take the off hour duties. However, you work even more hours and more erratic times than before. What's the advantage of being promoted?" He was certainly able to do a better job knowing that he wouldn't have to go through this every time he took personal responsibility for an off-hours follow up or a night call.

Now that he didn't have to explain any time he took away from home, at age 42, he was in the process of fulfilling a life long dream. He just needed a few more hours of practice and a final ride with his flight instructor and he could take the test for his private pilot's license. It was hard to work in the time to fly sometimes but he had lots of compensatory time off available for his extra hours and he could go out and fly during working hours if nothing was pending. Maybe he could take a couple hours off tomorrow and practice his landings.

As he shaved the next morning, he studied his face in the mirror. Blue eyes with dark brown hair, a speckle of grey at the temples. Not handsome but a pleasant face, firm and reassuring with just a few wrinkles to show maturity. Yes, he could picture it under an airline captain's cap. He laughed at himself. He was a lieutenant in charge of detectives after eighteen years at the department and wasn't about to start at the bottom in a new profession.

"Shall I call and say I won't be available 'til noon?" he asked himself. "I might as well use a little comp time and nothing much is pending today." He was just pulling on a pair of jeans when the phone rang.

"Carson."

"Lieutenant, there was a murder last night in the Hilton Hotel."

"Who is on it?"

"Ridley and Carnucci, sir."

"What room in the hotel?"

"Four fourteen, sir."

"I'm on my way."

Porter threw the jeans on a chair and took out a dress shirt and a pair of grey slacks. He tucked his gun in his belt, clipping his badge on beside it. A blue sports coat was in the little closet by the entry door. Locking the apartment, he went out to his official car, a Ford sedan retired from patrol and repainted a repulsive shade of dark green.

After starting the engine, he turned on the police radio before pulling out into Villa Street. At Los Robles Avenue, he turned south to the Hilton. He pulled into a loading zone behind a black and white unit and walked over to the main entrance of the hotel. Business people were coming out, starting their day, and no one seemed to know about a problem. When the elevator opened on the fourth floor there was a young, black, uniformed officer standing casually across from the elevator. He looked at Porter as if about to stop him, then his face changed.

"Good morning, sir. It's down the hall to your left."

"Thanks, Tyson," Porter congratulated himself, "I don't know how I came up with that name." He felt it important for the brass to recognize the young officers but he had trouble remembering names. They were all so young now. A lot of people had gone through the department since he started.

A young lady, looking very sharp in her well fitting uniform recognized him immediately. "Good morning, sir." She stepped to the door and opened it for him.

"Thank you, Flores. How are you this morning?" This one he definitely remembered.

"Well, thank you, sir."

Walking into the room, Porter first saw Detective Sergeant Virginia Ridley making notes. A very bright, hard working cop, she had just made sergeant at age 32. She was dressed in a beige sweater and dark brown slacks. Her brown hair was cut short. This way she rarely had to comb it and it never hung over her eyes. A very practical young lady who made no effort to show off her good figure. Her partner, Al Carnucci, was a dapper, slender man of 40. He had been a detective for years and had no interest in rising to the supervisory level, never even taking the exam for sergeant. His sharp featured, well tanned face was close to an opened suitcase, inspecting the contents.

"What have we?" Porter inquired.

"Looks like he offended a hooker," Ridley replied. "There are tooth marks which almost severed his penis."

"Do you know who he is?"

"His driver's license says Henderson Tilson. He lives in Modesto. That's all we know so far."

Porter turned toward where the body slumped, held partly sitting by an overstuffed chair. It was naked except for an opened shirt. A small pool of blood was between his legs. "Not enough blood for him to have bled to death. What killed him?"

"There is a little stab wound with minimal bleeding just below the xiphoid. We'll have to wait on the coroner to see where it goes."

"What have you done so far?"

"The coroner is on the way. We have found the victim's wallet. He is a chiropractor from Modesto. Don't know any more."

"Have you the hotel registration?"

"Not yet, we're just starting."

Porter went to the door. "Flores, go down to the desk and get the hotel registration. Find out who checked him in and I'll talk to her. See if you can find out why he is in Pasadena."

The detectives heard Flores respond excitedly, "Yes, sir." Obviously she was pleased to be participating.

The door opened again and the police lab technician appeared with a heavy case. "What do you want on this one, boss?" Porter didn't like being called 'boss' but ignored it as the tech was a character who went his own way, but did his job well.

"Photos of everything. Close ups of the body. Try for fingerprints around the body. We'll let the coroner's people check the wounds." He turned to Ridley, "You guys touch anything?"

"Of course not," Ridley sounded offended. "Except for opening the wallet with forceps to get the ID."

The tech had finished with his pictures when the coroner's tech and his assistant arrived. They received Ridley's report, took more pictures.

"Think it is possible to get the killers DNA from saliva on the penis?" Carson asked.

"Hard to tell. The bleeding may have diluted it too much. We'll sterile bag the penis and give it a try."

He got out a sterile plastic bag and carefully put it over the penis, taping it in place.

"OK to load him, Lieutenant?"

"Sure." He gave the tech a card. "Have them give me a call when the time for the autopsy is scheduled."

"You got it." They loaded the body on a gurney, covered it with a cotton blanket, and took it out to their van.

Flores appeared while the door was open. She handed Porter a paper. "The original registration. I made a photo copy for their records. A Janice McIntyre checked him in. She's off and will be back to work at four. Here's her address if we need her before four." She handed Porter another piece of paper. "He was here for a chiropractic convention held at the Conference Center. There are about 60 people at the convention."

"Good job, Flores. Hang around and we may have something else for you."

"Mike." He called the technician, "Make me up 10 sets of pictures with good full face and profile. Get the name and address from Al and put it on them"

"OK. I've got a little more time before I'm comfortable that the finger prints have been covered. I suppose you want the pictures yesterday?"

"First thing in the morning will do."

"I'll have them if you don't come to work too early."

"Do your best. But that's not as high a priority as getting everything covered here. Do you have good prints?"

"I took quick prints from the victim and most of what I'm finding are his. Common sources like faucets, door knobs, and the table have been wiped clean. Incidentally, he had a glass from the bar on the table but there had been another one which is missing."

"How do you know his didn't make several marks?"

"There are two different sizes. His was a whiskey glass whereas the other would fit a cocktail glass."

"Good observation. I wonder if she took her glass with her?"

"Seems likely. She must know that glasses are a fine source of prints."

"Thanks. Do what you need and let me know if you find anything." He turned toward the detectives.

"Ridley, tell the vice team to cancel their afternoon schedule and be over here. We are going to have to interview each of the attendees and see if anyone was with him last night or saw him in the hotel. I'll talk to the conference director about how to do it. You might draft Flores to help— she did a good job so far."

"Yes, sir. We'll ask the vice guys if it sounds like any hooker they know."

"Al, if Mike is finished with them, check, itemize, and pack his things. Sign it into evidence."

Porter went over to the conference center, two blocks from the Hilton. The center is connected to the historic Pasadena Civic Auditorium. Through a scenic break in the city mall, Porter could see the Pasadena City Hall and the Sierra Madre mountains beyond.

The conference director, Matt Griswold, was a supercilious middle aged man, flashily dressed and with a sneer for a dumb cop. Porter said, "Did you hear that Dr. Tilton was killed last night?"

"No. How did that happen?"

"We are trying to find out. He was stabbed in his room, probably by a girl he picked up."

"That's terrible. Why don't you protect us from such things when we have a convention in your town?"

"We try, but taking pick-ups to a room makes it hard to control." Porter was annoyed by the man's attitude. He told him, "We need to interview all the attendees and see if anyone saw him last night."

Griswold loftily said, "You can check the hotels in town and try to catch the conference attendees in the evening. We can't interrupt the conference."

"I'm not going to have to get warrants and go to all the hotels. I want to see them this afternoon."

"Well, we might be able to get the hotels and room numbers from the conference registration papers. I would do that for you."

Porter assured him, "We are going to interview them this afternoon."

"That won't be possible. The schedule is too important."

"I can offer you choices: we can schedule the most convenient time for you with several officers doing the interviewing or I can shut off the conference with everyone held under guard while one officer interviews them one at a time."

"You can't do that," Griswold insisted.

"I can and I will. And I'll hold you in a cell until we have finished the interviews."

Griswold finally got the message and they scheduled breaks for the various work groups to meet with the officers in the team. The two vice officers had reported in and Carson kept Flores with the group so there were six officers.

Al Carnucci was talking to a doctor from Santa Barbara. "We have no interest in your activities, Dr. Thomas. We only want to know about Dr. Tilson's activities last night. Did you know him?"

"Casually. We've met before at these conventions. We had dinner together last night. We had talked a little after the meeting and I suggested we go to dinner at the hotel. When we went to the dining room, the hostess started to put us at a small table but we saw five fellows we knew and asked to join them."

"Was there room at the table?"

14

"It was only set for six so they had to add another place. We talked about the future of our profession and had a very pleasant time."

"Who paid the bill?"

"We joked about it but in the end we each put some money on a pile. I think it made a good tip when it was all done."

"What did you do after dinner?"

"I walked out with Mike and asked what he planned."

"Who is Mike?"

"Oh, Dr. Tilson thought Henderson was a ridiculous first name and always used his middle name Michael with friends."

"OK. What did he answer?"

"He asked me if I knew he had been divorced and when I replied positively, he said that it was too public in Modesto to have an affair and he thought he would try to find someone to spend the night with."

"Did he do it?"

"That's the last I saw of him. I wished him luck and went back to my room."

Flores was interviewing a doctor from Needles. "Doctor, we just need help in finding out about Dr. Tilson's activities last night. Do you know him."

"I do. I had dinner with him."

"About what time?"

"Five of us went into the dining room about six thirty. We were seated and about to order when Mike came in with Al Thomas."

"Mike who?"

"Tilson always uses his middle name."

"Thank you for explaining."

"Sure. Anyway, he's a little pushy. They came over and said they would join us, not asking us. The waiter had to set up another place. It was pleasant enough but Tilson did more than his share of talking."

"What did he do after dinner?"

"He and Dr. Thomas walked off and the other five of us went to the bar and had an after dinner drink and talked some more. It was easier without Mike as the others have been friends for a long time. I didn't see him again and don't know where he went."

"Thank you very much, Doctor. You've been very helpful."

"You're welcome. Aren't you a little young to be a detective?"

Flores blushed. "I'm fairly new to the force and I'm just getting started."

"Well, you did a good job. You seem well trained."

"Thank you, sir."

When he went out, Flores rushed over to the lieutenant's corner. "Lieutenant Carson, I found someone who the victim had dinner with."

"Good work. Make careful notes and share it when we all get through. There are still several to interview."

"Yes, sir." Flores realized that this was all routine to him and he wasn't as excited by it as she was, so she went back to her next interviewee.

Porter's cell phone rang, "Carson."

"Sylvia. The coroner's office called. They've done the X-rays and external and Dr. Whiteman will do the autopsy at eight tomorrow morning, if you want to go."

"Thanks. I'll be there."

Five minutes later, Porter's radio said, "L3." Porter was the third lieutenant in the department.

"L-3 at the hotel."

"Call the station, 10-35."

"10-4." 10-35 meant important information, not to be disclosed over the radio or in public. He went out in the hall and called the station.

"Lieutenant, there has been a big fire with a disabled man burned and in the hospital. The fire marshal thinks it's arson and wants a detective to work with him. The address is 1023 North Hill."

"It's a bad time for something like that to come up. I'll send Sergeant Ridley. Thank you."

"Yes, sir. I'll tell the fire marshal that she'll be there."

Porter went over to where Ridley was finishing with one of the conference attendees. "Can I speak to you, sergeant?"

"I think we're all done with your information, doctor. You can go; thank you for being so cooperative."

"Glad to. Hope you get Mike's killer." He walked away.

Ridley turned to Porter. "Yes, sir."

"They just called from the station about a fire with a burned disabled man. The fire marshal thinks it was arson and wants a detective to work with him. It's too bad that these things come up at the same time but I guess it would be best if you went over to 1023 North Hill Street and I supervised the finishing up here."

"OK. It doesn't sound like too nice a case either."

"Do we ever get one that does? Thanks. I'll be at the station later so you can tell me what's going down. If you're late, call me at home. Thanks and good luck."

"I'll talk to you later." She left the hotel.

When they all finished with the attendees of the conference, Porter went to the office and wrote up a report on the findings so far. He went back to the hotel at quarter to four. Janice McIntyre was a middle-forties, considerably overweight, blonde lady. She was pleased to be able to talk to a police lieutenant and talk she did. When Porter finally got her turned off he had established two facts. One: the victim had done nothing unusual at check in. Two: she hadn't seen him again and knew absolutely nothing of any use.

"I appreciate your time, Mrs. McIntyre. You certainly do have full recall."

"Thank you, lieutenant. I try to remember everything of importance." She went off to work, smiling.

Porter met with all the officers before they went off duty.

He asked Flores to report first and she told about the dinner. She was obviously excited to participate in a detectives' crime conference. Then Al reported, "Yeah, I talked to the guy who joined him for dinner. Afterwards the victim told him that he was going to look for a girl and left."

The vice squad officers reported, "We don't have any record on a hooker that does that sort of violent thing. We each talked to one or two of the guys who were at the dinner. No one knows anything after dinner. Do you need us tomorrow?"

"I don't think I have that much to do so you can go back to your regular details. Thanks a lot for helping. Try asking any informants you have if there is anything about the one who did it on the street."

"Glad to, lieutenant. Be happy to work with you anytime. Nice to see a good clean crime, not all the sordid stuff we see regularly."

Ridley came into the station while they were meeting. "Do you have anything on the murder to report?" Carson asked her.

"I had only one response from the attendees. One man thought he saw the victim walking up the hall as he was getting off the elevator. He was with a girl, notable only for a short skirt and very black lustrous hair. She was about half a head shorter than the victim, making her perhaps 5-5. He saw only the back and wasn't even positive it was the victim."

Porter himself contributed, "The bartender was very busy and didn't notice the lady at all and couldn't remember serving the victim. I'll get to the dining room people tomorrow and confirm the dinner story but all of the group tell the same thing so there isn't much doubt. We don't have much, but your group did a necessary job. Al, keep on it tomorrow. I'm going over early to the autopsy."

When everybody was gone except Ridley and Al, he asked, "How about the fire?"

"It's pretty definitely arson. Don't know much more. The fire marshal is a sharp guy and we're trying to put it together."

"I guess you'll have a full time job working that."

"Yes. I have to start interviewing the neighbors. I haven't talked to the victim yet."

They were interrupted by the lab man who stopped in the room on his way home. "I did get some pictures made up." He handed Porter a packet.

"Thanks so much. That will help a lot for me to follow up in the hotel tonight."

"You're welcome, but you do owe me. Good night." He hurried out.

Carson turned back to Ridley. "OK. You follow up on that and I'll continue with the murder." Ridley went out to her car.

Carson said to Al, "We need to talk to everyone on that floor of the hotel and see if anyone saw them. I had the desk give me a list of the rooms on that floor and the tenants of those that are still here who were here last night. I'll work on it tonight and you can follow up tomorrow on the ones I can't find."

Al said, "Some may leave early in the morning. I'll stay a while and work them."

"You've put in a long day already."

"So have you. Actually I doubt if there will be much to find out so it should go rapidly. I'll start on one end of the floor and you can do the other."

"Well, I'm not going to turn you down. But let's not stay too late. I'll start on the low number end."

He went to the first room at the end. No one answered his knock. The next room was vacant according to his list. The third was opened by a man in slacks and an undershirt. "What do you want?"

"I'm Lieutenant Carson of the Pasadena Police. We had an unfortunate incident on this floor and I'd just like to ask a few questions."

"Well this is a real imposition but if it won't take over five minutes, go ahead."

Carson took out the print that the lab man had given him. "Did you see this man and a lady in the hall or on the elevator at any time yesterday or last night?"

He studied the picture a minute. "I think I saw him going down in the elevator at dinner time, but he was alone. I'm sure I didn't see him with a lady."

"That's really all I need. I appreciate your help."

"Good luck on finding him."

"Thank you, sir. Good night."

The next room belonged to one of the conference attendees so they had already talked to him. After another vacancy, there was a room with no one answering the knock. He moved on and found a middle aged couple. After he introduced himself and showed them the picture, the man said, "I think we went up with them on the elevator last night, didn't we dear?"

"I believe so. I didn't notice much about him but did notice the girl."

"She is the one we are interested in. Can you describe her?"

"Well, she was really quite attractive. She had shiny black hair and a round face with a slight turn-up to her nose. The thing I noticed most was how inappropriately I thought she was dressed. The skirt was so short that I don't know how she could sit down. She had no bra and her nipples pushed out in the blouse. And the man had his hand on her rear on the elevator ride."

The man added, "I noticed the skirt and I thought she was a pick-up that he was taking up to the room."

"Would you have time to spend a few minutes with a police artist tomorrow and try to come up with a picture of her?"

"Of course, if you think we can help."

He gave them his card and said, "Would nine o'clock be too soon to contact you?"

"No. Eight thirty might be better as we need to get off by mid morning to get home to Monterey."

"That would be great. I'll get him over first thing. Thank you very much."

Another empty and a salesman who had noticed nothing and he met Al. "Any luck?"

"One couple thought they might have seen their backs in the hall. Didn't notice anything but the shiny black hair on the girl."

"I have one that rode up on the elevator with them and will meet with the police artist tomorrow."

"Very good. That only took us forty minutes. Maybe we should do the other floors while we can."

"If you don't mind the time, I think that's a good idea. On this floor I have two that will be gone by tomorrow, one early and the couple who saw them by midmorning." They went to the desk and got lists of the occupied rooms. "I'll take two if you want to do three."

"Good enough. I'll meet you at the desk."

In another hour, they had talked to everyone who was in at that time. "Any more luck?" Al asked.

"Not a nibble. How about you?"

"Nothing. If you want to leave me the room lists, I can give the ones that weren't in another try in the morning."

"Here you are. I've marked off the ones that I did contact. Thanks for doing this. Have a good night."

"Thanks and the same to you." They tiredly went to their cars. When Porter walked into his apartment, again he thought, "It's nice not to have a constant pressure to get home on time." He found a few left-overs in the refrigerator, had a glass of wine and went to bed. It was lonesome in bed. He thought about the women he knew. He had seen two attractive women today: Flores was cute, with a fine figure but really she was hardly more than a teenager. He thought about trying to kiss her and getting a mouthful of bubble gum. He laughed to himself.

Ridley was younger than he was but she wasn't a child like Flores. She was attractive, partially camouflaged by her business-like working appearance. Well, they both were subordinates and that was a no-no. He hadn't seen an attractive girl out of the department for a long time. Then he thought, "I really haven't seen much of anyone outside the department except arrestees, witnesses, or victims." He went to sleep trying to think of how he would expand his social life.

Chapter 3

Fred Norton had grown up in Pasadena. His father, Paul, had started a family mortuary and had made a successful business of it. His mother, Mary, kept the records for the mortuary and also worked three days a week on the records of a nearby dry cleaning plant. They lived in the residential quarters of the mortuary and Fred had never known another home. He was a bright boy and did well in school. Both his parents were well educated and were active readers and he was challenged more at home than at school. At an early age he told his mother, "Jack hasn't ever seen anyone dead. Isn't that amazing?"

As he advanced in school, the kids occasionally teased him about living in a mortuary. "Fred rhymes with dead."

"So do you sleep in the morgue?" It didn't bother him and so it didn't continue.

Since the mortuary business often had periods with no work, Paul often did the cooking and other household chores. He also had time to take Fred to museums, teach him to shoot, and to help with his Boy Scout troop. Fred had watched both his parents cook and do the preparation. His job had been to clean up the dishes after dinner. When he was seven, he told his mother, "I'll fix dinner tonight."

"Do you know what you plan to have?"

"No, because I don't know what we have to cook."

"I was planning pork chops, boiled potatoes and carrots."

"OK. I'll cook that."

"Let me know if you need help or can't find something." She walked out and left him in the kitchen.

After an hour, he called his parents to dinner. "I thought I had watched everything but there were some things I didn't see. I hope it's OK."

The pork chops were burned on one side and red on the other. The potatoes were cooked almost to mush but hadn't been peeled. The carrots were still firm. Mary said quietly, "I know you have seen me leaving the potato skins on but we usually bake them with the skins and boil without. However, that's mostly habit and we can peel them easily when they are cooked."

They all ate the food and then his father told Fred, "There are fine points that you don't see just watching. If you would like, either your mother or I will be glad to tell you some of these as we do the cooking."

"Not too good, is it?" he asked.

"I've had worse at supposedly good restaurants. I think it was remarkable that you could do it all without asking where anything was. With a little practice you'll be a sharp chef."

Soon Fred was comfortable with cooking when needed and helped with the house.

In high school, Fred decided he would like to learn more about the fine points of cooking and signed up for food preparation in the home ec department. When the class met, he was the only boy. One of the girls said, "What are you doing here. Men can't learn to cook. My father would starve if my mother left for any time."

Fred answered, "If women are all such good cooks, why would he starve with a daughter like you around. Besides who are the great chefs of the expensive restaurants. Aren't they all men?"

After a couple weeks of class, it became apparent that Fred was the best cook of the class. The girls always wanted to be the ones to try his food and evaluate and criticize his work as the food was really very good. Some of them cooked so badly that it was a trial to evaluate their work. One of the boys made a remark about Fred in cooking and one of the girls from the class said, "You just haven't tried what he makes. I'd sure rather date a good cook than a muscle bound football player." That put a new viewpoint on it and the boys became interested in what it was like to take cooking.

Fred also grew up helping his father with the mortuary work. Having worked with bodies, he knew more anatomy than anyone else in his class. "What are women really like down there?" other students would ask. Fred ended up as the class authority on women and on dying. "Do bodies really get so stiff that they break if you force motions?"

"Does anyone seem to get dead and then get buried alive?"

Even the teachers sometimes utilized his experience. "Fred, can you tell us what the rules are about declaring someone dead?"

One evening his father said, "Fred, would you like to inject this in the vein?" The vein was large and he thought it would be easy to hit with the needle. But it wasn't easy. The needle would slide off the vein and the vein would move around. Finally Fred asked, "What am I doing wrong? You do it so easily."

"You've watched my right hand hold the needle and insert it many times but you've not noticed the left. The left is tightening the skin and holding the tissue firm so that the vein stays in place. I'll do it now and watch my left hand."

He was an excellent teacher and soon Fred was very good with veins. Other techniques were learned the same way and gradually Fred learned to watch all the parts of a technique rather than just the most obvious.

Occasionally one of his friends came by and when they were together, would ask, "Could I see what the dead room looks like?"

"Sure." Fred enjoyed sharing his knowledge and if they had a body from somewhere else that no one would know, he might even allow a quick peek at a body. A couple of his dates even wanted to go by and see the mortuary. He was a pleasant, happy boy and had a number of girl friends but none seriously.

When Fred was a junior in high school, his mother seemed to change. She tired more easily and had trouble getting going in the morning. This became worse and Fred and his dad would have breakfast before she arose. "I'm very worried, Fred. This isn't like your mother. She has always been full of energy. I suggested seeing the doctor but she puts it off. I'm going to insist that she go."

"Yes, she is different. I think that's a good idea."

Paul asked her to go to their doctor. "I don't really have anything wrong. I'm just tired."

"You are too tired for your age. I've made an appointment next Tuesday and I want you to go. Please!"

"I suppose I should. But I don't think he'll find anything."

She went to the doctor but he didn't find much definitely wrong. "I'm hoping the blood tests will give us some answers."

"Please let me know what they show."

When the test results were returned, he called Paul Norton first. "Paul, I have bad news. Mary has a rather acute form of leukemia. We can try to chemically put it in remission but the results aren't too favorable in this kind. Do you want me to tell her?"

"I was sure something was wrong. I think you must tell her. She will be sure that something is being held from her. It will be a blow, but she would rather know."

When the doctor called Mary, her first question was, "Does Paul know yet?"

"He does. I called him and he felt you should be told the truth. I talked with an oncologist and have made you an appointment for tomorrow. I think it is well worth trying a course of chemotherapy, though it doesn't always work on this type."

"I'll be there. But if it doesn't work, I don't want to continue to take medicine that isn't going to give me a decent life."

"That's fair. I'll be honest if it isn't working but I do have high hopes."

"Thank you, doctor. Please keep in touch even though I'm seeing the oncologist. I've known you long enough to feel you are a friend."

"Thank you. I feel that way about you and your family."

That night Paul and Mary were sitting together. Mary said, "I thank you for encouraging the doctor to tell me the truth. I'm sorry about all this."

"I'm sorry too, dear, but it isn't your fault. I felt you should know the truth. I would want to."

"What shall we tell Fred?"

"It will be hard for him but I think we should consider him a voting member of the family and tell him the truth too. We don't have to go into the details of the chemo."

"Would you tell him? I don't think I can handle that."

"Of course."

The next day Paul sat down with Fred. "Your mother has a bad form of leukemia. She is going to go on chemotherapy that we hope will lead to a remission but it is possible that it may not work."

"Oh, dad, how sad for all of us."

"Yes. You and I must do as much as we can so she can conserve her strength but try not to be obvious that you are doing more. And talk to her about school and happy things. Many families avoid a member who is severely ill and that only makes it worse."

"I'll do my best."

After a month of chemotherapy, Mary was weaker and was having small bleeding spots in her skin. The doctor called, "Mary, I'm afraid that this chemo isn't doing much."

"I realize that. I'm weakening a lot."

"The oncologist wants to try another type, but I don't think it has much of a record of positive results in this kind of leukemia and it does make you quite miserable."

"I'll refuse that. Can you arrange for hospice to help me?"

"Of course. Do you want to stay at home?"

"Unless I become too much of a burden on Paul and Fred."

Mary failed rapidly and died quietly and peacefully five weeks later.

Fred missed her sorely but his father tried to give him all the love and care of both of them. "Son, I know I can't do many things your mother could but you have learned a lot about keeping house as well as mortuary work. I hope I'm not asking too much of you at your age."

"No, dad. We both miss mom but I'm glad we can work together and keep on living together without having a housekeeper around all the time. I'm glad to do what I can and you are very good to me."

"I'm really not very active outside the business and you have become my best friend, Fred. I hope we can stay that way."

Fred was on the swim team in high school. He really wasn't very outstanding but was called the utility man. He swam whatever event the opposition was weak in and picked up thirds and an occasional second. He did well enough to get his letter in swimming.

When he finished high school, Fred entered the University of California at Irvine. He was home almost every week-end and spent the time with his father, working, hiking in the local mountains, or just sitting around reading and discussing their books.

Fred enjoyed college and did well. He dated some but had not found anyone of particular interest. He did go out for the swim team. After swimming a time it became apparent that he wasn't good enough to make the team in college. The coach approached him, "Fred, you like to be around swimming and are a well organized young man. Would you like to be the team manager? It would put you in charge of seeing that things were ready and planning for the away trips. You would work with both the men and women's teams."

"How much time would it take?"

The coach worked out a schedule that met his needs and Fred took the job. Things ran smoothly with Fred's efficient nature and everyone was happy with his work. Fred found that he could go into the women's swim office to see that the laundry was ready and frequently girls would wander in partly clothed or leave the door open so that he could see into the locker room. He took advantage of this as much as possible without showing that he was looking.

One of the girls came into the office in only a pair of panties, looking for something. "Oh, I didn't know you were here, Fred."

"Very nice." He reached out and touched her breast. She grabbed his hand and pulled it away.

"Damn you. I know you've been looking and I don't care but you touch any of us again I'll report you and you'll lose this job and maybe get kicked out of school."

"I'm sorry." Fred mumbled. From then on, he was very careful not to appear interested when he saw one of the girls.

In his junior year, Fred met Janice in his class on "Peoples of the Pacific". He walked across the campus with her after class and they found it easy to talk with each other. After a few classes and walks, Fred asked "How about studying together tonight in the library?" This was a productive session and soon they studied together twice a week. In another class there were projects and they asked to do one together. Once she came out to Pasadena with Fred to work on the project as they needed room to set up the posters. She enjoyed the trip and came out occasionally. One night they worked late and Fred suggested she could stay in the downstairs apartment. He took her into the school with him the next morning. Fred asked her about going to a movie occasionally but the timing never seemed right. After she had stayed overnight in Pasadena, Fred felt that they should have more social contact and was debating how to approach this.

Arriving home after school one evening, there was a formal envelope addressed to him. He tore it open and read: "You are invited to the marriage of Janice Hampton and Jules Rynerson." He was appalled. How could she do this? She must have been dating all the time that she had been studying with him.

The next day at school Janice came up to him, glowing happily. He started to say something unpleasant but she said, "Did you get the invitation? I so hope you will be there. You are really my best friend."

She seemed so happy and so warm to him, he couldn't say what he had planned. "I think I can. I hope you are very happy." He muttered and went to his seat. That night he lay in bed and thought. It had been a wonderful relationship. Maybe it was better to have that than to have the risks and potential unhappiness with a romantic relationship. He shed a few tears for what might have been and then slept through the night. He found that Jules had been a high school sweetheart and they were together only on week-ends. Janice continued studying with Fred and he was able to adjust himself to enjoying her happiness and be rewarded by the friendship.

One summer vacation his dad made arrangements for another mortuary to cover for him and the two of them spent two weeks exploring England. Fred was fascinated by all the history in the country. They visited Cambridge and he loved the picturesque old colleges. They visited castles and Fred enjoyed the ruins more than the better preserved ones that had been modernized. He was very intrigued by Stonehenge and by the prehistoric white horses carved into hills.

They visited Hever Castle where Anne Boleyn had lived. Paul had read widely in history and told Fred the story of Henry the eighth and his six wives. They looked at the furnishings of the comfortable little castle and wondered what Anne's life had been like. "I enjoy this one, dad. One can imagine living in it."

"That's one of the joys of travel. You see how other people live now or how they lived in the past. So many Americans think that our way of life is the best and only but there are many advantages in some other life styles. In this one, the advantages were only for the elite. The workers who supported them had a very poor life."

Fred had taken a number of history courses and now he started taking anthropology with an interest in how prehistoric people had lived.

The next summer they took a trip to France. Fred was excited by Paris and particularly liked the Musee de l'Homme, the anthroplogical museum. His father had planned to rent a car when they left Paris and they went to the Loire River and visited several chateaux. They were able to stay in a castle hotel by the river. Fred said, "Dad, it's wonderful to actually stay in one of these. I can picture how they must have lived, even though I know they have added electricity and changed the bathrooms."

"It's great. We don't have anything this old in the US."

"I'd be willing to spend the rest of our time along this river."

"No. I have us scheduled to go down to the Dordogne River. There one can see caves with paintings of primitive men. I think you'll like that area."

And Fred did. "Gee, Dad, I'm glad you didn't let me talk you into staying on the Loire the whole time. I've never seen anything as exciting as the chamber of the bulls in the reproduction of Lascaux Cave."

"And in Font de Gaume, we saw the actual paintings as the Cro-Magnon men did them. Also, this is wine country and we need to stop and taste at some of the vineyards."

"I'd love to come back here to work or to take more schooling."

"Maybe you can. We'll have to see what you want with your life."

Before Fred started his last quarter of college, he sat down with his father. "Dad, I would like to go to graduate school in anthropology."

"I am in favor of more education. I'll make you a deal. If you take a semester off, go to mortuary school and pass the state boards, I'll then finance you in graduate school as long as you want to go."

"Would I then work here while in school?"

"Just as you do now, except I could take off occasionally as I wouldn't have to supervise you. You are a big help now and you could handle it but the law doesn't allow you to unless you are state approved. I would hope we could continue working together as we do. Business is good and I'd like an occasional trip or time off but I plan to continue doing most of the work."

"It sounds fair to me. I do enjoy working with you, though I'm not sure I want to do it as my life's work." They shook hands on the agreement.

After passing the mortuary boards, Fred started graduate school at the University of Southern California. This was a big city school without a great deal of student housing and was only twenty minutes from Pasadena by freeway (except at rush hour) so Fred lived at the mortuary and commuted to school. This worked well as Fred was able to help his father when he was unusually busy and could cover in evenings, allowing his father to be more active in a couple of the local organizations. They continued to enjoy working together and became even closer friends. Anthropology was fascinating to Fred and he enjoyed telling his father what he had learned. Paul was interested in almost everything and was learning a lot of anthropology. "Fred, did your lecture today tell you whether the Neanderthal and Cro-Magnon people ever met?"

"Most specialists think they didn't overlap but they aren't sure. It's possible that the modern Cro-Magnon men pushed the Neanderthals to extinction."

In graduate school, Fred had even more flexibility in hours. Much of his time was spent in reading and he was able to do most of this at home. He could thus be available a lot of the time and yet not interfere with his studies.

During his second year in graduate school, Fred noticed that his dad was having increasing trouble with delicate details like threading needles into veins. He made an increasing effort to be around and help with these. "Have you seen a doctor in recent times, Dad?"

"Not for a while. I guess it would be a good idea."

"Mom kept putting it off. I don't think you should do that. See him as soon as you can."

A month later Fred came home and found his father sitting in the living room, staring into space. "The doctor says I have Lou Gehrig's disease and probably won't be able to work at all within a year."

Fred just hugged his dad silently. What else was there to say? Increasingly, Fred was doing the majority of the work. He lightened his load at school progressively and spent more time with his father. A few months later, his father could hardly move around and Fred hired a practical nurse to care for him during the day. He spent most of his evenings with his dad and watched with agony as he became less and less able to do anything.

His dad was still mentally alert so Fred read to him or they discussed books, travel or current situations in the country. Fred was able to keep up the work of the mortuary without problems. Finally his father was confined to bed all the time and could hardly move at all.

One night Fred woke suddenly, feeling that something was wrong. He went into his dad's bedroom. There was no sound of breathing. He sat by the bed until the sun came up. Then he called his father's doctor. "Dad stopped breathing about four AM. Do you need to see him?"

"Oh, I'm sorry, Fred. No. I'll sign the certificate. We know what was wrong. If I can help in any way, let me know."

"Thanks, doctor. I know the procedures pretty well by now."

"Will you keep the mortuary?"

"I haven't really faced that issue yet. I'm not sure what I'm going to do. I will let you know."

"Good luck either way. I hope you stay around."

"Thanks for all your help.

His next call was to Valentine Mortuary, a friendly competitor. Its owner was a Fred too. "Fred, this is Fred Norton. Dad died during the night. Would you handle the arrangements for me? He wanted to be cremated."

"Gee, I'm sorry, Fred. I didn't realize he was that bad. He was a fine man and a pleasure to work with. I'll be glad to take care of everything."

"Thank you very much. Some time I'd like to talk to you about whether to keep the mortuary but I'm not ready now."

"I'll be here anytime you want. I hope you do keep it."

Fred kept the business going but for a long time didn't decide whether to stay permanently. He kept thinking he would go back to graduate school but time passed and he just continued in the mortuary. People knew the Norton name and he was making a good living and finally drifted into considering himself permanent. He was able to keep up with the business but found the paper work unrewarding. There wasn't really enough for a full time worker but he could use some help. Disgusted with a pile of paper work, one day he called the city college and asked if they had a good student who would work a couple hours a day filling out forms, sending bills and keeping the books.

Chapter 4

Louise Hall was a bright girl but she had a sardonic sense of humor that could be very demeaning to others. Her father had died when she was in the seventh grade and her mother had a job in a bank that kept them in a small apartment in Alhambra. Her mother was consistently tired and wasn't able to give much emotional support to Louise.

There was another daughter who was eleven years older than Louise. She had married early, against her parents' wishes and had become estranged from the family. She had moved to upstate New York and was raising two sons in a small town there. Louise could hardly remember her but Helen did send Louise a note and a small check on each birthday. She didn't write their mother except a letter of sympathy when her father died. Louise was careful to write thank you notes and tell her a little about activities in Alhambra.

Louise dated occasionally in high school but her brains and sarcasm put boys off so that few came back to try again. Her best friend, Rose, admonished her, "You have to act dumb and grateful around boys. They don't like it if you can outthink them." Louise didn't pay much attention.

In history class, they had a contest to recognize dates. 1619—"The first legislature in Virginia." Louise said. 1861—"Fort Sumter." Gradually the others made mistakes and were dropped until only Louise was left. The teacher went on until finally: 1309. Louise didn't know. "Removal of the papacy to Avignon," the teacher said.

"You were awesome," Rose told her. "How do you remember all that?"

"I don't know. I just think of the number and it comes to me."

As they walked to the next class, Tom O'Reilly said in a stage whisper, "Smart ass."

One cool evening she went to the movies with Jack Carr. He was a big man on campus as well as a big man physically. He was second string fullback in football and felt that he was pretty special. He held her hand during the movie and patted her bottom as they walked out and back to his old car. The car started then died. He tried again to get it started but it wouldn't. "I didn't plan this," he said.

"I know that. If you had you wouldn't have done it on a busy street. If you push the darn choke in when it starts turning over, it'll run," she said with her usual sarcasm.

He looked at the choke in disgust and started the car. He had planned to park and try to neck with her but after her put down, he dropped her off without even trying to kiss her. He never asked her out again.

Louise had done well in high school but had not been at the top. She didn't even try to get a scholarship for college but when she finished high school, she started Pasadena City College, the local junior college. Her demeanor was about the same until near the end of the freshman year she met Bill Stout. She fell for him like a ton of bricks.

Bill was a year ahead of her in school. He was a small man with a rather pretty face and a dark complexion. He had dark brown hair which he wore carefully cut long. He had a self satisfied personality but could be charming and was to Louise.

She felt he was perfect and did everything his way. Her sarcasm was put away. They were very close for several months and were together most evenings and every week-end. Her mother said, "I think you are spending too much time with Bill. Your grades have dropped this semester."

"I'll try to study more. I just can't think of much else but Bill. I like him so much."

"If you want to finish college, you're going to have to get a scholarship. Your grades will make the difference in getting it."

Louise tried harder to concentrate on school but she was completely dedicated to Bill. One week end they drove up to Mount Wilson. They looked at the TV towers as Mt. Wilson was the source of most TV for the San Gabriel valley. They viewed the valley from the mountain. "It's lovely. One can see all the places we know from here," Louise said.

"A little hazy with the smog. It would be wonderful without that. Let's go to the park and have lunch."

Louise had packed a picnic and they went to an out of the way corner. Bill took a blanket from the car. After lunch, he kissed Louise and then lay over her. They hugged and he started undressing her. Finally they were lying nude together. Louise thought how much she loved him. When he started entering her she didn't protest but held him close. It hurt a little but was also exciting and she felt closer to him than ever before.

"That was good," Bill said after a few minutes. "Am I as good as others?"

"Bill, it was my first time. I love you."

After that, they didn't need movies or other excuses to be together. They had sex in the car, in parks, and even in the school yard after a school dance.

Louise had been trying to avoid sex during her most fertile period since Bill had stopped using condoms. She thought she should have birth control pills but didn't know how to go about getting them. One month her period didn't come and she began to worry. The next month there was no period and she began to feel nauseated when she got up in the morning.

They were sitting in his car one evening after a movie. "I'm pregnant," she said.

"Are you sure?"

"Yes. I'm two months off on my period and I feel nausea in the mornings."

"You're sure it's mine?"

She was deeply hurt by this. "Of course, I've never been with anyone else."

"How could you be so stupid? I don't want to be saddled with a brat."

He drove to her house, let her out, said "Good night," and drove off. He never spoke to her again.

When Louise finally told her mother, she was very upset. "I told you—" she bit off the words. She realized that recriminations would do nothing but drive Louise away. "I love you. It is going to change a lot of things but we'll work it out. I do love you and I'm sure I'll love the baby."

"I'm so sorry, mother. I thought I loved him and he turned out to be a rat. I guess I'll have to be out of school for a time."

"I think it would be better. I've read about programs of home study. Maybe you can make up the courses while you are home."

Louise took a semester off from school and went to classes for mothers at the local YWCA. She had an unpleasant pregnancy. "Mother, every time I feel bad, I think of what a fool I was with Bill. When the baby moves, it reminds me of him."

"Try not to think about him. Think of the baby. It will be all yours. Do you think it will be a boy or a girl?

"Some days I'm sure it's a boy, then it tells me the next day it's a girl. I just don't have any idea."

She had prenatal care at the Pasadena Dispensary, a low income offering of the Huntington Hospital. She was delivered at Women's Hospital, a small charity obstetrical unit across the street from the Huntington, manned by the interns and obstetrical resident from Huntington.

After the baby arrived, they named her Jane. Stout never asked her how she was or if she had the baby. He never offered to help but was busy chasing another girl at school. Louise went back to school, taking a couple evening classes when her mother could watch Jane. Louise now had a different group of friends. She had an occasional date, but no one came back after they heard about Jane.

One evening one of her teachers stopped her after class. "We've had a request for a part time office worker. The timing is flexible. I don't know if you are interested in working but you are efficient and good with numbers. I thought you would be good at this type of office work. Are you interested and do you think you could arrange a couple hours a day?"

"Thank you. I'll talk to mother and see if we can work something out."

"Let me know in the next couple days. I think it would fit well, if you need some work."

Louise broached the idea to her mother, who responded, "It would help with the expenses. I can be home by four. I don't know whether that would be too late. Maybe we could get Mrs. Henderson next door to watch Jane for an hour or so. Why don't you interview and see what the needs of the employer are?"

Louise interviewed with Fred Norton. He was very flexible and just wanted eight or ten hours a week to do the records and bills at the mortuary. Louise dropped one of her classes and was able to work out a schedule with Fred. He liked her sense of humor and found her a pleasure to work with. When he heard about Jane, we wanted to meet her and went by the apartment. Louise's mother loved Fred and he enjoyed her but he was entranced by Jane. Sometimes he would stop by the apartment just to play with Jane.

"It's wonderful how much Mr. Norton likes Jane." Louise's mother told her. "I find him very interesting too. He knows all sorts of things but doesn't act superior about his knowledge."

"Yes, he's very nice at work. He explains well what he wants and then lets me do it."

Louise really wasn't very fond of Jane. Every time she saw her, it reminded her of her hurtful experience with Stout and pointed out that she would probably never finish college. She enjoyed being at the mortuary and Fred was very good about her schedule.

One morning, Louise's mother said to her, "I don't feel well. My right arm doesn't seem to move very well." Louise rushed her to the hospital. She stayed quite some time in the emergency room and finally the doctor came and said, "It seems clear that you have had a small stroke. Your blood pressure is down now and I think you are out of immediate danger."

"Will I be able to return to work?"

"Physically I don't think you will be much handicapped. However, the stress of work is probably what sent your pressure so high. I think you should retire."

"I don't know how we will live."

"See what you can work out. I think it is either find a way to do this, or you may well not live after the next stroke."

She told Louise, "The doctor says I must retire if I want to live. My retirement pay will help but it certainly won't support three of us. I don't know what we are going to do."

"I'll have to get full time work," Louise said. "I'll probably have to leave the mortuary as I don't think Mr. Norton needs full time help."

She went to Fred and told him, "You know mother has had a stroke and isn't going to be able to go back to work. I'm going to have to find full time work. I hate to leave the job."

Fred thought a minute and said, "This isn't the way I had planned to present it, but will you marry me? The mortuary has a room and bath on the first floor for the on call person. We have never used it and your mother could live there."

Louise was amazed. But she did like Fred. She responded, "Are you sure you want me and aren't just trying to have Jane?"

Fred laughed, "Both. I'll love having her here. Your mother can help with her and you can finish up school."

"This is such a surprise. Let me think about it for a day or so."

"Of course. I hadn't planned to propose for a while yet, but the situation seemed to force the decision."

Louise went to her mother and told her of the offer. "Grab it. Fred is a wonderful, kind man and he loves Jane already. You'll never have another chance like this."

A day later Louise accepted and they were married quietly at a private chapel a few weeks later. "I'm so happy for you," her mother said, "I just hope we can all get along."

The three generations moved into the mortuary and it worked well. Louise's mother was able to do a lot of the care of Jane and freed Louise to go back to school. She finished Pasadena City College and they were planning to have her go to the Cal State University, Los Angeles the next fall. Shortly before school was to start, she told Fred, "I'm rethinking going to school."

"Why? I thought you were looking forward to it," he asked in surprise.

She smiled. "I think it will be a little too demanding as the baby grows."

"You're pregnant? That's terrific." Fred was enthusiastic. "It'll be wonderful to have another child. And it will be ours together."

This was a happy pregnancy for Louise and she was looking forward to having a baby she really wanted. One morning her mother didn't come to breakfast and Louise went down to her room. Her mother was lying quietly, not breathing. "Fred," Louise screamed, "Come down here." Her mother had had another stroke during the night and was dead. Louise was very upset and the night of the funeral she went into labor, after only six months. Fred took her to the hospital. "It'll be OK, honey. They can keep premature babies living now."

Louise delivered a dead male fetus and had severe complications. It was necessary to remove her uterus to stop the bleeding. In a week she had lost her mother, her much wanted baby, and the possibility of having another. She was extremely depressed as well as having considerable pain.

Living in his place of work, Fred was able to do much of her care and to take care of Jane. He hired a lady to come and help several hours a day. "Louise, you only have to do what you feel like. I want you to get stronger and back to your old self. I miss your happy company."

"What do I have to live for. I've lost our baby and can't have another."

"You have Jane and you have me. Don't think like that."

Louise kept complaining of abdominal pain to get more pain killers. The drugs seemed to make life a little better, though she felt foggy when she took them. She really wasn't having much physical pain but severe emotional distress.

Finally the doctor told her, "You can't have any more opiates. You're becoming addicted. You have to face the reality and stop taking refuge in drugs."

Her support taken away, Louise started drinking increasingly. Her caustic streak came back, but without much humor. She could hardly stand being around Jane. She was sharp tempered and nasty before she had a drink and afterwards she just didn't give a damn. Fred tried to get her to seek help, "Please, Louise, won't you go to AA or to the counselor that Dr. Browne recommended?"

"You think I'm just a drunk."

"No, dear. You are drinking a little more than you should. But that's due to the depression. I think they could help you out of it."

"It's just reality. The baby is gone. What do I have to live for?"

"Please, think of Jane."

"Every time I think of her I think of that bastard, Bill Stout. I don't even like seeing her around."

Fred was unable to get her to do anything and finally gave up.

Jane, now three, couldn't understand losing her grandmother who had done most of her care and also having her mother withdraw from her. Fred became her only support.

Fred wasn't going to divorce Louise but they really didn't have much social or emotional contact anymore. He couldn't get her to go for counseling and ended up just living along with her and putting most of his emotional investment in Jane.

Chapter 5

Porter was up at six, wanting to make sure that he didn't miss the timing of the autopsy due to LA traffic. The coroner's office is on the campus of LA County Hospital and he took the back way down Huntington Drive, rather than fight the freeway. He pulled into the last visitor parking space. "There's never enough parking in this place," he said to himself. He walked into the office where a large black lady was seated at a desk.

"Can I help you?" she asked.

"Lieutenant Carson. I'm to meet Dr. Whiteman."

"I'll have a guard in a few minutes to take you down."

"I know the way. Just buzz the door."

She thought a minute and then decided it was easier to comply. The door latch buzzed and Porter went in. He walked down a long hall and he was in the autopsy room when a man entered. "What are you doing here?"

"I'm Lieutenant Carson. I'm on the case Dr. Whiteman is doing first."

"OK. I'm going to get the body ready. You can wait outside if that bothers you."

"I'm fine." He found a small metal chair in the corner and sat down. The attendant got out the instruments and then moved the body into the room and onto the operating table.

Dr. Whiteman walked in. The doctor was a round faced, middle aged man who pleasantly introduced himself. He then said, "The X-rays were negative. The bite almost severed the penis and the marks have been photographed in detail. We are going to try to get a DNA on the sputum but it may not work with the blood washing over it."

He stepped to the body and uncovered it. "I'm going to make the incision to one side of center so as not to go through the wound and distort it."

He quickly and expertly opened the body. He dissected along the stab wound, having the tech make photos at each stage. Finally he got to the underlying heart. "The stab wound entered the right ventricle but she must have then pushed up on the handle, using the xiphoid as a fulcrum. There is a long heart wound, ripping open both ventricles. The immediate hemorrhage was so great it couldn't get out of the hole in the pericardium and formed a compressive hemorrhage in the sac. She either knows some anatomy or was very lucky in her stab motion."

Dr. Whiteman slid the heart out of the chest. "See," he pointed out, "This is the pericardium and it should fit close to the heart. Here it has a half inch layer of blood separating it from the heart itself."

When he opened the stomach, the doctor reported, "He had had dinner and by the look of it, about three hours before death. Probably a couple drinks later but I can't be sure."

Dr. Whiteman opened the partially severed penis. "I wondered if she had used the knife on this but it is apparently all from a bite. From the shape of the bite, it must have been quite firm at the time of the bite. That isn't a surprise, is it?"

"I'm afraid that is what we expected from the situation," Porter answered.

The remainder of the autopsy revealed no further information. Dr. Whiteman summarized; "The perpetrator was right handed. We assume female, but have no proof of this. She probably knows some anatomy. The knife is unusual—a very narrow, stiletto type. That's about it, not much help for you. I will do some microscopic exams but I don't think they are likely to add anything in this type case. If they do, I'll certainly make it available to you."

Porter thanked him and drove back to Pasadena. A lab report was on his desk. "We were asked to get DNA from the hairs found at the scene. They are from an expensive, well made wig and do not relate to the wearer."

Ridley met the fire marshal at the house at eight. Tim Eldridge was a big man: six foot, three. He seemed to move slowly but was methodical and efficient and the impression of slowness was deceptive. "Good morning, Sergeant," he said.

"Good morning, sir," Ridley answered. "Where do we start?"

"I'm going to examine the area of the fire now that it's cooled off. You don't have to do that with me, unless you want to see it."

"I think I should. I'm sure I can benefit from your experience and I should know as much background as I can."

"Fine. I have done a few of these. I've been in fire for almost forty years. I'm due to retire next year."

"I'm sure they will miss you."

"A couple of the younger guys are salivating for my job. They are tired of riding the engines at night. Let's go in. Be careful that your clothes don't touch anything in the burned area. It's very hard to get the smell out."

As they walked in, Ridley almost choked on the smell of burned wood and wire insulation. Tim noted her sudden holding of breath. "Fire smells are pretty acrid and hard to take at first. One gets used to it." He led the way for them.

"This is the utility room where the electric board was. You can see that the electrical equipment is all burned. It had a hot fire on the surface rather than from inside, showing that inflammable material, almost surely gasoline was poured on it. If the fire had gone on a few more minutes, no one could have determined this."

"So you would have written it off as an electrically caused fire?"

"Most probably. Now look along here. See the areas that are more deeply burned. They are irregular and not related to the material here on the floor. These areas are where he sloshed gasoline as he walked into the other room."

They walked along, following the areas of heavy burn. "Here next to the victim's room is an area of intense fire. This was heavily doused with gasoline and should have burned into the room very quickly. Except for the quick work of one of our off duty firemen, the victim would have been rapidly overcome by smoke and then burned to death."

"So you think this attack was aimed at the victim rather than at the building?"

"Almost surely. If they are torching a building, say for insurance purposes, the fire will be set to attack the main areas where it can spread to the rest of the building and center on highly inflammable materials. This was aimed in a particular direction with the most heat next to the victim. Obviously, he couldn't pour gasoline on a living, awake victim without raising an alarm so he centered on a hot fire involving the door and wall of the victim's room which would rapidly enter the room."

"So where do you go from here?"

"I'll continue to study the materials here and see if I can find out anything more but I suspect we know what the site has to offer. I have contributed where the fire was set and how and probably the purpose of setting it. Now it will be your job to find out about the victim and why someone wants him dead."

"Thanks for telling me all this. I guess the next thing is to see if the victim is able to talk to me. Then I'll start studying his finances, family connections, possible gambling or drug debts. Unless he can tell us something, motive is most likely to lead to the arsonist."

"Sounds like a good course. Will you keep me informed of what you find?"

"Of course. And you do the same for me. Thanks a lot."

"You're welcome and good luck."

Ridley walked thoughtfully out to her car.

Carson paged Sgt. Ridley. When she answered, he asked, "How's the fire going?"

"Not much yet. It was set in the room with the electric board and would have gone down as an electrical fire except that an off duty fireman happened to see smoke. He called the fire department and went in himself and rescued the disabled occupant. He was early enough so all the gasoline used to start it hadn't burned off yet."

"You keep working on that."

"I will. What have you found out on the murder?"

"Lab says the hair is from a wig. It's what people notice about her, taking attention away from the face."

"So much for our only identifying feature. Thanks. Anything from the autopsy?"

"She ripped the heart open. Dr. Whiteman says she was either very lucky or she knew some anatomy. He says the murder occurred about three hours after dinner. I'm going to work the hotel dining room. We'll keep at it."

Porter stopped by the lab to pick up more pictures of the victim and then drove over to the hotel. He parked in a 15 minute zone and put a police ID card on the dash. He stopped and said to the doorman, "I'm Lieutenant Carson from homicide. You've heard about the murder last night I'm sure. Here's a picture of the victim. Do you remember seeing him at all yesterday?"

"I think that he went out with a couple other fellows from the conference at lunch time but I didn't see him after that."

"What time do you go off duty?"

"Five o'clock. The evening man comes in about 4:30 if you want to catch him. He's a big Irishman with a reddish complexion. He is outgoing and often talks to people going in or out so he might have noticed him."

"Thanks a lot. I'll either come back then or have another detective talk to him. Alert him to what we want and he can think about it 'til we get there."

"Sure. Glad to help."

Porter went on in and up the corridor to the dining room. He found the manager. "I'm Lieutenant Carson from Pasadena Police."

"I'm Gloria Thorpe, the dining room manager. How can I help you?"

"Our murder victim had dinner here last night and I'm interested in finding the details. This is his picture. Maybe you can also tell me about the work schedules—who would have been serving dinner and welcoming the guests."

"I and two of the waiters come in at eleven thirty and stay through dinner. There are also two of the breakfast waiters that serve lunch and then leave. We have several part-timers who only work dinner. I don't remember seeing him but we were busy and there were several groups from the conference where I only talked to one individual so I can't say he wasn't here."

She stopped a passing waiter. "Henry, this is police lieutenant Carson. He wants to know if this man ate here last night." She showed him the picture Carson had given here.

"I'm sure I didn't wait on him. That doesn't mean he couldn't have been in the other areas of the dining room." He rushed off to a table where the customer was waving to him.

"One more possibility. If he doesn't know, the part time waiters don't come in until four." She looked and finally beckoned a waiter from across the room.

"Carlos, this police officer wants to know if this man was served dinner here last night." Again she held up the picture.

"Yes, he was at table fourteen. There were five at the table and this man and one other came in a couple minutes later and wanted to sit with them. It is a six table so we had to set up an extra place."

"Any women in the group?"

"No. All men and all had conference badges. I remember they had some good-natured joking about the bill. I don't know how they decided but there were a number of different value bills so I assume everybody chipped in. They did leave a good tip."

"Anything else you noticed."

"I don't think so. They seemed to be talking about how they were going to make more money out of what they were learning and they all walked out together."

"Thank you very much."

"Do you need to know what he ate?"

"No. The autopsy surgeon told me that."

"OK. I'm sure the food was more pleasant when I saw it." He laughed at his joke and went back to work.

"Thank you, Ms. Thorpe. That confirms what his table mates said and helps us set the time when he met the killer."

"You're welcome. So you could spend hours just finding out that he didn't meet his killer until after dinner?"

"That's what most detective work is. The solution doesn't come to you like it does in TV programs."

"Let me know if we can help in any way."

"Thanks."

Next he went to housekeeping. A young Hispanic lady was working at a counter, piling linen into individual room piles. "I'm from Pasadena Police. Could you tell me who takes care of Room four fourteen?"

"Yes, sir. That would be Helena Rodriguez. You're in luck. She's one of the few in housekeeping who speak some English. Should I page her?"

"Would you, please?"

She picked up a walkie-talkie. "Helena to the office. Helena to the office."

Then to Porter, "She should be here in a couple minutes."

"Thanks. Your English is certainly good."

"Should be. I'm third generation American. My parents spoke both languages so I know Spanish too. That's why I have this job. The supervisor has to communicate well in both languages. Actually I have a degree in hotel management from Cal Poly, Pomona. This is my start in the business."

44

"Really. I didn't know there was such a degree."

"It's almost required now to get anywhere in the business. Oh, here's Helena."

"Helena, this police officer is checking on the death in the hotel."

She looked at Porter expectantly. He asked, "You take care of room four fourteen?"

"Yes, sir. It was really a shock to me to see the body there."

"Was everything normal the day before?"

"Yes. He left everything neat and I did the usual cleaning."

"Then yesterday you went in as usual?"

"Well, I opened the door with my master key and started in but then I saw the body. I screamed and came down here where Ms. Hernandez called the police."

"You didn't see anything else?"

"No, sir. As soon as I saw the blood I shut the door and ran."

"Thank you for your help."

"You are welcome, sir." She looked expectantly at Ms. Hernandez who nodded and said, "Thank you. You can go back to work."

When she left, Ms. Hernandez asked, "Anything else we can help with?"

"I don't think so. Thank you very much for your cooperation."

Porter drove slowly back to the police station, trying to plan the next move. He went into his office and turned on the computer. He pulled up the victim on the state DMV records. They had previously looked at his driver's license but now he accessed his driving record. A couple of speeding tickets, two years apart, were his only black marks. Then he went to the court records. All he could find was one malpractice suit in which the doctor had successfully defended his treatment and won the case. This was pretty normal for any type of medical practitioner in California. Then in another data base he found a divorce from three years previously.

No help in a motive here. It certainly wasn't robbery. A fifty dollar bill and some smaller ones were still in his wallet. It certainly seemed as though he had made a casual pick-up. Why would she want to kill him? He wouldn't pick up a former patient who hadn't been pleased with her care. A religious or ethical punishment for him? He had read about such motivations in serial killers.

Suddenly he realized that if this was the motivation there would probably be other killings. "Oh, shit," he said, "All I need is a serial killer active in Pasadena."

Chapter 6

Jane Norton was eight when her step-father told her that he wasn't her real father. He never knew her father. It didn't really affect her relation with Fred Norton. He had been her father since age one and the only person who gave her love and respect. She did try to ask her mother about her real father but got the usual annoyed, curt reply, "None of your business. Forget it."

Jane had realized that her mother was unreasonable, short, and unpleasant when she was sober and uninterested and non-responsive when drinking, which was much of the time. She knew that Fred Norton owned and operated the small mortuary in Pasadena where they lived. Since Jane was a toddler, he had taken her to the embalming rooms, telling her stories while he worked. She had learned to bring him things he needed and generally help with the work. She was completely unconscious of any fear or concern around dead bodies.

Fred had discussed books he had read and many of his interests in history, anthropology, medicine, and other fields. Sometimes Jane seemed to know too much at school. In the third grade, one of the children sneezed and others said, "Bless you."

"Does anyone know why we say 'bless you'?" the teacher inquired.

Jane raised her hand. "The council of Nicea in the sixth century decided that the soul left the body with a sneeze and if no one blessed you, a demon might get in and prevent the soul from returning."

The teacher responded, "Very good, Jane." She didn't realize that Jane had remembered the wrong conference and date. The other kids felt she was showing off and called her 'Sneezy' for several weeks. Jane realized that one could offer too much information.

When Jane was in the fourth grade three other girls were planning a party and had Jane with them for the planning. Then one said, "But you aren't invited to come."

Jane came home from school and told her mother.

"Quit whining. That's the way the world treats us."

Fred took her arm and led her into his office. Sitting in a big chair, he took her on his lap. She started to cry and then when she stopped, he said, "Tomorrow we'll discuss how to handle the girls. For tonight all you need is to know that most of the people aren't like that. There are many good, caring people and lots of them like you." She put her head on his shoulder for a few minutes, then got up and went to do her homework.

About the time Jane was eleven, as they finished work in the mortuary, Fred asked, "Have you noticed that your breasts are growing?"

Jane nodded shyly and Fred explained the hormonal reactions at puberty. Another night he gently rubbed her nipples. "They do keep growing, don't they?"

She pulled back a little and he said, "It's OK. I'm helping you not to be embarrassed by growing up."

Another time he asked her to take off her blouse. He touched the nipples gently. "Don't be embarrassed by them. They have a nice shape and are becoming more attractive. Soon you'll be proud to have people notice them." Soon she was comfortable with taking off her blouse at the end of work sessions.

One evening Fred asked, "Are you beginning to get hair where your legs come together?"

"A little." She said shyly. He then explained more of the hormonal effects and warned her that she would have a little bleeding someday. A couple weeks later he asked to see how her hair was growing.

"It's OK. I'm your Dad and we're just helping you to adjust to being a woman."

She took off her panties.

"It looks a little ragged but don't worry. It will form a nice smooth tuft in a few months." The next time he inspected it, he ran his fingers through the hair and smoothed it.

"Growing in very nicely", he commented. "Are you interested in the difference between boys and girls now?"

"I don't think so right now," Jane answered.

"Let me know when you want to know," Fred said and dropped the subject.

A few months later she had a little blood on her panties. She went to her mother, "I think I've started a period."

He mother found a Kotex pad, handed it to her and said, "You'll figure out how to use this. Don't bother me with it."

She told Fred that evening. "Congratulations. You're growing up." And he explained the purpose and mechanism. "Sometimes the uterus cramps, particularly if the blood clots. You can take aspirin if it bothers you but don't let it scare you into stopping your activities."

Jane finished grade school. There was an honors program in which she became one of the winners. Her review of the *Autobiography of Benjamin Franklin* was outstanding. Her teacher said, "Not only did she summarize the book well, but she pointed out how reading it was a preview of the accomplishments of one of the great founding fathers of our country and a leading scientist on the world scene. She pointed out that his printing establishment was the country's first franchising program, as well as recognizing that he founded the first city library, the first city fire department and the University of Pennsylvania. And he invented bifocals. This required other reading of his life and makes a mature book review which is rare for a grade school student."

Fred and Louise went to the graduation ceremony. Jane had several friends in the class but she was hesitant to have them meet her mother, not knowing how her mother would respond. Finally she took her best friend, Estelle Davis, to meet her parents. Her mother tried and said, "I'm glad Jane could have you for a friend."

"Will you be together next year?" Fred asked.

"We don't know yet. They well send out letters next week about where we go."

The Pasadena schools were under a court ordered busing decree. Jane was bused to a different junior high school than many of her grade school classmates. Unfortunately, Estelle was assigned to a different junior high school. "I don't know why they had to send us to different schools." Jane complained.

"I'm afraid that's the kind of unfair, unintended consequence that happens when big government tries to solve local problems. I wish we had some recourse," Fred told her. "Maybe you'll find a new, very nice social group at McKinley."

In middle school, Jane met girls who became good friends. Heather Appleton and Felicity McReynolds made a threesome with Jane. Jane and Heather rode their bicycles to Felicity's house each Wednesday to swim in the McReynolds pool. After swimming, they were changing in the little pool house.

After coming out of the shower, Felicity said, "Jane, your breasts are bigger than mine but Heather is bigger than both of us together."

Heather responded, "But look how protruding your nipples are. I have a big dark area—"

"That's called the areola," Jane interjected.

Heather continued, slightly miffed by the addition, "The areola, but my nipples hardly stand out."

"Breast size is variable as we all know," Jane said, "but the age at which they develop is also variable. I've never read about it but nipple shape and areola size must be variable too."

"Well, I hope I'm a slow developer and will get some more before I stop growing," Felicity said.

"What about below? Are we different there too?" Heather asked.

"Well, my hair is blonde," Felicity said and the others looked at her tuft of blonde pubic hair.

"In spite of her light brown hair, Jane's is black," Heather said. "I'm black, as you would expect with my black hair."

Felicity and I grow hair only over the pubic bone while Heather's runs up almost to her belly button," Jane noted.

"How about further down?" Heather asked.

"I've tried looking with the mirror but it doesn't work very well," Jane said.

"Would you let us see yours, Heather?" Felicity asked.

Heather lay on the couch, spreading her legs. Felicity and Jane studied her pubic region. "Whose do I get to see?" Heather asked.

"I'll do it," Jane said and took Heather's place.

"They look the same to me," Felicity decided.

"I wonder how boys look and if they are different too," Heather commented.

The girls dressed and went on with normal activities.

Two days later Jane was in the embalming room with Fred. She said, "Fred, the girls were wondering about boys. I think it about time I learned about them."

"Sure, as soon as we finish this case."

When he finished, he took a pad of paper and starting drawing, meanwhile saying, "The first thing you need to realize is that while women have two openings, one for urine and one for sexual functions such as periods, men have both functions in the penis." He showed her the picture he had been drawing.

"The urethra runs from the bladder down to the end of the penis. Sperm from the testicles down here is fed into the urethra here. The penis is erectile tissue as are your nipples and clitoris. It grows firm and very much larger." He took down his pants and showed her the testicles and the flaccid penis. "Now put your hand on it and move a little." In a very short time it was erect. "Isn't that an amazing growth?"

"It really is," she answered.

"Another time I'll show you how it works."

At the next swimming day, Jane took the picture and showed the other girls, explaining the parts. "It's soft most of the time but is erectile like our nipples and clitoris and becomes very firm."

"What's the clitoris?" Felicity asked.

"Don't you know that little sensitive bump down there?"

Felicity felt herself. "No. I can't find it. Show me."

Jane put her finger between Felicity's legs and found the clitoris, rubbing it a moment. "There."

"Oh, that feels good. Rub it a little more."

Jane wasn't sure that she should do this, but she did rub it a little. Suddenly Felicity began breathing heavily. She gave a moan and a shudder. "That was wonderful."

"What happened?"

"I don't know. Suddenly it became very sensitive and a sharp sensation ran through me down there."

The others tried rubbing but didn't get the response.

Jane told Fred what had happened. "Is it bad for me to do that?"

"No. Many young people experiment and it's part of learning. Her reaction was what is called orgasm or climax. Some people just call it coming. Let me try with you."

Fred gently massaged her and she breathed faster. He gently touched her nipple with his tongue. She did come and afterwards said, "I see why she likes that."

Fred told her, "There are questions about the reason for the female orgasm but the male orgasm is to squirt sperm into the female in search of an egg. I'll show you how the penis works."

He had her rub his penis and he climaxed, squirting four feet across the room. He caught the rest with tissue, after she had seen the force of it.

Jane was impressed but couldn't think of any way to tell the other girls about it without telling what she did with Fred.

After a couple times rubbing her, he inserted his finger in her vagina.

"That stimulation should cause the vagina to lubricate." At a later time, he said, "I think it is time for you to see why the vagina lubricates." He had her lie down and pushed his penis gently against the vaginal opening. "Sometimes this hurts a little as the opening isn't used to stretching. Tell me if it hurts." He increased the pressure a little and finally it slipped in. "Does that hurt?"

"It did a minute but it's OK now."

"I'll leave it in a minute until your organ gets used to the stretching."

After a couple times of this he told her, "This time I'm going to move in and out. That will make me ejaculate. You remember what that is like. You will feel it inside you. It may feel odd but it won't hurt. Many women find it pleasant."

After this they had occasional intercourse. Jane was rather passive, but found it somewhat enjoyable. Fred explained how this caused pregnancy. "This is a condom. It catches the sperm so that you won't get pregnant. If you start going with boys, be sure they use one."

"What about you?"

"There is a tube that brings the sperm from the testicles to the urethra. I had mine surgically tied off to make sure I couldn't get you pregnant."

"Can girls be tied off too?"

"Yes. It's a bigger job on females because one must go into the abdomen to find the tube while a man's can be done with just a little skin cut."

One day Fred looked at her and said, "You are a very attractive woman. Your hair is nice, your face is pretty. Your posture is good and your breasts firm. I'm pleased with how you have grown up and I love you very much."

Jane didn't know how to respond and just nodded.

A few days later at the mortuary, a family member identifying a body fell apart emotionally. Fred felt he had to drive her home in her car. "Louise," he called to his wife, "Will you pick me up at 2430 Midwick in Altadena?"

"OK," she replied tiredly.

"Hold the fort," Fred said to Jane. She was doing homework and frequently was left to answer the mortuary phone.

"Norton Mortuary," she answered a call an hour later.

"This is Sgt. Carson, Pasadena Police. Who is on duty?"

"Oh, Sgt., this is Jane. Nobody here but me. Fred will be back shortly."

"I'll stop by in a few minutes."

"OK." She had seen Detective Carson at the mortuary. He was a very pleasant young man who had just made sergeant and she liked him.

Soon the doorbell rang. Jane opened the door. "Come on in, Sergeant. Fred should be back any time."

"I need to talk to you. I don't know any easy way. Your mother pulled out in front of a heavy truck and both she and Fred were killed. I'm terribly sorry"

Jane sat silently for a minute.

"Do you have any relative we can call?"

"Mother has a sister in upstate New York but I've never met her."

"I know that you will miss your parents terribly."

"My mother has been gone for years in an alcoholic fog but I'll miss Fred."

This would back up Porter's suspicion, to be confirmed at autopsy, that Jane's mother was heavily intoxicated. A neighbor had reported that she was very impatient, honking the horn repeatedly while Fred settled down the lady he had brought home. Louise was so angry when he finally came out that she pulled out without looking.

Porter didn't know what to do about Jane. "Do you have any close friends you can stay with?"

"No. I have two girl friends but I don't know that I could stay with them. I can stay here for a time."

"Do you know who Fred's lawyer is?"

"Andy Campbell."

He handed her a card. "Call me anytime if I can help. I'll check with you tomorrow."

In his patrol car, Carson called the station. "Find me the home phone number for an attorney, Andrew Campbell."

The radio gave him the number just before he reached home. He went into his little house and called, "I'm home."

"I've dinner in the oven, a little overdone as usual. Are you ready?" his wife answered.

"I must make a phone call first." He dialed the number. "Mr. Campbell, this is Sergeant Carson, Pasadena Police. Sorry to bother you at home."

"That's OK. What can I do."

"Are you Fred Norton's lawyer?"

"Yes, and a close friend."

"He and Louise were just killed in a car accident an hour ago. I told Jane and I'm worried about her there alone. Do you know if there are any arrangements for her? I hate to put such a bright, controlled young lady under the child protective services."

"Thank you for calling me. I agree about child services. I'll bring her here tonight and tomorrow start arrangements. Louise's sister is her next of kin."

Porter went to his dinner relieved. "You take care of everyone before your family," his wife said. He told her the story of the traffic accident and the now orphaned fourteen year old girl. His wife was still angry. "If you had kids of your own, you would probably still take more care of others."

"I don't think that's fair."

"So what's fair about being late every night. I work hard but I stop when it is time to stop."

Porter shook his head. There was no use in further discussion. He could see the marriage was doomed unless he was willing to give up his job. What else could he do? This was what he was trained for and he did it well. The police didn't pay high salaries but as a sergeant he did quite well. He certainly couldn't do as well starting in something new. And he wouldn't be happy just sitting in an office and shuffling papers somewhere. But he didn't feel up to going any further tonight. He ate in morose silence.

Andy Campbell took his wife and went to the mortuary. "Jane, we want you to spend the night with us. Tomorrow I will need your help in planning for you and the estate. Penny will help you get a few things together for the night."

Jane had been unable to come to any resolution of her new problems and was happy to have this direction. At the Campbell's home, Penny gave her some chocolate, a sleeping pill, and put her to bed with a hug. Jane slept late and came running downstairs. "I'll be late for school."

"I called them and said you wouldn't be in," Penny assured her. "Andy's gone to the office for Fred's papers and then we'll talk."

Soon the three were sitting at the dining room table. "I'm sorry to be such a bother and to sponge on you," Jane said.

"Jane, we would love having you under any conditions. Our house is lonesome with both our children gone. But I'll receive a substantial fee for handling the estate, so don't worry at all. You are a wealthy young lady. Fred had a trust fund for you and when I deposit the life insurance and sell the mortuary it will be considerably larger."

"I really don't know what to do."

"Of course you don't. We will help. Would you like to live with your aunt if they will agree?

"I think so. I don't really know them."

"Let me sound them out. You will be here a couple weeks while we make arrangements for your parents' things."

Penny and Jane went over all her parents' clothes and all the family possessions, deciding what Jane wanted to keep, what went to a consignment store, and what to the Salvation Army. Jane's clothes and books were packed and moved to the Campbells' home. In a couple days Andy announced that Jane's aunt would welcome her. The younger son had just gone away to University and it would work well. "We would love to have you live with us but it would take your aunt's release and a court order. In most instances courts feel it is best to be with family."

"Aunt Helen didn't get along with mother but she has always remembered my birthday and seems to be a nice person."

"That's good. She sounded pleasant over the phone. She sent me pictures of the house and her family. You will want them so you can feel a little more acquainted when you go."

"You don't think it will bother them to have me?"

"It would be something of a hardship if they had to support you as Helen's husband isn't well and their finances are a little tight. I have made an agreement that will reimburse them well. It should be a big help to them, so they should welcome you. Don't let them make you feel like a poor relation they have taken in. If you have any problems, call me at once."

Finally the Campbells put Jane on the plane for New York and her new home. "Goodbye, Jane. If things don't go well, remember that you are always welcome here. We hope you will visit us in the summer."

"Goodbye. Thank for everything." Mrs. Campbell gave her a hug and she walked down the ramp to the boarding area.

The flight was non-stop to Newark and Helen and John Waite had driven down to meet her. She recognized them from the pictures. "Are you Aunt Helen?"

"Welcome, Jane. We are so sorry about your family but glad to have you with us." She gave her a hug.

Chapter 7

She was putting on make up and she smiled at herself in the mirror. The Pasadena Star News had blamed the Hilton Hotel killing on the 'black widow', the spider that kills its mate. She looked at her nude body in the mirror. How would it look with a red hour glass tattooed on the abdomen, making her like the spider? She laughed at this fantasy, then picked a blouse and slipping to on, buttoned it. She took the stiletto from the drawer and carefully taped it to her hip. Then she pulled on a short black skirt.

She checked her purse—two twenty dollar bills and some change, her driver's license, and the car keys. She carefully placed the purse in a black carryall bag and walked out. After she had locked the door, she walked to the dirty Plymouth. In the driver's seat, she carefully put the motel key and the driver's license in the glove box. Starting up the car, she drove out Colorado Boulevard to Rosemead Boulevard and turned onto the 210 freeway. At the freeway end in LaVerne, she followed Foothill a few blocks, dropping down to Arrow Highway. At White Street she turned right and went through the Los Angeles County Fair grounds. At the end of the Fair, she went into the parking lot of the Sheraton Suites—Fairplex. There was almost always a convention here.

Entering the hotel bar, she took a table across from the bar. When the waiter came she ordered a Martini. With the Martini in hand, she looked along the bar. At one end, a couple were in deep conversation. Further over two casually dressed men sipped beer and watched baseball on the television. A mousy little man seemed about to leave. She sipped and waited patiently.

A young man entered the room. He seemed slightly ill at ease, looking around. His eyes settled on her. He came over and said, "Is this seat taken?" She could see that he was sweating and uncomfortable.

"Not at the moment. Won't you join me?"

"Thank you." He looked at her gratefully and sat down.

"Are you at the accountants' convention?" he asked.

"No. I live nearby and this is a pleasant place to relax. I come once a week or so. Are you an accountant?"

"Well, I'm studying to be one. I take courses and work at bookkeeping. This is my first convention."

"Where are you from?"

"I grew up in Sherman Oaks but now I'm working in Bakersfield."

"Isn't that terribly hot?"

"It does get bad but everything is air conditioned. I find it a pleasant place to live, though I haven't met many people outside the office. What do you do?"

"I teach fifth grade in Pasadena. I yearn for adult companionship after a week with those kids."

He had run out of conversation. He seemed a gentle little man, not at all sure of himself and wanting to be liked. This wasn't the type of man she wanted.

"Well, it's been a pleasure talking to you. My date will be here in a minute so I'd better be alone."

He looked like a kicked dog. "I'm sorry. I didn't know."

He got up. She said, "I enjoyed visiting with you. Maybe another time we can have an evening together."

"Thank you. That would be wonderful." He smiled as if given a reprieve and walked away.

She resumed her wait and patiently watched the men come and go.

A large black man, impeccably and expensively dressed came in and sat at the bar. He ordered a whiskey and looked around. His eyes paused a moment on her, then went on. Shortly they came back to her and he smiled. She gazed back and smiled. He took a drink and then looked back at her. She had uncrossed her legs and sat with them spread slightly so that he could see she wasn't wearing underwear.

In a couple minutes he came over to the table with a fresh whiskey and another Martini. He sat down, handed her the Martini. "How much?"

"I'm not for sale. It's my husband's poker night and I want to see a real man."

"You've found one. I'm Henry."

She held out her hand. "Rachael."

He took her hand and shook it firmly.

"Are you staying at this hotel?"

"Yes. I'm at the convention here."

"Then you must be an accountant."

"I practice in Santa Barbara. Lot of money there that people need help keeping track of."

"I always think of accountants as being small men."

"I suppose some small people go into it because they can't handle other jobs but big men can have the right brain for it too."

"It's impressive to have both your size and that kind of brain."

"I'm pretty lucky, even if I am black."

"Well, that can be a turn on for some people. And rumor says that sex size goes with body size."

"Not always true but in my case it is."

"Sounds interesting."

He nodded. "Shall we go?"

She took another drink, looked up and nodded.

In the elevator, he put his hand on her hip. She had turned a little so that he couldn't feel the knife. He led her up the hall and unlocked a door. In the room, she unbuttoned her blouse while he took off his coat. She turned off the overhead light and slid her skirt off. He took off his shoes and pants. "Shirt too, please."

When he was nude, he pulled her to him and hungrily kissed her. His skin was amazingly smooth. As he stepped back toward the bed, she looked down. His penis was huge.

"I like to warm it up orally but that'll be a tight fit." She said.

"I don't like that." He replied. "I just want it in. You'll find it more fulfilling than you have ever had. You may rip a little but it'll be worth it."

He pushed her onto the bed. His strength was amazing. This man frightened her. He pushed the massive penis against her. She felt it would split her and the pressure grew. She reached down and freed the stiletto. The pressure was becoming unbearable. She put the stiletto to his ear and shoved with all her strength. He had a momentary thought with the pain, "I can't be having a stroke at this time." Then the thought disappeared together with his life as she moved the stiletto back and forth, slicing the brain connections that make life possible.

She lay a moment, breathing heavily, and then rolled the heavy body off of her. Pulling the knife free, she looked down at the body. The giant penis was like a protruding mountain. "This is what this arrogant man was so proud of," she thought. She took hold of it with a corner of the bedsheet and quickly severed it with the knife. Then she threw it on the floor.

She wiped the knife with a towel and then wiped everything she could have touched to remove fingerprints. She dropped her drink glass into her bag, after emptying it into the toilet. She pulled out the maid's dress. After slipping into this, she bound up her hair with a scarf. Listening at the door, she let herself out and let the door lock behind her. When someone started to get off the elevator, she pulled open the door to the service stairs. Descending, she found an outside door across from the stairwell.

She slipped out the door, walked slowly across the parking lot to the Plymouth. Out of the parking lot, she dropped down a few blocks to the 10 freeway. Sure she was now safely away from the area, she took off the scarf, opened the window, to let her hair blow. The delicately coiffed wig started to ripple. She took it off and laid it on the seat beside her. Now her hair could be free to the breeze. This evening could easily have gone wrong. The strength of the huge man was formidable. She patted the stiletto gratefully. She must be careful not to let things get out of control. She was still breathing heavily when she pulled into the motel parking lot. She walked to her room and turned on the TV. She opened a coke and sipped it while she watched a ridiculous comedy until she calmed down. Then she went to bed.

She lay there and thought about the evening. What an arrogant prick the huge man had been. She wondered how many women he had damaged with his massive penis. Finally she drifted off to sleep. Again she felt relaxed when she awoke. "I think I'll just sit around the pool and read today," she told herself.

Chapter 8

Sergeant Tom Acker, head homicide detective of the Pomona Police Department, was just out of the shower when his phone rang. "Acker." He was a tall, slender man with a pointed face that could have been handsome but for the acne scars.

"This is dispatch. We have a death overnight at the Fairplex hotel. The uniformed unit looked and said homicide should come. They are preserving the scene."

"I'll be there in 20 minutes." Then he called to his wife, who was just getting up, "I've got an emergency. Can you fix me a cup of coffee and a piece of toast while I dress?"

"Sure. Will you be busy all day?"

"No idea. There was a murder last night at the Fairplex Hotel. I'll check it out and see what has to be done. I'll let you know if I'll be late." He pulled on slacks and shirt and tucked his small automatic in his belt with the handcuffs. He put on a sport jacket and went to the kitchen. He drank the coffee and ate the toast his wife had ready. He patted her on the bottom and said, "Sorry to rush but duty calls. I'll talk to you on the phone at your work when I find out anything."

He was in his car in ten minutes and was only one minute late for his estimated time of arrival. He parked behind the black and white in front of the hotel. Walking in, he said to the desk clerk, "Police. What floor are we on?"

"Three. It's room three twelve. Officers are waiting up there."

"Thanks." He pushed the elevator button. On three he turned right to where he could see two uniformed officers standing in the hall. "What's up, guys?"

"Big black guy dead in the bed. I don't see what killed him but someone cut off his dong and it's lying on the floor. Really a big one."

Tom opened the door and walked in. The kid was right; he was one big man. Then he saw the amputated penis on the floor. He looked at the nude body. There was only a little blood in the groin so the penis had been removed after death. There was a little blood running out of his left ear and he bent to look at it. There was a cut on the ear, running straight into the head. Tom went to the door and asked the cop, "Have you called anyone else?"

"No, sir. We didn't know in what sequence who was to come."

Tom thought, "Not only doesn't know but can't make a decent English sentence. What are the police coming to."

He pulled out his police radio. "S4." S stood for sergeant and he was number four.

"Go ahead," dispatch answered.

"This is definitely a homicide. Get the forensic crew out here and call the coroner. Room three twelve at the Fairplex. Send Detective Finley over as soon as he comes on duty."

"On the way, as soon as possible for all the above."

"Thanks. I'll send the uniforms back to duty."

While he waited for the others, Tom took out a pair of rubber gloves and started checking the drawers and the closet. A few extra clothes and some toilet articles but he didn't find anything that seemed significant. The two technicians and Detective Finley arrived within minutes of each other.

Finley was a small man for a cop but he had a strong, well-muscled body. His face showed the Gaelic white and red complexion and a pleasant smile. "Good morning, Sergeant," he said on entering. "Do we have something interesting?"

"Good morning." Then he said, "and to you also." as he realized that the lab techs had followed Finley into the room.

"Finley, try to get the victim's name and info from the desk." Then to the lab men, "I won't try to tell you how to do your job. However, don't step on the penis on the floor over there."

The lab men went over to look. "Hey, that's one hell of a big one. Maybe I should save it and have it put on me."

"Color won't match," said the other.

One started searching for fingerprints on the things that people usually touch. The other set up some lights and started taking pictures of the body and of the penis on the floor.

While they were working, the driver and an investigator arrived from the coroner's office. They measured the temperature of the body and took their own pictures of the scene. The penis was photoed and then placed in double plastic bags. They went down to their van and brought up a folding gurney. The body was placed in a body bag. "Boy. That is one heavy body. Would one of you give us a hand with the lifting?" One of the techs went over and helped them lift the body onto the gurney.

"I'm going to put in for back injury," the tech said.

"Ask the coroner's office not our department," Acker told him.

"Gee, sarge, just lifting the penis is enough to give you a hernia."

"Aren't you glad you don't have to carry one like that all the time?"

"I'm not sure. I've heard they make you more desirable."

"If you've got a sprained back, you couldn't do much with it."

The investigator chimed in, "It isn't the size but the drive behind it." He exchanged cards with Acker. "Probably autopsy him tomorrow. You want to be notified of the time?"

"Please let me know."

"Unless you need something more, we're out of here."

"OK. I'll hear from someone down there, I assume."

"I'll see that they contact you." They took the body out of the room on the gurney.

Finley was back. "I have the registration documents. Name is Henry Denver. Registered address in Santa Barbara. They remember him checking in but not much else. He received the convention discount so I will try to find out who at the convention knew him."

"Thanks. There isn't much here. If you'll help me inventory his things, we can send them to the station with the lab guys."

After they completed packing the belongings and checked all the drawers and cupboards, Acker asked the lab man, "Would you log these in at the station?"

"Sure" He took the package.

Then Acker said to Finley, "You follow up on his name and family. I'll go to the bar and see if anyone saw the pick up and then to the convention. You can check around the hotel if you have time."

When Acker had finished at the hotel room, he called the accounting office where his wife worked. "Strange case. I'll tell you about it later. We're having a meeting on it at four so I should be home for dinner."

"Thanks for calling. Good luck and I'll be interested to hear about it."

Acker went down to the convention area and found the man who was managing the convention. "I'm Detective Sergeant Acker of the Pomona Police Department. We had a murder last night in this hotel and the victim had registered at the hotel as part of the convention. His name is Henry Denver and I'd like any information you have on him."

"I'm Oscar Henderson. That's too bad. I'll get the papers." He went into an office. In a minute he returned, looking puzzled. "There isn't anyone registered by that name. I'll keep looking but I don't think he is part of our group. What does he look like?"

"A very large black man with heavy muscles and a big chest."

"He would have stood out in this group and I certainly haven't seen him. I'll look but I don't think I'll find him."

Finley came in and went up to Acker. "This is detective Finley, Mr. Henderson."

Finley nodded and said, "The name and address on the registration are false. I've fingerprinted the body and hope to find a match somewhere."

"Well, then I guess you don't have to look further for that name, Mr. Henderson. We'll have to see if we can find who he is."

Acker went to the hotel bar. A lone bartender was reading the papers and there were no customers. "I'm sergeant Acker with the police. Were you working last night?"

"I worked through the dinner rush and then went home. Rafael finished the evening. Can I help."

"We're looking for any information on a very large black man who picked up a girl last night."

"Oh, I remember him. The girl was sitting quietly drinking a Martini. She was attractive, with short cut blond hair, bright blue eyes, and a very short skirt. Then the black guy came in and sat at the bar. I fixed him a drink and was working the other end. He asked me for another and a Martini and took them over and joined the girl. In a few minutes they walked out. He dropped thirty bucks on the bar as they walked out. That was the last I saw of them."

"Can you tell us anything else about the girl?"

"I can describe the guy in detail. He was dressed very sharply."

"We have his body so it's the girl we are interested in."

"He was killed?"

"Stabbed in his room. The girl probably did it. What do you remember about her?"

"I think she was looking for someone to pick up. There wasn't anything very remarkable about her except the shiny hair and the blue eyes. And the skirt was really short, showed a good pair of legs."

"Here's my card. If you can think of anything else about her, give me a call. I don't suppose her drink glass is still around?"

"She took one with her and the empty went to the dishwasher early last night so there isn't a chance for fingerprints unless the second glass is in his room."

"Afraid it isn't. Thanks for your help."

At four o'clock the different people working on the hotel case met in the Pomona police station. Sergeant Acker asked Finley to report first. "What did you find out about the victim, Finley?"

"The name and address on the hotel registration are false. In spite of registering at the hotel with the convention discount, you found out he didn't register for the convention, either with the name he used at the hotel or with any other name. I've fingerprinted him and sent in the prints. I hope to have a file on him tomorrow."

"Then I guess we won't have to worry about the people from the convention knowing him."

"I guess everyone has heard that she cut off his penis. It was quite remarkable in size."

Acker made his report. "I spent most of the day at the hotel. I checked with the people running the convention but dropped that line after Finley found the name and address were false. I've interviewed all the people working in the bar. One noticed the victim sitting with a young lady. He couldn't describe her except to say she had short cropped, very blonde hair, bright blue eyes, and an unusually short skirt."

Finley put in, "If a bartender thinks the skirt was unusually short, it must have been short. Those guys get all the suggestive dressers in their bars."

Jonathan from technical said, "We have lots of fingerprints but most of them are the victim or hotel employees. We still have hope of getting one from the killer, but not much hope. The places where one might expect to find them, doorknobs, sink faucets, have been wiped clean. We are analyzing a few hairs that were found on the bed."

"If that's all, everyone keep working and we'll talk at the same time tomorrow. I want to say good job, Findley. It was great to get the fingerprints out immediately. Thanks to all of you. I go to the autopsy tomorrow. We'll see what they have to say."

Acker was down at the coroner's office on time and went into the autopsy room. Dr. Whiteman was doing this autopsy also. "Morning, Sergeant."

"Good morning, doctor."

"We've done the usual X-rays and external exam. Nothing of interest except the missing penis and the cut on his ear. As you thought, the penis was removed after he was dead. I'll do the head first as that is the area which is most likely to interest you." He carefully dissected around the ear and followed the cut inward. "There is some fracturing of the bone in back of the cut. Something was pushed into the brain through the ear, with considerable force. We need to see the injured area from the inside." He turned back the scalp and cut off the skull cap with an electric saw.

"That makes a lot of noise. Ever cut yourself with it?"

"It's a Stryker saw. The circular blade moves back and forth with very small amplitude rather than rotating. It cuts rapidly through hard material like bone but won't cut you if you actually put a finger to the blade. The soft tissue moves back and forth with the blade."

"Interesting. No one ever told me that before."

After a few more minutes of working, the doctor said "The path is fairly narrow and is cut rather than torn. I think it was a long narrow knife that was inserted. This was a bar pick-up case?"

"Apparently so. He was seen in the bar with a somewhat flashy blonde girl in a very short skirt."

"We had a bar pick-up case from Pasadena earlier this week in which a long, narrow knife—probably it would be classed as a stiletto—was pushed into the victim's heart and then moved down, cutting the heart open. I'll have to study the brain to be sure but I bet this was inserted and then moved to cut off his basic brain functions. We can certainly say that he was killed by stabbing the head through an ear."

"That's pretty unusual, isn't it?"

"I've never seen one like it. I think she knew what she was doing. This is probably all you'll get from the post mortem. If you want to go back to work, I'll call you if we find anything else."

"You're very helpful, doctor. I appreciate it."

Later in the day the group met and again Sergeant Acker led off. "I went to the autopsy. The perpetrator shoved a narrow blade in his ear, rotated it around and scrambled his brain. As you know, she cut off his penis after he was dead. The autopsy surgeon thinks the blade is the same one used in a heart stabbing in Pasadena. I met today with Lieutenant Carson of Pasadena P D. Both killings were bar pick-ups. The same knife was probably used. However, in Pasadena she bit his penis and when he jerked forward, caught him in the chest with the knife. She then pushed it down, ripping open the heart. They found no useful fingerprints. They did find some black hairs that turned out to be from a wig."

Jonathan spoke up, "You have preempted my report. We studied the blonde hairs and found that they must be from a wig. Our fingerprints have gone nowhere."

Finley was anxious to give his report. "The fingerprint reports on the victim are back. He's really Elijah Washington, a registered sex offender. He has a long record of rape and beating up women. I think he must go to conventions under another name so he can do his thing without the authorities finding out that he is breaking his probation. He's one mean son of a bitch and maybe we should get a medal for the killer."

"That's amazing. If you think he was doing that, we should send out a notice to all agencies. If they have unsolved rapes, we can get them his DNA record. Can you take care of that, Finley?"

"Glad to. I don't have his DNA profile yet but we will soon. In the meantime, they can look over their files."

"We're setting up a joint task force to meet with Pasadena every couple days and compare progress. There will be two of us on it. So far it doesn't look like either department has any real information about the killer, except that she wore a wig, black in Pasadena and blonde here, and no one notices anything else except the short skirt."

"She really has balls to take on someone this size with just a knife. If we find her it'll be interesting to see what kind of person she is and how she got into this." Finley had obviously been thinking about the case.

Acker responded, "The longer you're in this business, the less you understand how murderers' minds work. She hasn't taken anything, so robbery isn't a factor. When, not if, we catch her, I'll let you work on the psychodynamics. See you tomorrow."

Acker went home to tell his wife about the case. She was a good listener and very discreet. He probably told her more than he should but he found that telling the story sometimes ironed out the sequences for him and she often had female insights that helped him in the investigation.

Finley went to his little apartment and took a beer out of the fridge. He sat down to think. This was his first real homicide case since he had been promoted to detective and he would really like to solve it. What did he know about it? Not much really. A girl with a very sharp knife had killed a guy. She hadn't left a useful description, any fingerprints or any other information. After going over the case several times, he didn't have any idea what to look for next. Maybe he wasn't ready to solve major cases yet. He would see how Sergeant Acker went about finding the next clue.

He resignedly fixed himself a frozen dinner and sat down to eat it on the couch, turning on the ball game on TV.

Chapter 9

Jane's new family took good care of her, though there was little demonstrativeness on either side. She continued to do well in school. She didn't let boys get close, either physically or emotionally. She did have some good times with her older cousins when they came home to visit. They teased her like a little sister and gave her a taste of masculine contact. Her uncle was older and rather withdrawn. He was pleasant enough but had little emotional contact with her. Her aunt tried to be motherly but she didn't want to hear about Louise and Jane's previous life. She introduced her to her friends' girls and tried hard to get her integrated into the junior high school.

Andy Campbell sent her a quarterly report on her trust with letters of encouragement. He said in a letter at the end of the first year after her parents' death, "I hope it has been a good year and you don't miss them too much now." This led her to think of the family. She certainly didn't miss her mother. She thought occasionally of working in the mortuary—what else did she and Fred do? Her mind had completely blocked it out.

Jane went into high school and made a good record. She had several girl friends but rarely dated. She did babysitting for the neighbors occasionally. One day her aunt said, "Jane, you know that you have your own money. You don't have to baby sit. It isn't as though you were taking it from us."

"I realize that. Many of my friends baby sit and I like the feel of doing something. I meet some nice kids doing it."

"That's fine as long as you don't feel it is something you have to do."

A year or so later Jane decided to try for a job. She went to the local mortuary and introduced herself to Henry Cavanaugh, the owner. "Do you need any part time help in office work or answering the phone? I did this at my step-father's mortuary and know pretty well how to handle the different things that come up."

Mrs. Cavanaugh asked her husband, "Wouldn't it be nice to have someone answer the phone on our night away and you wouldn't have to take all those unnecessary calls on your cell phone."

"It would." And then to Jane, "We take Thursday evenings off and have dinner out and sometimes go to a movie or play. Would you like to sit the mortuary for five or six hours each Thursday night?"

"That would be fine. I don't want to work more than a day or two a week."

"Baby sitting pays about five dollars an hour now and this would have more responsibility. I would think about eight dollars an hour would be fair. Does that sound OK to you?"

"That would be just fine."

"You could use the kitchen to fix supper if you want and there is a TV in the office with a desk to do your school work. Let me show you around."

They showed her the office. "There is even a couch if you want to take a nap."

The kitchen was attached to the reception room and was used for serving after funerals held at the mortuary. "We have a smaller but more generally equipped kitchen upstairs but this is certainly adequate for anything you would need. Do you want to see the actual mortuary rooms?"

"Please. I spent many hours helping with the work." It all looked familiar and she saw the refrigerated room where they had spaces for six bodies.

Jane started the next Thursday. The Cavanaughs gave her his cell phone number and left with a little worry. When they returned home about nine thirty, Jane reported. "You had four calls. One is social for Mrs. Cavanaugh. The number is here. One wanted to know the prices on funerals. I told him you would get back to him tomorrow. One asked if an emergency ambulance service was available. I told him not this evening. I didn't think you ever did, but I wasn't sure."

"No. We don't do any ambulance work. We have a hearse but only to pick up after they are deceased."

"The last was a kid who wanted to know if we had the body of Elvis here. I told him that he had been here but had walked out yesterday without paying the bill. He laughed and hung up."

"You handled all that very well. We won't worry about the place next time. I was a little concerned for someone so young but obviously you have had experience with this. Thank you very much." He paid her for the evening and said, "Shall we see you next Thursday?"

"If you wish, I'll be glad to be here."

Jane worked there almost every week. She enjoyed the time and was able to study undisturbed most evenings. She told her aunt, "Even though it's my money, I feel a little better actually doing something for part of what I want to spend. I feel freer to waste some if I want."

"That's good. Our boys always had part time jobs and I think it was helpful in learning to handle money and also to take responsibility. As long as you enjoy doing it, keep on. If you get tired of it, stop."

Glenn Thompson was in Jane's biology class. He had crushes on a couple of the girls in school, but they didn't last long. Now he had one on Jane. He came over to her seat and talked to her whenever there was a break. "Can we get together to study the biology some evening? You seem to know a lot and it would really help me."

"I don't think it's a good idea. I study better alone."

He kept after her and finally one day she accepted. "I work Thursday nights at the funeral home, watching the office. I don't have much to do and can study there. Come over about seven."

He arrived on time and she let him in and led him to the office. They studied a time but his heart didn't seem to be in it and he kept taking her hand or patting her shoulder. He suggested, "Maybe one learns biology best by the Braille system."

Finally she said, "If you don't want to study, let's go in another room."

He agreed and she led him down the hall. She opened a door and turned on the light. There was a shining steel table in the center with cases of instruments all around. He gasped. "This is for the bodies, isn't it? What are we doing here?"

She walked to another door and pulling hard, opened it. A gust of freezing air came out. "What is that?"

"This is the room for the bodies. I thought you wanted to study biology by the Braille system. We have a couple here that won't mind."

"Holy Jesus. You're crazy. I'm not a medical student. Let me out of here."

"Turn left into the corridor. The first door goes out to the parking lot."

He dashed out.

When the Cavanaughs returned, Jane told them, "I had a fellow student over to study since you said it would be OK. He turned out to want to study my anatomy so I took him down to the embalming room. He went home quickly."

Mr. Cavanaugh laughed. "Good thinking. You didn't let him in the cold room?"

"No. I wouldn't let anyone in there. Since I knew there were no bodies, I opened the door a little and when the cold air hit him, asked if he could smell death. I doubt if he will bother me again."

"I like the way you handle things. See you next week."

In biology class the next day Jane walked by Glenn's desk and dropped his notebook on the desk without a word. He just glared at her.

Jane was at a party at a friend's house when her friend Michelle's father called. They couldn't find Michelle so he spoke to Jane, "Michelle's mother had an attack and I'm taking her to the hospital. She must come home to stay with her little sister who will be alone. Please find her, Jane."

Jane was looking around the house for Michelle and opened a bedroom door. Michelle was nude on the bed with Mike, one of the football team. Jane saw his huge hairy body moving up and down over Michelle and his large penis between her legs. She shut the door, went to the nearby bathroom and vomited. How could Michelle do this?

In a few minutes Michelle appeared. "Why did you open the damn door?" she said to Jane.

"Your father called and wants you to come home to be with Susie. He took your mother to the hospital."

Michelle's anger suddenly deflated. "Oh. What's the matter with her?"

"He didn't say."

Michelle hurried home and they never spoke of it again. Her mother had her gall bladder out and was soon home, as good as new.

One day Ron Woodson asked Jane to go to the movies with him. He placed his hand over hers but nothing more. After the movie they talked for a long time. He was a quiet, scholarly type and had many of the same interests. He asked her out again and they often went together to school activities. He was always gentlemanly and never went further than a small kiss on the cheek as he said goodnight. They became an item in the view of others and one of Jane's friends said, "I'm glad you finally found someone to date. Ron is a nice, smart guy, even if not too exciting."

Ron asked Jane to the Christmas dance at school. While they were talking he said, "Jane, you are probably not going to like me anymore but I have to talk to you."

"Of course I'll like you. What is it?"

"I think maybe I'm gay. I just can't think of having sex with girls. I don't really know any boys I'd like but maybe sometime."

"Oh Ron. You don't know how relieved I am. I've lain awake at night, wondering what I would do if you insisted on sex. I couldn't face it but I don't want to lose your friendship."

"You don't care?"

"No. I went to find Michelle when her mother was sick and found her having sex with Mike. His huge, naked body was awful. I went to the bathroom and was sick to my stomach."

"Do you like girls?"

"Not that way. Can we just stay friends like we've been?"

"That's what I've been hoping for. It would make me very happy."

One evening Ron was picking Jane up for a school party. As she walked toward him, he held up his hand, halting her. "You've rounded a little."

"You mean I've gained weight."

"Not at all. You've lost that gangly presentation so many high school girls have. You are an attractive woman."

"I don't think so."

"Jane, many men are going to compliment you, in hopes of getting you in bed. We settled that long ago and I think I can be objective. You have a pretty face, set off by the elfin cut to your glossy brown hair. Your eyes project honesty and interest. Your smile is charming. Your breasts have filled a little, giving you a fine figure, enhanced by your good posture. Yes, a most attractive woman."

"I don't know what to say. I don't think of myself that way."

"Just say, 'thank you.' It is rude to contradict some one and say you aren't. On the other hand, you don't want to seem self satisfied. Thank you just says you appreciate his opinion and essentially closes the subject."

"Where did you learn all this?"

"Here and there. I've read a lot of psychology."

They continued the friendship through the last year of high school. Some of the other kids tried to find out how far they were going on dates but neither would talk and the curious just gave up. Ron won a prize for some poetry while Jane's science fair article, "Early endoscopy: Removing the brain of Egyptian mummies via the nose" won the prize for the most original article. Each took pride in the other's achievement and reinforced their friendship.

Her last year in high school, Jane applied to several colleges. She thought she would like to live in New York City and applied to several colleges there but also to Cornell, Yale, and Princeton. She was accepted everywhere but Princeton and was offered a partial scholarship to Columbia, which she accepted. She graduated from high school with honors and spent the summer as a volunteer page in the local newspaper. In the fall, she moved to New York and into student housing connected with Columbia. She signed up for a major in biology with a minor in broadcast journalism.

She met Jack Harwell in one of her classes. He was a large young man who wanted to be a football star but wasn't quite up to the practice and work it took. She dated him a couple times and one day he invited her to come to the frat house to study with a couple others from the class. When she arrived, he took her into a small sitting room and shut the door. "Where are Tim and Claudio?" she asked.

"They aren't coming. It's just you and me." He pulled her to him and started kissing her.

"I think I'd better go."

"I think you'd better stay. We can have some real fun." Again he pulled her to him. She pushed him away but he pulled her close again. She slapped him in the face.

"You shouldn't have done that. Now I'm going to put you in your place, you teasing bitch." And he hit her on the side of the face so hard her ear was ringing. He pushed her down and the couch and started pulling off her sweater.

Two young men opened the door and walked in. "Oh, excuse us," one said and they started out.

"Don't leave. Would you please take me to my dorm?" Jane asked. One young man looked at Jack with distaste.

"It seems the lady isn't as interested as you are. Of course we will take you home. Let her up."

Jack looked at them furiously. The second man was as large as he was and seemed to be completely in agreement with the speaker. Jack slowly moved away from Jane and she got up, pulled her sweater down, and walked to the other men. "Thank you." And she started for the door.

Outside the frat house, she said, "He said there would be two others from our class and we were going to have a study session. I'm certainly glad you came in."

"I'm glad too. He should be kicked out of the college. I'm Henry Cantor."

"And I'm John Ulrich," the previously silent one said.

"It's a pleasure to meet you both."

The next Monday, Jane signed up for a class in martial arts. After two weeks she found there was a woman's group, including a number of women in law enforcement, specifically teaching women self defense. She transferred to this and developed considerable skill. One of the lady cops asked her, "Why are you doing this? I work with scum bags all the time and need protection."

"I found there are scum bags in the classes in college and I need the protection too."

She now felt more confident dating. She dated several young men who turned out to having nothing in common with her and it ended very quickly. Tim Henderson, a quiet dark complexioned young man in her basic English class asked her to the movies. The next week they went to a dance. After the dance, he put his hand on her breast. "I don't do that," She said and pulled it off. He put it back and pulled her to him, trying to kiss her. She jammed her knee into his crotch. As he exhaled in agony and bent forward, she kicked him in the knee cap. He lost his balance and as he fell she slammed the edge of her hand into his neck. She looked at him writhing on the ground. "Bastard," she said and walked off.

Jane was very pleased with how well her training actually worked. She told her cop friend, Maria Duarte, about it at the next class. "Good for you. If you have on heavy shoes, kick him while he's down."

She had found the response to Tim very satisfying and did the same to a couple other boys who pushed her too hard. One told her later, "I'm sorry. I would have backed off if you had said something. You're pretty eager to hurt someone, aren't you?" She realized that she really did enjoy putting the men down.

One day in her second year, one of her professors approached her. "One of the TV stations is looking for a young person with science experience to do some brief interviews with scientists for a youth program on vocational choices. I think you would be ideal. May I request an interview for you?"

"Thank you, sir. I never thought of such a thing but it sounds interesting. Why not try?"

A few days later she was at one of the local TV stations. They called her into the interview room where she found a young man and an older woman. The woman spoke, "I'm Gloria Laktis, director of personnel and this is Tim Johnson, producer for special programming." They both shook hands with her. "Tell us about your school work."

Jane told them about her science courses and that she had also taken classes in journalism. Tim spoke, "I want you to interview Gloria briefly. Find out what is interesting in what she does."

Jane started, "In personnel you have the chance to meet lots of people. Which do you find more memorable: the good ones that you hire or the ones who have problems that preclude hiring?"

"An interesting question. I think maybe the ones we don't hire. The others have what I expect them to but one finds all sorts of interesting but often negative things in the others."

"Is the paper work just dull or are you able to picture the people from their records and think about the individuals?"

"Often I think of the people as I do their paperwork. I will sometimes have insights into feelings I had that something was wrong but I couldn't place. And I get ideas about how to have them do a better job."

Tim spoke again, "Those are good questions and not the usual type. I'm impressed. We do have a couple other people to meet and I'll give you a call in a couple days. Thank you so much for coming."

Jane went home pleased with his comments but waiting impatiently for the call.

She was chosen and turned out to have a knack for interviewing others. She picked various professors at the school, representing physics, chemistry, and biological science. The programs were so enthusiastically accepted that she branched out to an award winning microbiologist at Cornell medical school and an Egyptologist at New York University. She found the contact with these successful people very stimulating and was now sure that she wanted a career in broadcast journalism.

One day Jane was called to the personnel office of the TV station. She wondered if she was going to be taken off the vocational project. Had she done all the areas that could be offered? The director of programming said to her, "We would like you to become a part time member of the station's regular staff while you finish college."

Jane was thrilled and immediately accepted. "I would love to. It is a fine place to work and I find the work challenging and enjoyable." It did prolong her college time for a semester. She developed quite a reputation for her science interviews and was offered a job working for the network as well as with the station.

One of the station news anchors invited Jane to a media party. He was an attractive man in his late thirties and had a huge ego. Jane felt honored to be noticed by him but after the party he drove her to his apartment. "Come in for a drink. I've invited several others over."

In the apartment he offered her a drink. She was only twenty and didn't approve of illegal drinking. "Only a coke, please."

He sneered as he gave her a coke. "Haven't you grown up yet?"

"No. I'm still a student and don't feel a full adult. Who else is coming?"

"No one. Just you and me for some fun together."

"I'm going home."

"We are going to the bedroom. After that you can go home or wherever you want—to hell, maybe?"

"I'm leaving." And she started for the door.

"Not now you aren't." He grabbed her by the arm and pulled her to him.

She kneed him in the groin, grabbed his arm and twisted it back until he was down on his knees. She pushed him forward and he fell to the floor.

She kicked him in the nose and as the blood gushed into the carpet, she walked out. "I'll sue you," he screamed as she slammed the door.

He did file a complaint and a detective came to interview her at the TV station. She told him the story and that she had had training with Maria Duarte in self protection. He threw back his head and laughed loudly. "Maria is good at that stuff. I'm glad you knew how to do it. No court in this country would do anything but congratulate you. Forget about it."

A couple days after her twenty first birthday, she decided to go to a bar and see what people liked so much. She ordered a Martini but found it burned her throat and didn't drink much. A pleasant young man next to her at the bar started a conversation. She talked to him a couple minutes and then decided to go home. He followed her out and took her arm. "Let's go to my place."

"I'm not interested. Let go of me and go on about your business."

"I'm interested. Come with me." He pulled her along.

"I will not go to your place or anywhere else with you. Now let me go."

He pulled a small knife out of his pocket. "You are coming or I'm going to ruin you looks."

She hit the arm with the knife with the back of her hand as she kicked him in the shins. He looked startled and then gasped with pain. She elbowed him in the solar plexus, and hit him in the back of the neck as he bent over. After he fell to the ground, she kicked him in the ribs and then in the face. She picked up the knife. "I could cut your balls off but I hope you have learned a lesson." She threw the knife in his face and walked off.

The next day she began to wonder. "Am I becoming addicted to beating up men? Does it satisfy something in my psyche?" She decided to avoid getting involved with this type of man in the future.

Shortly before she graduated she was asked to come to the biology office. The secretary took her into the department head. "I'm Paul Hellman, head of biology." He offered his hand.

"Yes, sir. It's good to meet you. Of course I know the name and position."

"The department looks with favor on the work you have done in your courses and in the research project you undertook. We would like to offer you a fellowship for graduate study. It would pay most of your expenses and would only require that you spend two afternoons working in the lab of the introductory biology class. You can take further courses and become involved in research of your choice."

"I'm honored, Dr. Hellman. I would find it very interesting. I think I will be offered a full time job in broadcast journalism and I will consider both. May I postpone an answer until next week?"

"Of course. That's an interesting contrast with your work in science."

"They do go together. I've been working part time, doing interviews with scientists to give ordinary people a little picture of what you do."

"I didn't realize that. Certainly that is a useful function too. Let us know what you decide."

The next day she was at the network offices and went to the producer of the programs she had done. "Mr. Coffey, I don't want to seem pushy but I've been told I would probably get a full time job offer from the network. I've been offered a very favorable graduate fellowship so I don't want to turn it down and not have a job. Is it possible to find out the plans for me?"

"That's a reasonable request. I certainly hope they plan to keep you on. Let me do some checking."

"Thank you very much."

Two days later she received a call from the personnel office at the network. "We are offering you full time employment in your present position, with a 10 % increase in your hourly rate over your present pay. It will include full pension and health benefits."

"I accept. Will you forward the contract?"

"If you could come in and sign it, we would like to go over the benefits and the withholding with you."

"I'll be in tomorrow."

After signing the contract, she went to the biology department at the school. She told the department secretary, "Will you please thank Dr. Hellman for me and tell him I am unable to take the fellowship?"

"Wait a moment. I'll tell him now." She went to the chairman's door and in a moment Dr. Hellman came out. "I'm sorry you can't be with us. Let me know when you are doing a program on biology. I would like to watch. Good luck to you and let me know if the department can help you."

"Thank you very much, sir. I will keep you informed about programs. It is very good of you to be so accepting."

"Good luck." He said again and went back to his office.

Chapter 10

Palmer was just turning base leg for a landing at El Monte airport when his phone rang. He went on and landed and when the plane had slowed enough, he pulled off the runway onto a parking area. He looked at the phone and saw his office number. He called it, "Sylvia, it's Carson."

"Lieutenant, the coroner's office just called. They had another autopsy that might be related to your case. He suggests you talk to Detective Acker at Pomona PD." She gave him the number and he punched it in.

"Acker."

"This is Lieutenant Carson from Pasadena PD. The coroner tells me you have a case that might fit with one of ours. Could we get together?"

"Sure. I'm free now. Where could we meet?"

"Twenty minutes at the restaurant at Brackett Field?"

"That'll be fine with me. See you."

Carson called the El Monte Ground on the aircraft radio. "Cessna 4762Kilo at parking. Taxi for take off."

"Taxi to runway one niner."

As Carson reached the beginning of the runway, he changed to tower frequency. "Cessna 4762Kilo. Ready for takeoff. I'd like a left turn departure for Brackett."

"62Kilo cleared for takeoff. Left turn approved at the freeway."

"62Kilo rolling."

It's only a few miles to Brackett by air and after getting the Brackett weather, he called the Brackett tower. "4762Kilo four miles east for landing with Zulu."

"62Kilo cleared to land on runway 26 left. Make left traffic."

Palmer repeated the instructions and landed on the left runway.

"Destination?" the tower asked.

"62Kilo for transient parking."

"Taxi to transient this frequency."

He parked, shut down the plane and hooked chains onto the wings in case of gusty wind.

Detective Acker was standing in the waiting room at the little terminal. He was thinking to himself, "I wonder where he was that he thinks he can get from Pasadena to here in 20 minutes." He saw a nice looking, well postured man walk in, wearing jeans, a flannel shirt and a baseball cap saying, "USS Pasadena, SSN752."

He questioningly said, "Lieutenant Carson?"

The lieutenant held out his hand, "I'm Palmer."

"Tom Acker. I'm a sergeant and do the homicides. Our department is small enough so I do other things also."

"We have the same situation. I'm called homicide detective and I have a sergeant and a detective but we do most of the detective work except for vice."

They walked up to the little restaurant. "Shall we sit outside?" Palmer asked.

"Fine with me."

They ordered coffee and Palmer said, "I didn't get breakfast. I'll have some eggs and toast. You want anything?"

"Coffee's fine. Where were you to get here so fast?"

"I was just off the runway at El Monte."

"You flew out? Police plane?"

"Yes, I flew. Not a police plane. I'm just working on a license and was practicing on some comp time."

"How about the hat?"

"The Navy named a sub after Pasadena so of course we adopted it. It was in San Pedro and we had most of the crew up to Pasadena for dinner and I coordinated the transport. The ship's crew gave me the cap."

"You had a hotel murder?"

"Gal went up to his room with a guy from a convention. Doing fellatio on him and almost bit his penis off. When he bent forward, she stuck a blade in his chest and cut his heart open. We have almost nothing on her."

"Ours started the same. He was on her and she shoved a blade in his ear and scrambled his brains. Afterwards she cut his prick off. It was huge— the biggest I've ever seen. And if you want to know about my data base,

I've seen a lot. I was a medic in the Army for a couple years. The only information we have was from the bartender. He remembers a female trolling the room. Shiny blond hair, bright blue eyes, and a very short skirt. We're still working on people who were at the hotel but I'm not optimistic."

"Ours had striking black hair and a short skirt. The hair turned out to be a wig from the hairs we found at the scene. I bet yours is too. With the unusual hair and the short skirt no one looks at her face enough to remember it."

"The coroner thought the blade was very similar in the two cases and is unusual. It sounds to me like we are chasing the same person."

"I agree. We got a little description from someone who saw them on the elevator but she really couldn't come up with a picture. The short skirt and shining hair are too much. I'll bet the bright blue eyes are contact lenses too. Our witness didn't notice them so she probably added them. No fingerprints or other evidence so she seems to have some forensic knowledge."

"The coroner feels after two cases that she has some knowledge of anatomy."

"That cuts the possibilities from 50% of the population of LA County to 5%. Still a hell of a lot of people."

"Let's keep in touch if we find anything and talk in a day or so anyway."

"Good idea. Maybe we should set up a joint task force of all working on it and get together for information exchange and sharing ideas. I must admit I don't have many to share right now. And I think we should send an all departments note to every department in the county to let me know if they have a hotel murder."

"Yeah. Why don't you do that as you have more rank than I do. You might send it to San Bernardino County departments too as we are right on the edge of that county."

They shook hands and Porter went back to his airplane. After starting he asked ground control for taxi permission. At the runway, the tower cleared him for take off. He knew the way to El Monte very well and was flying almost subconsciously. He was thinking about the murder in Pomona and suddenly realized he was about to pass El Monte airport. "I've learned one thing today. I've got to concentrate on my flying. It isn't safe to try to solve cases when I'm in the air." He called the El Monte tower and landed.

When the plane was parked he went to his car and then allowed himself to start thinking about the case. "The Pomona case certainly seemed to have the same perpetrator. Is this the start of a serial killing spree? I was worried about that possibility. I wish we had something but we'll just have to wait." He went home, changed clothes and drove down to the police department.

Chapter 11

She stood in front of her mirror. What would she be tonight? The blonde or the black wig. She picked the blonde one and put it on. She dressed in her usual short skirt and blouse and picked up the tote bag. She checked to see that she had everything. The door keys and driver's license would stay in the car. Her wallet had a little money but no ID. The car keys would go in the tote bag. The knife was in place. She locked the door and walked to the car.

Tonight she would try the Westin—the old Doubletree from when she had known Pasadena. She found parking on the street a block north. Slowly she walked down the street to the hotel and then into the bar. She found a small table and sat down. When the waiter appeared he said, "May I help you, miss?"

"Let me have a Martini with lots of ice."

When it arrived, she smiled at the waiter and then sipped slowly. She watched the people as the bar gradually filled. A young man stopped at her table. "Would you mind sharing the table, miss? There aren't any empties."

"Of course, sit down."

He was a tall, slender man in his early twenties. He wore black rimmed glasses and his sandy hair needed cutting. He had on a sport shirt and slacks rather than the dressier clothes that people at conventions usually wore. "Do you live locally?" she asked him.

"Yes. I'm a grad student at Caltech and work part time at the Jet Propulsion Laboratory. My work there will be my thesis topic for my doctorate. Incidentally, my name is Homer. "

"Good to meet you, Homer. I'm Rachael. You must work very hard with all that."

"I do. I rarely drink but I had an important test today and did very well. I felt that entitled me to an hour of relaxation.'

"Congratulations. What is your field?"

"I'm in chemical engineering but I'm working in a broader field. My project is for a new mechanism of transfer of fuel within rocket engines. It will allow more efficiency and thus require less fuel and allow a larger payload for the rocket."

"Would this be for space flight or more for military type rockets?"

"It would apply to either. Of course, there would be modifications depending on the size of the rocket and the operating altitude but those are easy to make once the basic mechanism is accepted."

"So this work is for JPL but you can also write it up for your thesis. Is that a common way of doing your research?"

"Very much. A lot of Caltech students work at JPL and apply their work to their studies. Since Caltech operates JPL, it makes for easy transitions."

This polite, earnest, hard-working young man was not the type she was looking for and she needed someone who was staying at the hotel but she was not one to waste an encounter. Who knew when a knowledge of rocket research might come in useful? She might even do a program on the subject. "Tell me how rocket engines work so that the fuel flow makes so much difference in efficiency."

Ten minutes later she had a fair knowledge of the workings of rocket engines. "My, you are a good listener and you understand very quickly. Have you had scientific training?"

"I have a degree in biology and did some research work but now I teach high school. I hope I can stimulate young people to be interested in science."

"That's great. One teacher can make all the difference. I had a teacher in freshman physics who changed my interests and inspired me to do well in school. Without him, I probably would be nothing special. A college degree but nothing learned that would be of value to me or to the world."

"I'm glad to hear that story. It makes me more hopeful that I do make a difference to some of the kids."

"I'm sure you do. I thank you for sharing your table and for listening to me. I think I must get back home and to work now. Please excuse me."

"It's been a pleasure to meet you. Good luck on your degree."

"Thank you. Good night." He walked out of the bar.

She ordered another drink and sat quietly for some time. She was musing on the workings of rocket engines when a man spoke to her. "Excuse me, miss, the room is full. Would you mind sharing your table for a few minutes?" She looked up to see a heavy set man appearing to be in the early forties. He had dark brown hair and a mustache that was beginning to show gray. She thought irrelevantly, "Why when the mustache grays before the hair don't men shave it off?" He was accompanied by a small woman in her thirties. Both were conservatively dressed."

"Not at all. Sit down. I'm Rachael."

"I'm Justin and this is Marina. We are at a conference on William Morris at the Huntington Library."

"Morris the English designer?"

"Yes. I'm glad you have heard of him. Many haven't. He was really a remarkable man. Did almost everything. When he published a book, he set up an in house press so he could control the font, the paper, everything."

"Do you work at the Huntington?"

"No. I teach English history of that period at Princeton. Marina teaches at the Art Center School of design here in Pasadena and she has been showing me Pasadena. Are you local?"

"I grew up in Pasadena but now live in northern California and teach high school biology. We used to go to the Huntington when I was a kid but it has been a lot of years."

"You should go again," Marina said. "It keeps adding galleries and new acquisitions. It's a remarkable place."

"Tell me more about Morris."

They had both learned a lot about him in the conference that day and were only too happy to recount much of it. "This is obviously an evening for learning rather than action." she said to herself.

Soon it was past ten thirty. "The conference is coordinated with an exhibit the Huntington has on the work of Morris. You really should go and see that while it's on," Marina suggested.

Justin thoughtfully looked at his watch. "Oh, my. Look at the time. The conference starts early tomorrow. I think we should really call it a day."

"It's time for me to go too." They paid their bills and walked out together.

"Goodnight. Thanks for educating me about Morris. It was very interesting."

"It was a pleasure to be with someone who has an interest. Good night."

She walked up the street, climbed into her car, and drove to the motel.

Last night had reminded her that in spite of her compulsive mission, she could have some vacation time too. She ate cereal and a Danish at the motel, read the paper and then prepared to go out. She dressed conservatively and fluffed her light brown hair. She packed her tote bag and went out to the car. She drove on the freeway to La Canada and took the off ramp to JPL. She couldn't go in without a pass but she could see the buildings against the foothills. She drove up to the gate, turned around and then went back to Pasadena by surface roads. She drove by the mortuary. It was now the home of a private nursery school and she didn't stop.

The street also took her by the Valentine Mortuary. It was still in operation. She wondered if the Valentine's were still there or if another generation had taken it over. She had stayed with the Valentines for a week end when Fred had gone to Sacramento for a meeting. Mrs. Valentine was a lovely lady who wrote poetry along with raising her family. She would like to have stopped but not this time. She drove on past the Caltech campus and out to the Huntington Library. She parked and walked to the entry and paid her admission fee.

Fred had taken her to the Huntington several times. They had seen the exhibit on George Washington and she remembered one on Audubon's birds. The size of the bird pictures was enormous for a book. She walked through the library exhibit. One Audubon picture was still on display. Seeing the Gutenberg bible, she remembered how Fred had used that to teach her the importance of the development of moveable type in printing to the spread of literacy. She gazed in awe at the illuminated paintings in medieval books. Fred had used these to tell her how knowledge had been preserved by monks making hand copies of books.

She went to the little tearoom by the rose garden and had lunch. Then she went to the old Huntington mansion, now the art gallery. On the upper level, was the temporary Morris exhibit. Here she was thrilled by one of his designs. She had taken up needle-point to pass the time while waiting in airports and one of her favorites had been called the strawberry thief—a bird with strawberries. She hadn't known where the design came from but here it was. Morris had used it in decoration and even in wall paper.

Finally she was back at the motel and rested a few minutes to prepare for the evening.

Chapter 12

The first meeting of the joint task force of Pasadena and Pomona was held at the Pasadena Police Department. Prior to the meeting, Carson called Sergeant Ridley. "How's work on the fire going?"

"I'm coming slowly. I've talked a little to the victim but he was sedated. I have to go back and I'm working on his finances and family."

"The joint task force is meeting this afternoon. Do you think you could take a half hour away from the fire and present our findings, since you did so much of the work?"

"Sure. I can do that. I'd like to keep in touch with that case since it's so unusual."

"Good. See you there."

Lieutenant Carson, Sergeant Ridley, and technician Hoffman represented the host department. Sgt. Acker wanted to take Detective Finley but Sergeant Diehl, the head of special services, had gone to the Chief and suggested that he be the other representative. Lieutenant Carson opened the meeting. "Would you like to start off, Sergeant Acker?"

"Sure." He proceeded to summarize their findings.

"I'd like to add something," Sergeant Diehl spoke up. He spoke several minutes on the possible role of special services if they had a barricaded suspect.

"I'm not sure this is relevant until we have some chance of finding the suspect," Lieutenant Carson said. "Sergeant Ridley will summarize our findings."

Diehl interrupted several times with questions such as, "What type of fingerprint save was done."

"Our technical people know the best ways and I don't ask them how they did it," Carson said, exasperated.

They discussed future plans but no one had a new idea: just keep up regular detective work. The meeting broke up with a plan to meet again in two days.

Sergeant Acker came up to the lieutenant after the others had gone. "Sorry. I wanted to bring a bright young detective named Finley but Diehl convinced the Chief that he could represent the department better as he is senior to me. Should I try to go to our Chief and see if I can get him off?"

"It isn't your fault. And I don't want you to make trouble in your department. Leave it to me. I think I can generate some real horsepower in our department to present to your Chief.

Lieutenant Carson went to Captain Crane. He was the titular head of detectives, among other services, though he left running detectives to the Lieutenant. After being told of the problem, Crane said, "I think you should go direct to our Chief. Tell him I told you to do so and give him the story."

The Chief saw Carson immediately. "Are you having any luck with the sex murder? What can I do for you?"

"Very little progress, sir. She has been very careful not to leave us any clues. Have you heard about the sex murder that Pomona has?"

"Yes, but not much."

"The coroner thinks the same knife was used, I talked with the detective sergeant handling the case for Pomona and we have set up a joint task force with them to exchange information."

"Good idea. I'm glad you will take responsibility for something like that."

"My problem is that one of their senior sergeants, who knows nothing of the case, had the Chief make him a representative of their department. He is very disruptive, asking irrelevant questions and giving little speeches about his possible involvement."

"What's his name?"

"Diehl, sir."

"He won't be there next meeting. Keep up the good work."

Carson got up and left with a "Thank you, sir."

First thing the next morning, Carson had a call from Sergeant Acker. "Boy did you do it. Thanks."

"It worked out OK and you didn't get involved?"

"Yes and no. Diehl asked me yesterday morning if we were meeting with you today and I said, 'No. tomorrow.' After lunch he came over looking like a thundercloud. Said to me, 'Something's come up and I can't go tomorrow. I guess you'll have to take Finley.' The chief must have been really firm about it."

"That's great. We'll look forward to meeting Finley. You want us to come out there this afternoon?"

"Sure. Can you fly into Brackett again?"

"No. I can't carry passengers yet. I have my flight exam scheduled for this week end and after that I can take someone, if I pass. We'll have to drive. Shall we meet at your department?"

"It's a long way from the freeway for you. Why don't we meet at Brackett anyway? That's a nice little café and we can sit outside if the weather is good."

"Done. We'll be there at three. Incidentally, I'm not going to bring the lab man this time. He hasn't anything more to offer. We have a young lady patrol officer who was first on the scene and has been helping a little. Maybe I'll let her come and give her a thrill. She really gets excited by detective work. I won't let her pull a Diehl."

"Whatever works for you. We'll see you at three."

The Pasadena group arrived a few minutes early. Porter had Flores drive, thinking a marked patrol car would make the freeway a little more comfortable. As usual the traffic avoided the police car like the plague, not distinguishing between the Pasadena car and a Highway Patrol car.

Porter led the others to the porch on the little restaurant at the airport. Several tables were on the porch, where they overlooked the runway and they sat at the largest. It was only three minutes until Sergeant Acker came with Detective Finley. Finley and Flores were introduced to the others and Finley quickly grabbed a seat beside Flores.

"A pleasure to meet you. Are you working detectives in uniform?"

"No. I'm just a patrol officer. I was first on the scene at our killing and the lieutenant has let me help some. He's a great guy to work with."

The waitress appeared and asked, "What will you have? Do you want to see the menu?"

"No," Porter responded. "I think just coffee. Anyone not want coffee?"

Flores asked, "Could I have a diet coke?"

Acker said, "I didn't have lunch. Bring me a hamburger, please."

She brought the drinks immediately and said to Acker, "It'll be a couple minutes on the hamburger."

"That's fine."

Porter said, "We don't have a great deal to offer. We have pretty well set the time when he met her but that doesn't help much."

Acker turned to Finley. "Why don't you tell them what we know. I'm waiting for that burger."

"The bartender did remember the girl a little. Striking blonde hair and you were right. There were a few blonde hairs in the room and the lab people say they are from a wig. The other things he noted were the short skirt and the striking blue eyes."

"I bet those turn out to be contact lenses," Ridley offered.

"She has planned it well to make those things that can be falsified the most noticeable. We'll never get a description of her facial details. And the short skirt makes the judgment of her height difficult," Porter said.

Finley continued. "The most interesting thing for us has been the identity of the victim. He registered at the hotel as part of the convention but wasn't registered at the convention. He is however a registered sex offender on parole. We think he uses conventions as a cover for finding women. We have notified all area departments of his modus operandi and that we have his DNA. We already have requests from two departments for his DNA pattern and more details. It isn't going to help this case, but may solve a number of unsolved rape cases."

"That is interesting. Keep us informed. I'm afraid that won't help us find his killer, though it may make us a bit more sympathetic toward her," Porter said. "We are going to have a detective wandering around the bars at convention hotels in case she plans another assault."

Acker ate the last of his hamburger. "Now I feel more like facing crime. We'll all continue to work on this. Shall we meet after the week-end again? Do you want to wait until we have more information?"

Porter responded. "I think it is helpful to meet, even if we haven't uncovered any new material. It helps to know that we are all in this together and someone may come up with a brilliant idea. At our department meeting room on Tuesday at three thirty OK?"

"We'll be there. I'll try to get lunch first," Acker said.

As they walked out, Finley walked beside Flores. "Could we meet for a drink this week-end some time?"

"I work Saturday. I could Sunday late afternoon if you like. My phone is 795-3413. Give me a call Sunday if you still want to. I should be home from church a little after noon."

"I'll call you then. Thanks."

As they started back to Pasadena, Carson said, "Flores, I think you made an impression on detective Finley."

"Yes, sir, I think so. He already asked me for a date this week-end."

"You going with him on short acquaintance?"

"In a public place. Police officers are safe aren't they?"

"Maybe Ridley can tell us."

"Horniest bastards around. Don't trust one for a minute."

"My, Sergeant Ridley. You shouldn't pull your punches for this poor girl."

The subject was dropped and they discussed the case, wondering if there were any cases in Pasadena files that could be attributed to the latest victim.

Early Sunday afternoon Flores' phone rang. "Maria Flores," she answered.

"This is Frank Finley. You still willing to get together?"

"That would be nice. Where shall we meet?"

"Do you want me to pick you up?"

"It's a long way. Why don't we meet in between somewhere? There's a little bar and restaurant just off the 210 freeway on Myrtle in Monrovia that's nice and not too noisy."

"That sounds good. You have to work tomorrow?"

"I'm afraid so. I'm sure you do so let's make it an early evening."

"OK. I'll meet you there at six."

"I'll be there."

Finley was early and found a relatively quiet, secluded table. He watched the door and stood when Flores entered. She went over to the table. "Good evening, Maria."

She smiled and sat down. "Good to see you again."

"You know I didn't know your first name until you answered the phone. The lieutenant always just called you Flores."

"He's very professional. But your first name didn't come up either. Does your middle name start with an F also?"

"No. My parents weren't quite that single minded. My middle name is Randall. It's an old family name of my maternal grandmother."

"Where did your family come from?"

"If you mean recently, we moved to California from Ohio when I was six years old. Further back, we are English on both sides. I've checked a little and found the name of the village that most of them came from. Some day I'd like to visit that part of England and see if I can find some distant cousins. How about your family?"

"It's odd. People ask if I came from Mexico but my family was in California when the first Americans came. My great, great grandfather was a foreman at the Mission in Ventura."

"Do you speak Spanish?"

"Not too well. The family rarely uses it but I did take it in school and can get along with questioning non-English speakers. So many people think that all Hispanic named Americans can speak Spanish. Most of my friends with Hispanic names don't speak any."

"That is interesting. We do tend to lump them all together and wonder if they are legal or not."

"How did you become a cop?"

"I grew up in Whittier and went to Rio Hondo College. As you probably know, criminal justice is one of its specialties. I took those courses and then went to the Rio Hondo police academy. When I graduated, Pomona was interviewing and I went with them. I worked a patrol car for four years and continued to take courses at Rio Hondo. When a detective opening came up I had already had most of the training so I got the promotion. How about you?"

"I finished an AA at Pasadena City College with courses in sociology as well as a couple criminal justice courses. I didn't know where to go next and saw that Pasadena was hiring. I applied and they sent me to Rio Hondo. They used to have their own academy but it got too complicated and expensive and now they use Rio Hondo. I've been working patrol for just over two years but I would like to be a detective. I think you met Sergeant Ridley. She is my ideal of a police officer. She's young enough to be approachable and is always helpful."

"If you solve this case, it ought to get you a promotion."

"I don't know how to go about that. The girl seems to know all the angles and doesn't leave any clues."

"She is a smart operator. I bet we have another killing before the week is out."

"Do you think so?"

"Once a serial killer gets started they tend to form a pattern. I don't know how we can prevent it but just hope she slips and leaves us something to work with. Tomorrow however, I'm going to start working on possible cases involving the victim of our killing."

"He sounds like a real mean guy."

"That isn't the half of it. I'll bring his rap sheet to the next task force meeting and show you. He has a terrible record and he was huge. The coroner measured him at six foot four and two hundred ninety pounds. He was all muscle. I would hate to have to deal with him and it's amazing that our suspect didn't get hurt badly."

They ordered another drink and had some hors d'ouvers and continued to talk. Flores looked at her watch. "Oh my gosh. Where did the time go. It's past ten and we both have to work. We'd better get home."

"I enjoyed it so much I had no idea it was getting so late. Can we do it again?"

"I'd like that. Give me a call."

They walked out together and he walked her to her car. He gave her shoulders a squeeze and held her door. "Goodnight. I'll call you in a couple days."

"Goodnight, Frank."

Chapter 13

Jane had worked on a number of projects around the United States and was praised for her high quality reports. She decided that she might branch out and have a new experience at the same time. She had heard from one of the scientists that she had interviewed that there was to be an international conference on the future of supersonic transport aircraft, to be held at the University of Bologna in Italy.

She felt this might be of enough general interest to merit reporting. She pulled up the sponsoring organization on the internet and found the topic of the conference and the schedule of speakers. After printing this out, she called a professor at MIT who she had interviewed. "Dr. Miller, this is Jane Norton. I'd like to ask a favor."

"Sure. Anything within reason. You did a nice job on editing my interview and managed to make me sound quite intelligent. I appreciate it."

"It wasn't hard to make you seem intelligent. I just had to show the real you. I have a group of names of presenters at a conference and I'd like to know something about them. Particularly if their work is important and good quality and if they would interview well."

"I'll tell you what I can. Do you have the names listed?"

"I do. I'll read about a dozen to you and you can pick out the ones you know."

She read the list of ones that were giving papers she thought of interest.

"Yes. Those are all leaders in the field and I know most of them." He proceeded to give a summary of the people and evaluated how they would come across in a brief interview.

"Thank you very much. That's exactly what I needed. I'm going to try to go to the meeting in Bologna and do some interviews. You've been a big help."

"Glad to anytime. There are two of them that I feel comfortable having you use my name in meeting, if you want."

"That would be great."

He gave her the names and said good-by. She wrote up a proposal to go to the conference and report on it. She would include interviews with several well known figures, including an ex-astronaut who was now doing supersonic research with Lockheed-Martin. She also included some extra time to pursue possible contacts in the Vatican in Rome.

The idea appealed to the network management and they asked her to come in to discuss the project with the programming manager. She had met him before and he had always seemed pleasant and interested in her work.

"Have you ever traveled overseas?" he asked.

"No. But I've done a lot in this country. I don't have any worries about the trip. I'll make arrangements for someone who speaks English to get me started."

"Actually, we have an office in Rome with both American and Italian bilingual workers. They can certainly translate for you. How do you feel interviews would work out with translation?"

"Well, many of the scientists and engineers at the conference will be American and most of the ones from other countries speak some English so much of the conference will be in English. In addition, most of the ones I want to specifically interview are American, with one important Brit."

"That certainly makes it more workable. I'm impressed with your grasp of the potential of the various scientists. Most reporters give the names but go on fame rather than the actual material they might obtain. I'm happy with the arrangements for that part. Now what about the Vatican possibility?"

"There has been so much talk recently about the role of women in the church that I thought something could be made of it. I'm not sure how hard it will be to get anyone to talk. And to be perfectly honest with you I want a chance to see Rome."

"I'm glad you admitted that. I would want to do that too. I don't see why we can't let you have some tourist time and if you get a couple of interviews on attitude toward women in the church, that should justify the time. You could even interview your tour guide in Rome. I'm going to approve the application and I don't think there will be any problem at other offices. When would you be going?"

"The conference starts the 26th of next month. That will be six weeks from now. I'd like to get there a day or so ahead so I can be familiar with the surroundings and ready to go when they open."

"Good. Everything should be arranged by the end of this month. You can continue with the job you are doing now but take enough time to get ready properly. Any reasonable draw for the money you need can be handled by the office in Rome. I'll see that you are placed in contact with them."

"Thank you very much."

They rose together and he said, "Do enjoy Italy as well as doing the job."

"Thank you again. I'll report on the results."

Time passed too rapidly. Jane met with several people to get details of transportation, how to handle getting Italian euros, and other details. She talked on the phone with the Rome office and followed up with e-mails making arrangements for her time there. In no time at all she was on the Alitalia jet out of JFK airport.

Her seatmate, Rosa, was an Italian lady who had married an American. She was returning to Italy for her mother's seventieth birthday. She loved her home country and was happy to talk about it to Jane. "Rome is so historic. Even though it's touristy, you must see the Coliseum and the Roman forum. And walk on the Via Veneto. The shops are unbelievable. Cars are now forbidden in old downtown Rome and it is a great place to walk."

"Do you know Bologna?"

"Not so well. I've visited there briefly. The university is quite an important one. Is that where your meeting is going to be held?"

"It is. I don't know more than that but it shouldn't be hard to find it."

"It's not as big a city as Rome or Milan. You should be able to get around it without trouble. I really don't know what to see there."

"That won't matter as I'll be working most of the time there. My sight-seeing will be in Rome."

"That's a good choice."

Jane told her about the possibility of some interviews in Rome and Rosa told her, "The priest at one of the small churches was a friend of mine in school. I'm sure you could get him to help you with what you need." She gave Jane the name and address.

When the attendant got ready to serve dinner, Jane took a relaxing pill and after dinner was able to sleep much of the short night on the plane. In the early morning light she was able to see the hills of Rome as they came in to land. She was met at the airport by a young Italian lady from the network office.

"I'm Carla. We go this way to get your bag. Did you get any sleep on the flight?"

"Actually, I got over four hours so I feel pretty good."

"The time change will get to you in a few hours. We have a room for you in Bologna tonight and I'd suggest we see a little of Rome and let you meet the people from the office this morning and after lunch I'll get you on the train to Bologna and you can get a nap before you have to do anything there."

"You're very kind. I'd like to see a little and getting settled early in the hotel sounds good to me."

Carla drove her by some of the sights. She explained, "Access to the city center is very limited for vehicles. Another time we can walk and see different areas."

At the network office Jane met Luigi, the resident manager, and the American who was the second ranked in the office, John Pochard from St. Louis. They were all anxious to help and her plans were approved. John said, "It would be easier for her not to have to meet someone new in Bologna. Carla, would you be willing to go with her overnight and see that everything is set up?"

"Certainly. Should I stay the whole time?"

"I don't think you need to. Get her settled and find someone speaking English to show her anywhere necessary. Stay as long as you feel is necessary to get things working right. Is that OK with you, Jane?"

"That's fine. I'm sure I could get along but it will be a more efficient use of time if she does help me get started. I think Carla is a whiz. She organizes everything in short order."

John went with Jane and Carla to lunch at a small restaurant near the office. "How long have you been here, John?" Jane asked.

"Seven years this time. I came over for graduate school and fell in love with the country. When I went home and took the network job I volunteered to come back to Rome as soon as I had finished my probation. I started as a scut boy but have gradually worked my way up. I love living here."

"And you're a native, Carla. Where did you learn English?"

"I started with English in school but really learned to talk it when I had a two year stint in the London office. My first teacher had an American accent so the mix leaves it hard to tell which kind I speak."

After lunch, they went back to the office and picked up Jane's bag. Carla led her to a taxi. "I'll have to leave the car at the office. Even if I could keep it, there is no parking at the station."

On the train, Carla pointed out things they passed and discussed some Italian details that Jane would need to know, though now Jane's energy had waned and her head kept nodding. At the hotel when they had checked in, Carla left Jane at her room. "Take a bath and a nap and I'll pick you up about seven for dinner. I'll call fifteen minutes before to make sure you're up."

They had a leisurely dinner and talked about Italy and how Jane would do her assignment and then returned to their rooms. The next morning, after breakfast at the hotel, Carla went with Jane to find out about the conference and to locate things at the University. She then told Jane, "I found a cab driver who is trustworthy and speaks fair English. Here is his number. If you need to go somewhere, call him ahead and he'll pick you up. Some cabbies will take advantage of foreigners but he is OK."

After lunch, Carla said, "Is there anything else I can do for you?"

"I think you've done a great job of getting me up to speed. I do appreciate it."

"I'm going to take the afternoon train to Rome and leave you on your own. You have both the office number and my cell phone. If there is a problem, call me and we'll work something out. Ciao."

"Good-by and thanks," Jane called as she walked out.

Jane found a student attending the meetings who was bilingual and paid him to sit with her and to accompany her to interviews of foreign scientists. She found little need of him as most technical people spoke

English but he did help her with Italian courtesies and in learning to navigate the area. The meetings went well and Jane found a lot of material that could be newsworthy. She did several interviews but the one with the retired astronaut went particularly well. When the time ran out, he said, "I've some more things that might interest you. Could you meet me for dinner tonight?"

"That would be a pleasure."

At dinner, he talked for a time and then began to change the subject. It became apparent that he wanted her to spend a different type of time with him. "It's been very interesting," she said, "I do have another appointment."

"Are you sure you can't postpone it?"

"Definitely not."

"How about tomorrow night?"

"I'm afraid I'll be heading to Rome."

She saw another couple from the conference just getting up from a nearby table. "Let's walk back to the hotel with Dr. Henderson. I'm getting the bill."

"Of course not."

"The network has given me an expense account for just this purpose, giving meals for good interviews." She called the waiter and gave him euros for the bill with a good tip. Then they caught up with the Hendersons and went to the hotel. Jane said goodnight to the astronaut in the lobby and went to her room with a sigh of relief.

Arriving back in Rome, Jane went to her hotel and gave Carla a call. The next day they went to the church of St. Raymond and met the priest friend of her seatmate on the way over. Father Dalton was a gentle, slender man with grey hair. "Oh, I remember Rosa well. Such a slender pretty girl."

"I'm afraid she's gained a little weight since you were in school," Jane told him. He talked freely about the variations in opinion within the Catholic church on women in the priesthood, contraception, and celibacy. He suggested a couple of church figures on either side who would probably be willing to present their views to her.

Jane was able to arrange interviews over a period of a week and talked with the suggested church leaders. After a morning interview, Carla suggested they go to the market. Jane was fascinated by all the variety and color. At one table there was a display of knives. One section had very narrow knives, sharpened on both sides. "These are the traditional weapon of Sicily and are used in blood feuds and honor killings."

Jane found one with a particular pattern attractive. The vendor said, "You have a good eye. That one may look a little worn but it is one of the old ones. These new modern ones may be pretty but they aren't as serviceable as the old ones." Jane bought the old one and tucked it into her purse.

Jane finished her interviews and had seen most of the sights, usually with Carla.

They had become good friends and enjoyed their time together. The night before Jane was to leave, Carla met her for dinner. Afterwards she said, "I'll be over about eight to make sure you get off to the airport OK. Have a good night."

"The same to you and thanks for everything."

Jane packed and found she was restless and not sleepy. She decided to take a little walk in the hotel neighborhood, a local area that she found charming. She walked several blocks and then started back. Few people were on the streets and she found the old buildings charming in the weak light. As she passed a corner, a man stepped up and grabbed her arm. "Are you charging or are you just out for fun?"

"Let me go. I don't want even to see you."

He grabbed her more firmly. "You are coming with me." And started pulling her along. She pulled back and then suddenly let herself be pulled to him. This threw him off balance and she took the arm, jerking it around until the shoulder dislocated. She pushed him to the ground. In an impulse she grabbed him by the ear and took out her new knife. She made a sweeping slash and then caught herself. The blade just crossed his ear and made a half inch slit. "My God. I almost cut his ear off. I don't know what the Italian courts would do for that. The dislocated shoulder is self-defense and shouldn't be a problem," she said to herself. A chastened Jane walked back to the hotel.

In the morning she told Carla the story. "Yeah, you can bang him up in self-defense without trouble but cutting his ear off would be armed assault and could get you three to five years. Good move not to do that."

Carla took her to the train to the airport and gave her a hug. "I've enjoyed the time with you. Keep in touch and come back if you can."

"I've enjoyed it too and I really thank you. You must come to New York."

The flight back was uneventful and soon Jane was back at work, editing the interviews and preparing presentations.

Chapter 14

Officer Flores had done a lot of thinking while driving her patrol car. She had enjoyed the brief challenge of finding out about the victim and had been very impressed by the detectives. Ridley would be her model. Lieutenant Carson was the ultimate in her hierarchy but he was too far above. She could identify with Ridley.

She had thought about the killer and had been even more stimulated by hearing about the case in Pomona. Then there was another killing in Pasadena. She drove by the hotel but was unable to find a way to take part in the investigation. Not only did she want to be a part of the case but she was thinking, "Wouldn't Frank Finley be impressed if I were to find the widow?" So she started trying to think like the killer. "Would I do this in a town where I lived?"

"Absolutely not. Someone would recognize me or find that I had changed my schedules. I must go somewhere else to do it." Then she must have a place to stay. She wouldn't stay in the big hotels where too many people would see her. She wouldn't stay in someone's home—that would be too limiting. So she must be in a motel. When things were quiet on patrol, Flores started stopping by the motels.

"I'm not going to cause you any trouble and I don't have a warrant. I'm just looking for a young lady who was staying in the same place for a couple weeks. Could you just tell me if you have had anyone like that in the past three weeks?"

Mostly the motel keepers were accommodating and she had found a couple possibilities but they both checked as there for some other reason. She had also been checking the motels in Arcadia on her way home to her rooming house in El Monte.

She stopped at a motel near Rosemead in Pasadena, the Starlight Motel. The man at the desk looked at her uniform and said, "What do you want?"

"Just a little information. I don't have a warrant but I'm trying to find someone."

A customer walked in. He looked at the uniform and hesitated.

"She's just checking on some motel information. No problem," the desk clerk said. The man dropped a fifty dollar bill on the counter and the clerk handed him a key.

The clerk turned to Flores. "No one here you want to know about."

"I haven't asked my question yet."

"Well, don't bother until you get a warrant. And it had better be for the right questions."

"It won't hurt to hear what I want to know."

"Yes it will. You make customers nervous. Good bye."

Flores walked out to the patrol car. She saw the man who had paid for the room a few doors up, opening the door for a woman. When the woman saw Flores she turned away, hiding her face. "I think I'll talk to the guys in vice about this place," Flores said to herself. She decided to make her approach even more low key. She didn't want a motel owner to report her to the department.

She continued to work the motels in the area. She tried the Red Roof Inn Motel the next day. Once again the motel operator was friendly and willing to be helpful but had no recent residents meeting the description. As Flores walked along the row of room doors towards her car, she heard "Help, HELP, HE -." then a sudden silence. This had come from unit 17 and Flores went over to the door and listened a minute. There was a scuffle type noise and then a feminine voice said, "No, please."

Flores knocked on the door. "Police officer."

"We don't need you. Go away," a male voice responded.

"Come and open the door," Flores said. Then with no response she said, "Open this door or we'll break it down." She pushed the transmit button on her radio. "P7. Call for help in unit 17 at Red Roof Inn, 2734 Colorado. I'm knocking and checking. Back-up, please."

"Dispatch to P7. Back-up on the way. Report entry."

"P7. 10-4." Flores knocked again. "Open this door, now."

"OK. OK." In a couple minutes, a young man opened the door a crack. He was handsome in a dark, flashy way but with a weak chin. He seemed in the early twenties. "We're OK. No problem," he said.

Flores peeked around him. A young girl sat beside the bed, pulling a blanket around her. "I'm coming in to talk with her," Flores told the man.

"Do you have a warrant?" he asked.

"No. I don't need one. Let me in."

"The hell with this. I'm leaving." He threw open the door.

"What do I do now? Try to stop him or go to the girl?" Flores thought to herself. "I want you to wait until I see her," she said in a loud voice.

"Screw you. I'm out of here," he responded.

Flores was debating whether to stop him when she heard the voice of the shift sergeant behind her. "Hold it right there, guy. You aren't going anywhere."

He brought the man back to the door. "What's up, Flores?"

"I don't know, sir. I heard a call for help that was cut off and I just got him to open the door."

Sergeant Tommy O'Reilly was a big man with a typical Irish complexion and red hair, looking about forty. He looked at the girl. "Go ahead and talk to her, Flores. I'll keep him here."

Flores went over to the girl. "It's OK now. I'm a police officer. Tell me what happened. You can get up now."

The girl stood, trying to keep the blanket around her. Flores saw a bra on the bed and a pair of jeans on a chair. She picked up the clothes and said, "Let's go in the bath and you can get dressed." She added a blouse from the chair. When the girl was dressed, Flores took her out and let her sit in the chair. "Now relax and tell me what happened."

"I feel so dumb."

"Don't worry about that. Just tell me how you got here."

"He approached me a couple days ago at the Pizza Hut where our group hangs out. He said he was a scout for TV shows and I would fit a part perfectly. He was going to talk with his director and tell me what the director thought today."

"He didn't bother you the first time?" Flores asked.

"No. He seemed very professional. Today he said the director was interested and would meet us at this motel for a short interview. When we came, his phone rang and he said the director was calling that he was held up in traffic. In the meantime, he would check me as they had once hired a girl for a swimming pool scene and found she had a big birthmark on her leg. He got me to take off my jeans and blouse."

"So he hadn't touched you?"

"Well, then he asked me to take off my bra to check me there. I told him that if I had to appear that way I wasn't interested in the job. Then he said, 'I want it off' and grabbed me. That's when I yelled help. He said, 'Shut up.' And hit me across the face."

Flores looked and saw a red mark on the right side of the girl's face with a drop of blood at the corner of her mouth. The girl continued, "He undid my bra and then you knocked at the door. I was so frightened."

"How old are you?" Flores asked.

"Fifteen."

"What's your name?"

"Judy Lancaster."

"Where do you live, Judy?"

"3740 Mayfair Drive. I go to Pasadena High School."

The sergeant had been listening to the story. "OK, Flores, take her to the station and get the story recorded." At this point the man started to move away rapidly. Before his second step, O'Reilly had cuffed one hand and was pulling the second arm behind him for the other handcuff. "I'll take him in and meet you at the station."

Flores took the girl to her patrol car. "You'll be OK. I'll take you home after we record your story." They settled in the car and Flores keyed the radio. "P7 enroute to station with one female victim. Mileage 62743 point 8."

She heard the sergeant's voice on the radio, "Sam 1. 10-15 with one male suspect. Mileage 4926 point 1. Please call a vice officer to meet Officer Flores at the station."

Flores pulled into the station and reported on the radio, "P7 station, mileage 62748 point 1."

One of the vice detectives was waiting. The sergeant came in and told him, "Help Flores get the story recorded but let her do the interview unless you see something left out. She seems to have rapport with the victim. If your partner is here, he can book this suspect for me. It's Flores' case but I think it is more important for her to be with the victim than with the suspect."

The detective called his partner and then led Flores and Judy to an interview room. He set up a small tape recorder. "Judy, I just want you to tell me what you told me before. It's just the same except we will have it on tape," Flores told her.

"I've never talked to one of these," Judy said.

"Don't worry. Just ignore it and talk to me like we did at the motel."

Detective Hal Mason was a small, quiet man dressed in a generic grey suit. He sat quietly to the side where Judy wouldn't see him while she talked. When Flores had finished recording July's story, he asked, "Did any of your friends hear him telling you this?"

"A couple were there but I think they were talking to each other and doubt if they heard what he said."

"But they did see him at the pizza place and knew he approached you?"

"Definitely. We discussed his offer after he left."

"Can you give us their names? I may need to ask them about him"

"I hate to have them know how dumb I was."

"I won't tell them anything about what happened. I'll just confirm that he approached you and that he was at the place."

"OK then." She gave him the names of her two friends.

"You did a fine job telling the story. Officer Flores can take you home now. If you think of anything else or have any questions, you can contact either Officer Flores or me. You won't hear anything for a time but you will probably have to tell the story in court. We will try to put him away for a time so he won't bother anyone else."

Flores took Judy out to the patrol car. Judy was now comfortable with Flores and asked her how the radio and the siren worked on the police car. Flores showed her how to key the radio as she said, "P7 returning victim to home. Beginning mileage 62748 point 1."

"Wasn't I dumb to fall for his line?" Judy asked.

"Most girls want a chance to act and the hope overcomes their common sense all too frequently. I'm glad I was close by."

"Oh, I am so grateful. It would have been horrible without you. I don't even want to think about it."

"I bet you will evaluate things a little more carefully next time."

"I certainly will. How hard is it to get to be a police officer? You're so efficient and so attractive in your uniform."

"Not too hard. It takes two years of college. Study hard in high school and you can make it with no problem. It's rewarding but it can be hard work. One has to work different shifts and getting used to sleeping can be hard with shift change."

They arrived at the house. "Would you like me to go in and help you tell your mother what happened or can you handle it?"

"She's really very understanding. I can do it. Thank you so much."

"You're welcome. I'm glad I could help." Flores turned to the radio as Judy entered the house. "P7 at victim's home, 3740 Mayfair Drive. Mileage 62753 point 4. Time eleven fourteen." She drove off and back to her patrol area.

At the end of the shift, Flores went into the station. The sergeant was doing paper work. He looked up at Flores. "Good job with that girl, Flores. Would you have stopped the guy or gone to the girl if I hadn't showed up?"

"I'm not sure. I was just debating that when you came. I think I would have tried to stop him because she wasn't going anywhere."

"Good decision. What were you doing at the motel?"

This was the question Flores had dreaded. "I had just talked with the manager about another case where I thought the person might have stayed there. He didn't however."

"Well, it's lucky you were there. That scumbag is going to get a couple years in the pen. Will the girl be OK?"

"We were just in time. He bruised her face and scared her but didn't really damage her. I think she will be fine and a lot more careful in the future."

"Occasionally we really do earn what the city pays us. This was one of those days. Points out that a lot of police work is luck. If you hadn't been nearby we would have a complicated case and probably no result. See you tomorrow."

"Yes, sir. I'll be in tomorrow. Thanks for your help."

Chapter 15

Officer Flores had talked with Ollie Linton, one of the two detectives that were working vice. Ollie was a small man, wearing hair too long, an irregular mustache and dirty jeans. He purposely avoided looking clean and neat. "I stopped at a motel and the manager was extremely rude and wanted me out of there. Some man came in while I was there and paid for a room with cash, not registering. He went into the room with a woman who turned and covered her face so I couldn't see who she was. Do you think that's a little strange?"

"I can tell you the motel. We know it's a hot pillow place. That's where couples cheating on their spouses go for a quickie. Sounds like he's getting a little too brazen. We'll check on it in the next few days. Thanks for letting me know."

He talked it over with his partner. "It's hard to do anything about the hot pillow business but I think he might be going a little further. Let's see if we can get him procuring."

They went by the motel several times, noting license numbers. When they found the same car there a second time, they ran the license and found the owner's name: Karl Compton. Later they went to the motel in separate cars. Ollie went in and spoke to the manager, "Hey man. My buddy Karl brings his girl here a lot. I need some too but don't have a girl. Do you know where I could find one?"

"You a friend of Karl's? What's his last name?"

"Compton. Sure am. We do a lot of things together."

"I might be able to find out something. Sit a minute." He went in the other room and then returned. "Yeah. I got it all set up. You owe me thirty bucks for the room for an hour."

Ollie counted out thirty bucks. "How do I know she'll come?"

"She'll come. You go to room 12 and wait. You have to make a deal with her and pay her directly."

"OK. But she better come." He walked to the room. Inside he pulled out a small radio. "Hal, the girl's on the way. When I bust her, you go in and take the manager. I have him on a wire."

"Will do."

Ollie sat down on the bed. Vice cops were particularly good at waiting. Finally a gentle knock and an attractive black woman came in. "Hi, honey," he said, "How much."

"Depends on what you want."

"Just a regular roll in the hay."

"Forty bucks. If you take longer than 15 minutes it's more."

"Sounds fair. Come over here."

She walked over to the bed. "Turn around slowly and let me look at you."

She turned and when her back was to him he slipped a handcuff on one wrist and as she turned, grabbed the other and cuffed it.

"Damn you. That's what a girl gets for trying to be nice and do someone a favor."

"Afraid so. However, if you're willing to tell us about the guy at the motel, I think you can get off with just a warning not to do it again." He took out his radio and said, "Go, Hal."

"I don't owe him anything," she said. "I'll talk about it."

He took her outside as Hal came out of the office with the manager in handcuffs. He and the girl looked at each other. "Damn you too," she said. "I didn't need this today."

The officers put the prisoners in their separate cars and took them down to the station for booking.

Ollie talked with the girl as he booked her. "What's your name?"

"Joy Ronson."

"I haven't met you before. Are you new in Pasadena?"

"No. I have a job in a book store. It doesn't pay much so I turn a trick occasionally. My girl friend gave this guy my number and told me that he's reliable."

"Is this the first time he's called you?"

"The second. Once it worked out OK."

"And you're willing to tell the court that he called you?"

"Yeah. I'll do that if it'll get me out of this without jail time."

"Well, you go to the court first thing in the morning and we'll tell the judge it's the first and see what we can do."

In court the next morning, when her case came up, Ollie told the judge, "This is the first time we've seen Joy and she has a regular job. She is willing to testify against the man who set her up in this and I'd recommend a warning."

The judge had worked often with Ollie and trusted him so he said, "Joy, I'm going to warn you that another offense will be treated more harshly and that if you don't appear when needed for testimony that you will be prosecuted."

"Thank you, your honor, I'll be there."

"Case dismissed."

The man, William Tasman, was held for trial. He had a well known attorney representing him, who was known for appearing for organized crime figures. He arranged bail and took Mr. Tasman out of the court.

Two days later, Ollie was sitting at his desk. The dispatcher called him on the phone. "Detective Linton, we have a shooting up on Summit Street. All the other detectives are in the field. Could you go up and see what's going on? I know you're used to that area."

"Sure. I'll sort it out and see who I can pass it to."

He went out to his beat up car and drove over the freeway at Marengo and over to Summit. This was the center of the criminal element of the black community in Pasadena. He slowed when he saw a marked police unit parked and pulled over in front of it. There was a crowd gathered in front of a nearby house. He saw a young black patrol officer in uniform and walked over to him. Someone tried to block his way but when the officer said, "Oh, detective. I'm glad to see you. The ambulance is on the way but I'm sure she's dead." Ollie walked over to the front of the house, where a body was lying on the ground. He looked at the girl.

"Jesus, that's Joy." There was a massive amount of blood which had come from the center of her chest, where two bullets had torn the clothing and underlying tissue.

There was the sound of a siren approaching. The ambulance pulled up and the paramedics jumped out. They went over to the body. One checked her pulse and then looked at the chest wound. "She's gone. We have to take her in and make it official." He approached the uniformed officer. "Do you think there's anything to be learned from the scene or should we take her in and then pass it to the coroner?" The officer looked at Ollie.

"Take her in. See if the bullets passed through or if they're still in her before you go."

The paramedics turned her over. "No exit wound. They must still be there."

"Then we won't have to look." They loaded the body onto a gurney and took it to the ambulance.

Ollie said to the uniformed officer, "Talk to anyone you can here and see if anyone saw the shooter. You'll have a better chance at getting some information than I will. When you've done what you can stop by detectives and let me know. I'll write the report if you would like."

"I'd appreciate that. I'll see what I can find out and see if anyone saw the shells."

"See you later." Ollie got into his car and returned to the station. He pulled up the information on Joy. Her address was at the house on Summit. He ran her driver's license on the computer and found no infractions. He had previously looked for a police record and had found none. The next thing would have to be finding out if she had a family and who lived at the house with her. Others would have to do this as he wanted as few people as possible to know he was a cop. He shouldn't have gone to the crime scene but he didn't expect to have to identify himself as police. He was just going to drive by and see what had happened.

Officer Brown came into the detective office. "White guy in a black Buick was parked in front of the next house. Nobody knew who he was. He came a few minutes before it was time for her to go to work. When she appeared at the door, he pulled out a long barreled revolver and shot twice. Before anyone came to see about the shots, he took off at high speed and disappeared. One guy wondered how new the car was before the shooting and noted that the license started with 5 Frank which makes it about a year old. He didn't note the rest of the number."

"Well, if it was a revolver there's no use looking for brass. Did you check at the house?"

"Yes. Rooming house with five people living there. The owner says she was pleasant, quiet and he doesn't know much about her. Doesn't know if she has any family."

"You did a good job. Keep your ears open and let me know if you hear anything about the shooting."

"Will do. However, I don't think I will. Everyone I talked to was puzzled. It doesn't sound like the local gangs and no one had any idea why the victim was picked."

"I arrested her two days ago for her first prostitution bust. She was willing to testify against the guy who set her up and so we let her go with a warning. It makes you wonder if he had something going that he didn't want investigated."

"I would think that's a more likely possibility than someone in the neighborhood. I'll keep in touch."

"Thanks."

Ollie thought about the license plate. "Two letters makes about 600 combinations since they don't use I or Q as the first letter. A thousand numbers with each makes over half a million cars." He called the DMV office of analysis. "This is the Pasadena Police Department. We have the first two digits of a license plate that was used in a murder. Can your computer sort the plates starting with these and find out how many black Buicks are in the group?"

"Is it a sedan?"

"Yes."

"I can tell you without sorting that there will be over 25,000 Buicks in the group. About one in six cars are black so we're talking five thousand cars."

"That sounds like a little too many to check out. But is it possible to do it if we get desperate?"

"It would take some programming but I think we could do it."

"Thanks very much. I'll work on finding another letter if I can."

"That would make it a number that one might handle."

"I'll be in touch if we have to have it."

He called Lieutenant Palmer's number. "Palmer."

"Lieutenant, this is Ollie. This afternoon they couldn't find another detective so they asked me to drive by the site of a shots fired call and tell the patrol officer what to do. It turned out to be a planned shooting with a dead victim."

"We need to know all you know about it. We're meeting to update on cases in about an hour. Why don't you tell all of us about it at that time?"

"Good. I'll be there."

As Ollie went to the little conference room the detective department used, he followed Al into the room. Palmer and Ridley were already seated at the table. "Thanks for coming, Ollie," Palmer said. "Have a seat." When Ollie and Al were seated, Palmer said, "Why don't you tell us about the new one before we update the others, Ollie."

Ollie recounted how he was given the call. "A group were gathering about the patrol officer and I thought we needed to get going. I stopped and went over to see a body. A twenty five year old black girl that I had arrested for soliciting two days before. She was new to us and we let her go if she would testify against a motel owner that we also arrested. She was clearly dead with gun shot wounds to the central chest. The paramedics came and took the body. I had the patrol officer interview people at the house. She is a quiet girl with a job and no one knew she was selling."

"What did you do then."

"As soon as they left with the body I got out before anyone else could see that I was a cop. The patrol officer was a sharp black guy and I left him to check with the people around. We need to get more information from people in the area but if I start asking questions there I might as well give up undercover vice."

"Any ideas who shot her?"

"No. However, he was parked nearby waiting for her to come out so it wasn't random. The thing that worries me is whether the motel owner is important enough to need to stop her testimony. If so, he's doing something besides run a hot pillow motel."

"Well, let's get up to date on the other cases and we'll decide how to divide the work. I can tell you now that we haven't a damn thing on the widow. I don't even have much idea of anything else to check. How about the arson case, Ridley?"

"When I heard it was in the home of a disabled person, I thought of some elderly person smoking or forgetting the oven. However, the fire marshal says there is no question that it was arson. And the disabled person turns out to be a man of forty who was recovering from a gunshot wound which was reported as a hunting accident. He has no apparent means of support and has kept some bad company. I talked to him in the hospital and he says the fire must have been an accident. He's hard to get information out of. It was only the chance presence of a fireman near by that kept him from being burned to death. I'm now going into his background and finances. I'm convinced he is a crook of some sort but I don't have the evidence yet."

"I think you had better keep working on that, Sergeant. Al, you are going to have to do the leg work on Ollie's murder and see what you can find. Ollie, maybe you can help both Ridley and Al by working up computer information on the two victims."

"May I make a suggestion, sir?"

"Of course, Ollie. What is it?"

"Summit is a bad area. Officer Brown is black, a sharp young man, and has worked that area. I think if Al could get his help he'd be both safer and a lot more likely to find something out."

"That sounds good. I'll talk to the patrol lieutenant about making him available when Al is up in the area. Ollie, would you write a report that Al can use as a start?"

"Sure. I have a brief one of what I did but I'll add the suspicions and Brown's information in an informal one to you, Al."

"I'll try to coordinate all this so if you find something useful let me know and I'll pass it along. I'll also keep digging at the widow."

"Ollie, while you are digging info could you get a warrant and then have the phone company give us all the records of the house where the arson was?" Ridley asked.

"If you do that, how about getting the phone records for the motel also?" the lieutenant added. "I'll have patrol pick up the log books at the motel and bring them in to you."

"Sounds like I'll be doing a bunch of fishing."

"They didn't tell you about the time you get for fishing when you applied to be a detective, did they?"

Chapter 16

Jane had developed a considerable reputation as an investigative reporter on TV. Much of her work was with science materials but she had broadened her field and was doing other areas of interest. She found the work fascinating and was almost totally engrossed in it.

Gradually she became more nervous about contacts with men and was increasingly fatigued. One day she was in a nearby bar with two friends after work and they met several men. One seemed interested in Jane and after talking a while, he placed his hand on her thigh under the table. She felt increasingly threatened and closed in. Suddenly she rose from the table and rushed from the room, saying, "I'm sick. I've got to go home."

Another day, her boss called her into his office. "You seem distracted and not up to your usual ability. Is something wrong?"

"I've been really tired and haven't been able to concentrate as well as usual. Maybe I'll take a little time off."

"You certainly deserve it. I don't know when you had a vacation without working most of your supposed time off. Try one and I hope you feel better."

In spite of his apparent understanding, Jane knew the business well enough to know that if she continued with sub-par work that she would no longer have the freedom to do her own choices of projects and maybe not even a job. "I think I'll go back to Pasadena," she told herself. "This problem seems related somehow to my time in California."

The next day she stopped to see Hector Rodriquez. He worked in the printing department but did all sorts of specialty work. He was a Columbian who had been a document forger for one of the drug cartels. When he was sent to the United States to study American documents, he never went back. He had made calling cards with various names for the news people on investigations.

"Hector, I need some special favors."

"I'll do anything I can for you."

"I want some business cards for Rachael Compton, consultant, at some non-traceable address in Silicone Valley."

"That's easy."

"I also need a California driver's license for the same name and address."

"That's a little harder. California is more complicated than New York but I think I can find a way."

"Since it's easier, I'd like a New York license for Amy Gregory, address some dead place in the Bronx."

"Well, honey, you're going to owe me a couple for this."

"That's fine, as long as you don't blackmail me and try to take my virtue."

Hector was gay and completely safe so he and Jane had developed a joking relationship that she had with no one else.

"I think I can get this done by Thursday. Can you stop by that afternoon?"

"See you then."

When she went home, she made a reservation for the Friday night flight to Los Angeles for Amy Gregory. "And what credit card do you want to use?"

"I had my identity stolen and don't have credit cards. Is there someplace I can pay the amount in cash? Or I can mail in a money order."

"I can put it on will call. This means you have to pick it up an hour and a half before the flight. You can pay at the airport that way."

"That will be fine. Thank you very much."

"Your reservation number will be 357824JL."

"Thank you."

Thursday before she went home she stopped at the printing department. Hector had her materials ready. "I hope you have a project that will make all this worth while."

"I hope it works too. What do I owe you? This is a private project which the company hasn't said they will pay for."

"Don't worry about it. I can put it under some budget or maybe I won't and I'll force you into being a woman of ill repute."

"You couldn't make my repute as bad as it is with some politicians now. Thanks a lot. I hope I can help you someday."

"Be careful. I'd miss you. You're the only one here who likes my sense of humor."

"I'll be sure and come back. What do they say? The bad ten thousand dollar bill always comes back?"

"I'm not sure that is the exact quote but I know what you mean."

She waved to him and walked out.

She packed a few clothes and then picked up her knife. This was the stiletto that she had picked up as a souvenir in Sicily. It was long and narrow and very sharp. Both sides had cutting edges. It was the traditional weapon for settling blood feuds in Sicily. She looked at it a minute and then tucked it in the suitcase. She had planned to carry on but this would mean she had to check the suitcase. She found a tote bag and put a book, her cosmetics and the new identification materials in it.

The next morning she took a written request down to personnel, asking for two weeks emergency leave for a family crisis. There was no problem with this as her boss had already advised her to take some time off. She left no forwarding address or phone. Then she went to the bank and drew $20,000 in cash from her trust account. She stopped at a wig shop and bought a black and a blonde wig.

After work she went home and distributed the money between her tote, her suitcase and a money strap. She added the wigs to the suitcase. Then she called a cab and went to JFK airport.

She checked in using the Amy Gregory license and paid for her flight in cash. She checked her bag and took the tote on the plane. There was a movie but she put on a mask to cut out the light and slept most of the flight. Arriving in Los Angeles, she retrieved her luggage and went and studied the yellow pages. There was a Rent a Wreck car rental near the airport. She took a cab there and presented the Rachael Compton driver's license.

"I want a moderate sized, dark colored car with little personality."

"I have just the thing. A two year old dark blue Plymouth sedan. It doesn't look it but it runs like a top."

"Sounds good."

"What credit card will you use?"

Again she used the identity theft story and offered a cash deposit of $2000. This was acceptable so she signed the papers and took the car with the promise to return it in two weeks. "Do you have a map showing the freeway net?"

He handed her a map. "Don't get lost."

She got in the car and drove to Pasadena. Coming off the Pasadena Freeway, she jogged up to the new 210 freeway across Pasadena. She exited at the Madre turn off, went down to Colorado Blvd. and drove into the Best Western Motel.

Going into the office, she asked for a room. "And what credit card will you be using?" the clerk asked.

"I had to cancel all my credit cards as I found my identity had been stolen a couple weeks ago. I don't have new ones yet. It's really a terrible experience. In view of this, I got some extra money from the company before I came. Will you take a cash deposit of a thousand dollars?"

"It must be awful. So many things you have to change or look into. Did they find out who did it?"

"Not yet. At least he can't use it any more as all the companies know about it. It's amazing how surprised people are when you pay cash now. We really won't need money before long. Will the cash be OK?"

"Of course, a cash deposit will be fine. You don't need that much."

"Well, I'll be staying a week or more so that will be fine." She signed in as Rachael and paid the thousand dollars in cash. She took the card key and walked to her room. It was right across from the pool which would be pleasant. Going in she looked around and found it clean and comfortable. Then she unpacked her things. She sat in the chair and set the knife on the table. Looking at it, she wondered, "Now what?"

She hadn't consciously made a plan but she realized that she knew what she must do. She would go to hotels where there was a convention and make a pick-up in the bar. The wig and a short skirt would be noticeable and people wouldn't be likely to be able to describe the rest of her. She must watch for fingerprints or for anything that could be left behind. When she left, it would be better not to have the short, revealing skirt on.

The next morning she took the car and drove to Penneys in the Arcadia Mall. She went to the young women's department and bought a couple of very short skirts. She wouldn't be seen in New York in such a skirt for any reason. She then went to another department and found a maid's dress.

She bought one slightly large so it would slip on over her clothes easily. She took her purchases back to the car and then went to Borders and picked up a couple travel books that she could read during the days.

Back at the motel, she hung up her purchases and went out to sit by the pool.

Chapter 17

Parker sat at his desk most of the morning. He was looking through various crime data bases on the computer, trying to find something related to the widow. They didn't have a decent clue of any kind.

Sergeant Ridley came in from the field and stopped by Parker's office. "Any luck?"

"Nothing. I'm out of ideas about where to look further."

"Yeah. Makes one wonder if she's in law enforcement. She seems to cover all the bases. There's something fishy about the guy in the arson case. I'm glad Ollie is working on the phone calls. What are you going to do next?"

"I've been writing a summary of what we know and will send it to the FBI for profiling. They have people who can tell a lot about perpetrators just from their methods."

"I'm going to start helping Al on that shooting up on Fair Oaks this afternoon. It won't be as interesting but maybe I can get somewhere."

"The problem there is that people in that area aren't going to talk to the cops. I'm sure some of the folks know who did it. But we have to try. Good luck."

"Thanks. What do you plan?"

"I'm scheduled for my flight test tomorrow morning so I think I'll take the afternoon off and practice the maneuvers. Tonight I'll be studying the paper work."

"Good luck on the test. I know this means a lot to you."

"Yeah. Can you see me with an airline pilot's uniform?"

"Not nearly as impressive as the police uniform when you get those bars on the collar."

Ridley wandered back to her office and Parker picked up the paper work on his desk and then told the secretary that he was taking the afternoon and the next morning off on comp time.

Mike Henley was in the lab, looking at a bullet under the microscope. "Take a look at this," he said to Sid. "This is the one that killed the gal up on Summit. Twenty five calibers are fairly rare and this type dumdum bullet is even rarer. It's not a usual caliber for an assassination but it must have been one of those marksman revolvers."

Sid looked at the bullet. "You know, I saw a bullet from the hospital taken from a guy in a hunting accident. It looked a lot like that. Let me get it." He went to a storage drawer and came back with a bullet in a plastic package. He placed it on the microscope in the position used for comparing bullets. Mike looked in the scope.

"Well the bullets aren't in very good shape but they are certainly the same size and caliber. There are a few similar markings. I think they came from the same gun but I can't be sure yet."

"It's hard with those bullets that deform so much when they hit."

"Yeah. That deformation is why they use them. As they flatten out, they do more damage."

"What the hell would anyone hunt with that kind of gun and these bullets? The hunting accident doesn't make much sense to me."

"I can't believe it was a hunting accident. I think the detectives should go into it a little further. The fact that we have two similar bullets in a short time is unlikely to be a coincidence."

"I think we'd better let the detectives know about this. You were working on the bullet. Why don't you go and tell someone?" Sid asked

"OK. I'll talk to the lieutenant if he's in and if not, to Sergeant Ridley. I saw her come into the department a few minutes ago." He got up and walked out.

Ridley was eating a sandwich at her desk when Mike came in. "I thought someone should know about this. The hospital sent over a bullet a few days ago from an accidental shooting while hunting. Sid looked at it and filed it. This morning I got the two bullets from the homicide on Summit from the coroner's office. Sid looked at the shooting ones and thought they looked familiar so he pulled the one from the hospital. They are the same type and from a similar gun. Those twenty five caliber marksman pistols are fairly rare as is this type bullet. The markings were beat up enough so I can't be sure but I think they came from the same gun."

"Really? That's pretty amazing and it's very good work on your part to connect them up. This is going to tie the arson case to the shooting. Thanks a lot."

"I didn't think you were going to believe me. Glad we could help."

Ridley went over to Ollie's office. "Ballistics thinks the bullets in the shooting and that from the hunting accident in the arson case victim are from the same gun."

"Hard to believe that would be a coincidence. Are you thinking of tying the two cases together?"

"Seems logical, doesn't it? When you're looking at phone numbers, try to see if any duplications occur between the two lists."

"OK. I'm working on numbers now. I've only worked on the ones from the arson house. There are an amazing number of relatively local numbers. Occasionally there is a repeat but many different ones. And they are mostly ingoing. This is really suggestive of a gambling book. All the people are calling up and placing bets."

"That might suggest possible motives for the arson and also for the 'accidental' shooting. But what's the relation to the motel?"

"I sure don't know. But the other interesting thing about the phone calls is that there are quite a few to and from Las Vegas. If he's running a book, maybe he's placing off the big bets to the gambling group in Las Vegas."

"Well, you might try a Vegas reverse directory and see where some of the calls went."

"Yeah. And I'll check out a few of the local ones. Here I would expect to find either homes or small businesses. Places where gamblers could safely call from."

"OK. Keep at it. When you do get to the motel phone note if any of the same numbers come up."

"That's not easy to do with so many unless I enter them all in the computer. But I'll see what shows up. This will keep me for some time. Would you like to take the motel registration book and see what it shows?"

"Sure. I suspect most of the customers didn't get entered with that type of hot pillow clientele but I'll see what I can find. Thanks, Ollie. I'll check with you later."

"Shall I tell the Lieutenant what I'm finding or will you?"

"He's off this afternoon and until noon tomorrow. He's finally going to take his flight test. I don't think we have to worry him until tomorrow afternoon."

"That's good that he's finally doing it. I hope he doesn't get unbearable if he passes."

"I'm thinking of buying him an airline captain's shoulder boards. Maybe if he has those he'll take us for a ride."

"I think I'll wait until he's had a few months experience before I go."

She walked out with the somewhat dog eared registration book from the motel. Maybe it was time to talk to the arson victim again. She went over to the Huntington Hospital and parked in a red zone reserved for police. She hadn't had lunch yet, so she stopped at the employees' cafeteria. She picked up a plate of pasta and walked through the tables. Finally she saw a nurse she had met and asked, "May I join you?"

"Sure. Good to see you again, Sergeant. Have a bad guy in the hospital?"

"I'm not sure. I did see you on the floor where our arson victim is, didn't I?"

"Yes. He's coming along. I don't think he'll be here much longer."

"I'm not going to ask about his medical condition but I'd like to know what sort of person he is. Does he talk about himself?"

"No. He is very close mouthed and hard to get anything out of. He also isn't a particularly pleasant person. Fairly demanding and not at all appreciative. Never shows any interest in anyone else. I'll be glad to get rid of him."

"Did you know that he was home because he was recovering from a gun shot wound?"

"It was on the record as a hunting accident. I asked him what kind of hunting he did as my father did a lot and I grew up with it. He was rather rude and asked why I cared. I apologized and told him I came from a hunting family. He just grunted and changed the subject. I doubt if he really was hunting at all."

"I doubt it too. It doesn't sound like he's telling very much."

"Not at all. I haven't asked him anything more."

"I have to go and talk to him and he probably won't tell me anything more than he did you. It's good to see you again and I hope you have some patients that are more pleasant."

"Most people are really very nice, even when they feel bad."

"That's encouraging to know. See you later."

As she took the elevator up to his floor, she thought, "No real information but the nurse's impression fits what I think. Something's wrong about this guy and we'll find out what it is."

Ridley went to the room where Mr. Maldenado was. The door was open and he was lying in bed, looking at a sports magazine. She knocked at the open door. He looked up. "Hi. It's Sergeant Ridley. May I come in?"

"I suppose I can't keep you out. What do you want?"

She walked in. "Just checking up on how you're doing and have a couple questions."

"Always asking questions that aren't of any use."

"Well, I never know when something might fit together. Was it your gun that you were shot with in the accident?"

"No. It was my partner's."

"It's a fairly rare type gun. Could you give me his name?"

"No. It has no relation to what I'm in here for and it's past history."

"Can you tell me where you were hunting?"

"I'm not telling you anything. Go back to your office."

"Do you have any idea who could have poured the gas on the house and lit it? I would think you might be interested in that."

"I don't have any idea."

"You were off work because of the gunshot wound. Where is it you were working before that happened?"

"That's none of your business. Scram."

"It seems to me that if I'd had two failed attempts on my life I would want some help and protection against the next try."

His eyes opened wider but he responded, "I haven't any idea what you are talking about. Why would anyone want to kill me?"

"That's what I'd like to know. Tell me why."

"I'm not even going to talk to you anymore." He turned away from her.

"OK. I'm out of here but I'll be back before you go home. Think about it and see if you don't want me to help."

Ridley picked up her car and went back to the police department. She sat down at her desk and made some notes about her interview with Mr. Maldenado. She thought for a few minutes and then shook her head. She was getting nowhere. She picked up the motel register and started looking at it.

It wasn't just a hot pillow motel. There were quite a few registered guests. She went down the lists for several weeks. There were a scattering from around the state but the largest single source was Las Vegas. Most of these seemed to have stayed two or three days. She noted down some names and found that two or three of the Las Vegas visitors had been there repeatedly. How did they come?

One had repeatedly come in a Lexus with a Nevada license. Another apparently flew in and rented cars as there was a different California license each time. She was looking at the licenses and something stirred in the back of her mind. She wasn't sure what but there was something. She went back down the numbers. The most recent trip had license number 5FNK417. A 5F number. She looked at the make—Buick. Color—black. BINGO.

She ran the license on the computer. The car belonged to Budget Rent a Car. She called the Budget central office and found the car to be based at Ontario Airport. The Budget office at Ontario found the car was on the lot at this time. "Do not rent it tonight. We think if may have been involved in a crime and I will be out in the morning with the laboratory people to check it."

"Suppose we need it today. Will the department pay to have it remain here?"

"No, but if you can't promise to have it there in the morning, I'll have it towed to the police impound lot now. Then you can go pick it up in a few days."

"We'll keep it here tonight."

"Thank you. We will be there first thing and will try to get through quickly so you can use the car. I also want the rental papers."

"Very well."

She called the lab. "Sergeant Ridley here. I think I've found the car from the Summit street shooting. I'd like you to go out to Ontario Airport tomorrow morning with me and examine it."

"Do you want to go with us or meet there?"

"I should have my car and you guys need the stuff in your van, don't you?"

"Never know what we'll need so we'll take it all."

"Good. I'll meet you out there about eight thirty."

"It may be a few minutes later by the time we get all the equipment organized, but we'll be there."

"Thanks very much."

She went back to searching the register but found nothing more interesting. She took the address on the visit involving the Buick and called Las Vegas Police Department. Asking for detectives, she said, "This is detective sergeant Ridley of Pasadena. We have a rental car probably used in a crime that was rented to a Mr. Ted Amalfi at the following address. Can you tell me anything about the address?"

"Yes. Even without looking it up. That address is a so called social club which is the hang out for many of the mafia types who run some of the gambling here. They use it as an accommodation address and they may live anywhere. I don't remember an Amalfi but they often use different names. There are also a bunch of mid level thugs who float around from different cities."

"Thank you very much. We have some more checking to do and I may be in touch again with more information, if you don't mind."

"Glad to help."

Ridley wrote a set of notes on what she had found out and then went home.

In the morning she drove out to the airport. A few minutes after she arrived at the Budget office, the van from the lab appeared. By this time she had copied the rental papers for the car. Sure enough, the renter had used a different name from the one at the hotel; T. A. Malone. The address was the same location in Las Vegas.

The two lab men were taken to the car. "I think this may be the car used in the Summit shooting. Check the car generally but I'm particularly interested in knowing if a gun was fired in this car. Can you determine that?"

"Sometimes. It depends on where the gun was and how close to the car itself. Do you know where the gun was when it was fired?"

"According to witnesses, it was fired out the front passenger window by the one man in the car, who was sitting in the driver's seat. I don't know if the gun was completely outside or if he used the car as a prop for the gun. I'd also like you to check the renter papers for finger prints."

"I'll start on the car and you do the prints, Sid," one of the techs told the other.

Ridley waited while they worked. Then Sid said, "There are a few prints on here. One is partially covered up by another. I would guess that the covering one is the employee here and the earlier one the renter."

"Take the papers with you to the department and see if you can get photos of the prints. They can keep the copy here."

"I can get a better look at them there."

Ridley said to the Budget employee, "We're going to take the originals to the department for finger prints. You keep the copy and we'll return the original later. Do the papers say who handled the rental?"

"Yes." He studied the copy a minute. "Melissa Block."

"Is she working today?"

"Yes, she's in back. I'll give her a call." He spoke on the phone and in a couple minutes an attractive, light colored black woman in her thirties came out.

"Something you need?"

"The police are interested in a rental you did."

Ridley told her, "We are trying to get the fingerprints of the renter from the rental papers. Would you mind if we took your prints so that we can rule those out. You must have held the paper."

"I'm sure I held the papers. Sure, you can take my prints."

"Can you do that, Sid?"

"I'll get some print materials from the van and do it."

Ridley showed the copy of the rental agreement to Melissa. "Do you remember anything about this rental?"

"Yeah. He was a slick looking guy probably in his forties. I remember him because he gave me a credit card that didn't match the name he had given. When I asked about it, he told me it was a friend's card he had picked up by accident. He had about six or eight cards and looked for one with the right name."

"You didn't ask any more about the cards?"

"No. I wondered but it really didn't seem to be any of my business. I did make a note to check this card and the office made sure that it was valid."

"Could you identify him if you saw him again?"

"I'm not quite sure but I think so."

"Thanks much for your help. We'll get the prints and then may be in touch again."

"You're welcome. I probably should have called you but he seemed like the type that would raise hell if he was checked."

"No, you can't check out everyone who has lots of credit cards."

Ridley went out to the car and asked Mike, the other tech, "Have anything useful?"

"There are some traces of nitrates from gun firing on the sill of the passenger door. The gun wasn't on the sill, so they aren't strong but they are definite. I don't think any prints are useful. It's hard to get prints off the kind of plastic they use so much of in cars these days."

"Should we impound the car for the nitrates?"

"No. I have the test results and pictures of them and pictures showing the license. I don't think there's anything more we can do. I think this would stand up in court well."

"I appreciate your coming out. You'll take care of the rental agreement with the prints, won't you."

"Sure. We'll work on it in the lab and see if we can isolate a good one."

"Good job. See you later."

"Don't get us in any more trouble, Sarge. We have enough work for a couple days."

"I'll try to avoid anything that will require you. You guys did a great job on the bullets."

"Sid has a good memory for connecting up different things. I don't think I would have put that together."

"Well, you're a good team."

Ridley went to her car. She called and ordered a pizza and picked it up on the way back to the station. There was always someone who needed lunch and sometimes it was a good way to get a chance to talk to some of the other officers.

Chapter 18

Al had asked Officer Brown to meet him at the Summit address. "Good morning. How are you today?" Al asked.

"I'm OK. The sergeant gave me permission to spend as much time with you as you need. What do you want to do first?"

"Let's take a look at her room." They entered the house and an elderly black lady greeted them, "Good morning, Officer Brown. Who is this with you?"

"Good morning, Mrs. Jackson. This is Detective Carnucci. Could we see the room where Joy lived?" The house was old but well kept. She led them to a second floor room. It was large but a portion had been taken to make a tiny bath and kitchen. Then there was room for a table with two chairs by the kitchen, a bed in one corner and a small settee in front of a television in the other.

"Not a lot of room but she has used it efficiently and decorated it with good taste," Al said. "It seems quite homey."

"Yes, sir. She took good care of things and was an ideal tenant," Mrs. Jackson said.

Officer Brown told her, "Thank you for showing us. We need to look over her things and see if we can find something about a family. We don't need to keep you for all that. I'll tell you when we leave so you can lock up."

"That's OK." A smile broke her wrinkled face. "Stay as long as you need to. I'm not going anywhere." She left them in the room.

"You've developed a good relationship here. I'm sure she wouldn't be so helpful for me," Al told Brown.

"That's for sure. It took me a long time to get some of these people to trust me. Some never will."

"Well, let's see what she had here." Al went into the little bath alcove. The bath had a shelf with soap and cosmetics. In the kitchen there was a tiny refrigerator with milk, ham slices, and left over pasta. A shelf held cereal and condiments. A bar behind a sheet held hangers with a couple jackets, skirts, pants, and a coat. The only place that seemed to hold any promise of information was the chest of drawers by the bed. The top drawer held underwear and costume jewelry. The next had blouses and sweaters, neatly folded. The next drawer held miscellaneous folded clothing items. "Do you want to pack her things?" Brown asked.

"No. We don't need all that for any reason. If we find something with information, I'll take that."

The bottom drawer was apparently her filing cabinet. There were credit card bills, showing them paid up. There was a payment book for car payments. Al showed this to Brown and said, "I hadn't heard anything about a car."

"Nor had I. We'll have to ask about that."

Brown was going through a pile of papers and said, "Here's something. A letter from her mother in Alabama with a return address."

"That's one of the things we need. I think I'll take all the papers down to the station and do some follow up on the computer and phone."

"Will you tell me what you find? I've become involved with this case."

"Absolutely. I need to interview in the area. Would you be available tomorrow morning to work with me?"

"My sergeant told me to do what you needed so that will be fine. Where and when?"

"Why don't I go with you from the station rather than getting two cars up here. Would that be OK?"

"Sure. I come in at seven forty five for briefing and will be ready to go about eight."

"Good. I'll be there. Thanks for today."

"You're welcome."

Al went to his car with the papers placed in a folder. At the office he had the phone company find a phone number for the Alabama address. He called. After four rings, a voice said, "Hello."

"Is this Mrs. Martha Adams?"

"Yes, it is. Who is calling?"

"This is detective Carnucci of the Pasadena, California police."

"Is Joy in trouble?"

"I'm sorry Mrs. Adams but she died two days ago."

"I knew no good would come of her going out there. What happened?"

"She was shot by an assassin. We haven't found him yet but are looking. We think it was because she had said she would testify against a man who seems to be connected to the mob."

"She didn't learn to mind her own business. I'm sorry but not too surprised. Was it quick?"

"Very. I'm sure she didn't know what hit her. Do you want me to send you her clothes and things?"

"No. It's not worth it. And I can't afford a funeral, just have her buried out there."

"You don't know anyone who might have wanted her dead, do you?"

"Maybe that crumb Ronson that she married but I really don't think he cares. He left with all the money and their car, leaving her the car payments since she had signed for it. No one here has seen him since. They foreclosed on the house and the disappointment and the car payments led her to go to Los Angeles in hope of making more money. If there was any left from her pay, send that to me. You have the address?"

"Yes, mam. I found your last letter in her drawer and that's how I found you."

"Thank you for calling me, officer."

"Oh, you're welcome. I'm sorry to have such bad news."

"At my age, you get used to it. Goodbye."

He continued through the paper and found some pay stubs from the book store where she worked. He called them and asked for the manager. "This is Mrs. Serano. May I help you?"

"Detective Carnucci from the PD. Sounds like we might come from the same part of the world. My family is from just north of Naples."

"Mine came from Sicily."

"Do you have an employee named Joy Ronson?"

"Probably not. I put in to have her fired. She hasn't shown up for two days and didn't call."

"She was shot and killed two days ago, so she has a good excuse."

"I'm so sorry to hear that. She was really a very nice lady and it wasn't like her not to come to work."

"You don't know if she had any enemies do you?"

"I didn't know her life that well but I wouldn't think so. She was quiet and helpful."

"Did she have friends there?"

"She was a very private person and didn't share with anyone what she did in off hours, even where she lived."

"Thank you for your help. If anyone should think of any information call me at the detective division, 795-3456. I will send you her mother's address in Alabama so that you can send any money she's owed there."

"We'll take care of that. Goodbye."

In a little notebook, there were a few phone numbers. Al recognized one as the book store. He called a couple and no one knew a Joy Ronson. He wondered if she had met men who might want her later but they didn't seem relevant. He wrote a report on what he found and went home.

In the morning he met Officer Brown at the station. "Good morning, Detective Carnucci."

"If we're going to be working together, I'm Al."

"And I'm Henry. Everyone calls me Hank. Sounds like a baseball player. I wanted to be one but found I couldn't hold onto the ball."

"This is a much better career in the long run. Shall we go and see what we can find out?"

In the car, Hank asked, "Find anything in the papers?"

"I talked to her mother. She came out here after her husband left her, taking all their money and leaving her the car and house payments. That explains the car payment book. Mother doesn't know anything about her life here but expected trouble when she went to that big, evil city, Los Angeles."

They talked to the people at the rooming house. The story was always the same. She was pleasant but distant. No one knew her well and they couldn't see any reason why anyone would want to shoot her. They talked again to the man who had seen the black Buick but didn't get any more information. One other neighbor responded to a question, "I did see that white dude in the Buick sitting there before it happened. I wondered what he was doing parked in this area and wondered if he was one of you cops. I didn't see the license but I'd know him if I saw him again."

"What did he look like?"

"One mean looking son of a bitch. I don't think cops look that bad. He had black hair that was sorta greasy. Long nose that was reddish."

Brown said, "Would you work with a police artist and try to come up with a sketch of the guy? We don't want him preying on our people around here."

"Yeah, I could do that. We have enough black bad-asses here without adding white hoods."

"Good I'll make the arrangements for the artist to see you. Give me your number and he can call and find what time would be good for you to go down there, or would you rather he came here?"

"I'll go down. Just as soon not have the neighbors know I'm working with the police."

"Thanks a lot."

Brown spoke, "These people aren't easy for the police to get information from but I'm impressed with what we have. No one seems to be holding back and they are puzzled by the shooting. They are also a little frightened because they don't have any reason. Could this guy get one of them next?"

"They certainly have been more cooperative than other times I've been in this area. I appreciate your help. I'll buy you lunch and then have you drop me at the station, if you will."

"Glad to help. As I'm sure you remember, patrol can get a little boring and this has been an interesting break. Where do you want to eat?"

"Do you like Japanese food? There's a nice little place in the Colorado Arcade."

"That sounds good."

Ridley had just settled at her desk with the pizza box and Ollie had come over. They were putting pieces of pizza on paper towels when Lieutenant Carson walked in with a glowing smile. "Looks like you passed the flight test, Palmer." Ridley said. "Was it hard?"

"Everything went just right. I'm now a licensed pilot," he said happily.

"I'd offer a celebratory lunch but we're all set with pizza. I think there's enough for three. Did you have lunch yet?"

"I had a mid-morning donut with the examiner but I'd like a little pizza."

"Pull up a chair and grab a piece. Lots of progress. You want to be updated over lunch or have a regular conference?"

He took a piece of pizza. "If you've found out anything let's have it now."

They all took bites and Ridley said, "Ollie, tell him about the phones."

Just as he started, the door opened and Al came in. "Sorry, Al, but I don't think this will go four ways."

"I ate with Officer Brown. Want a report?"

"Sure, Ollie just started but you can be next. A lot of progress but the big news is the lieutenant is going to astronaut training next week."

"I'll bet on it. You did pass the test, sir?"

"I did. I'll tell you all about the flight test but we should get up to date on work first. Go ahead, Ollie."

"I spent hours going over the huge number of calls to the arson house, mostly incoming. They are from a wide variety of residences and business over the general Los Angeles area. I called a couple and asked if they had any bets outstanding. That he was in the hospital and I was trying to clean up his back log. No one denied they'd been betting with him so he definitely was running a book."

"Not enough evidence to book him."

"No. I was mostly trying to work out a motive for the arson. The other group of calls were Las Vegas calls, both to and from. Several numbers were repeated. I looked up some of the numbers and they are mostly little business names like Sunset Janitorial Service. On going over the numbers from the motel, there were quite a few Las Vegas numbers, both from the office and from rooms. Some of the numbers were repeats of those from the arson house."

"OK. Good job. Think the Las Vegas numbers are the reinsurance for the bets?"

"Probably. I wonder if they aren't mob related as the motel had some of the same and I don't think there was gambling there."

"Tell us what you have, Al."

"Actually very little. We had pretty good cooperation for that area and no one knows the killer or why anyone would do Joy. By all accounts she was a very pleasant lady and caused no problems. No close friends but we did find a letter from her mother in Alabama. Called the mother and she hadn't heard anything much from her. She had left Alabama for Los Angeles about eight months ago after her husband left her, taking all their money."

"Well, that makes it look like it might have been related to her willingness to testify. And what do you have, Ridley?"

"Quite a bit. First thing, the lab thinks that the bullet sent over by the hospital from the hunting accident is from the same gun that killed Joy."

"Really. That ties things together. I didn't suspect that at all. What else?"

"Beside the hot pillow business, the motel also had quite a few people from Las Vegas who stayed there one to several nights. One of them had a black Buick rental car with 5F license. We tracked it down to Budget at Ontario and the lab found evidence of gun fire out the passenger window. The lab is also working on fingerprints on the rental papers."

"Now that is interesting progress. It sounds like you have the murder car. The crime sounds like a mob hit and if the shooter is from Vegas, that makes it more likely."

"Yep. I called Las Vegas PD with the address of the renter. The address is a sleazy social club that is used as an accommodation address by mafia types. I interviewed the arson victim again and he won't say much but he doesn't know anything about hunting and won't say where he was when shot. I think it was either a missed attempt on his life or a serious warning to him."

"Anybody have any ideas about where we go from here?"

Ridley answered, "I think we're out of our depth. We don't have the personnel or the experience to go to Las Vegas and try to track down a mafia hit man. Do you suppose Las Vegas PD has enough interest to run with it?"

"I doubt it. They work around these people all the time and I don't think our little episodes would impress them greatly unless they were trying to get something on a particular group. The FBI has an ongoing interest in some of these gang problems. My first impulse is to go to them."

"I think that's a good idea, Palmer. If we could find a reasonable agent, without the ego some have, and just present what we have and see if they would like it or have suggestions of where to go next."

"I worked a while back on a case with the agent who is now the assistant agent in charge. He was pleasant to work with and maybe I could go and present our case to him."

"That sounds like a good plan. Now tell us about the flight test."

Palmer briefly told them how the preflight portion required him to plan a flight, get weather, and then check the airplane. "The planned flight was started but after a few miles, the examiner had me demonstrate an engine failure response and then do various maneuvers. Then he asked me to demonstrate landings in various conditions and configuration of the airplane. We landed and I expected more questions but he signed me off." He showed them his temporary certificate as a private pilot.

He changed to police mode. "I'll try to see the FBI man tomorrow. I'm going to call him now. Follow up on the good work you've done and be sure everything including the lab material is carefully documented. If the feds decide to come in with us on this, we want to show them good police work up to this point. They won't judge on our findings but on the reports of those findings."

Palmer went back to his office and called the Los Angeles office of the FBI. "This is Palmer Carson, chief of detectives at Pasadena Police. I'd like to reach agent Paul Nichols."

"Can another agent help you? Chief Nichols is quite busy."

"I've worked with him before. Please ask him if he will speak with me."

"How are you, Palmer? What can I do for you?"

"We have a homicide and an arson case with attempted murder that are connected and that apparently involve gang figures from Nevada. I'd like to present these to you and see if they might come under your area of interest and if not, get some ideas as to where to go with them."

"I'd be glad to go over them with you and discuss them. I can't guarantee that we have an interest."

"Of course not without knowing the cases. As long as you give me a hearing, that's all I expect."

"I'll do that certainly. Could you come over here tomorrow or should I go to your department?"

"I'll be glad to go over to your office. What time would be convenient for you?"

"Why don't we do it first thing before other problems come up for both of us?"

"That's perfect for me. I'll be there about eight thirty or do you start before that?"

"I usually get to work about that time. That should be fine. See you then."

Chapter 19

The Westin Hotel on Los Robles was hosting a small convention of one of the big insurance companies. She decided to give it another try after she bombed out the last time. No, she hadn't wasted the evening. She had learned a lot about rocket propulsion and about English designer William Norris. She drove near the hotel and parked on the street. Entering the hotel, she walked to the bar. She managed to find a seat at a small table when the previous occupant got up to go to dinner. Tonight she was being a little different. "Bourbon and water." She directed the waiter.

Several roving eyes stopped on her. A slender man, probably forty, sat down at her table with a quick "May I?" and without waiting for a reply. "I'm Powell."

"Rachael. Is Powell first or last?"

"First. It's an old family name."

"You work with New York Life?"

"Yes. I've been an agent with them for twenty years. I'm now the senior agent in the Fresno area."

"As you become senior, do you get extra pay or have supervisory duties?"

"We're totally on commission. One gets a good commission when you write the policy and then a small percent of the premium as long as the policy is in effect. Those mount up as I'm still getting payments on some I wrote twenty years ago. As they accumulate, your income is more stable and one can live comfortably without selling new policies."

"I didn't know that. That really ties you into the same company, doesn't it."

"It's possible to leave and keep payments under some conditions but it certainly is easier to stick with the same company."

"How do you decide what company to work with. I assume you can only work with one."

"That's right. One life company. One can also have another company for other products but most don't as that dilutes the basic work on life. Most people don't actually decide. They are looking for a job and meet a recruiter for a company somewhere, maybe a job fair. They decide to try it and then they are, as you realized, pretty much locked into that company."

"Did you know the company when you started?"

He shook his head. "I just lucked into one of the top companies and one with good personnel relations. I had no idea of the work when I started. They do pay you a salary until you get started."

"Did they give you training?"

"Oh, yes. This company has a very good training program and I wasn't turned loose until I had learned most of what was needed. Of course, there are always things one learns on the job later."

"I think that's true in any field. Certainly an education degree doesn't give you the key to interpersonal relations with students."

"Are you a teacher?"

"Yes. I teach high school biology here in Pasadena."

They conversed casually a few minutes. He seemed a quiet, pleasant person. "Could I invite you to my room?"

She was about to say no. He didn't deserve to die. But then he added, "I guarantee that you'll have a wonderful time. My technique is vastly superior to most of those pick-ups who are just quickie types."

"He just signed his death warrant," she thought, "Another arrogant jerk."

"Sure," she replied to him, "I'd enjoy that."

She leaned against him in the elevator. He kept his hand on her butt as they walked up the hall. In the room, he pulled her to him and kissed her. She responded by running her tongue into his mouth.

"Unbutton me," she ordered. He was so excited that he could hardly handle the buttons. When she slipped off the blouse, he kissed her nipples. Then she unbuttoned his shirt. He slipped out of it, then sat to take off his shoes and socks. He dropped his pants and stepped out of them. Standing in his shorts, he kissed her again and ran his hand up under her skirt. Feeling no panties, he said, "Oh, boy."

"No. I'm a girl." She laughed and then said, "see, I'm ready for you."

She dropped the skirt and then peeled down his shorts. She knelt in front of him and said, "Let me see if it's ready for me."

She took his erect penis in her mouth and moved her tongue over it. He gave a pleasured moan and then suddenly, "What are—" as she bit hard. He jerked forward with the pain, only to impale himself on the point of the knife. As she pulled the handle upward, he fell forward. She stepped back and when the body had stopped moving turned him over with a bare foot and pulled the knife out. She wiped it on his shirt. She put on her clothes and then took the maid's outfit from her bag and slipped it over them. She carefully checked the room and then let herself out into the hall.

Halfway down the hall, she saw the elevator door opening and a couple got off. She continued walking, staying close to the wall where the light was less bright. She turned into the stairway just before reaching them.

At the foot of the stairs, she took off the maid's costume, went out into the lobby to the exit door and walked to her car. She went immediately onto the freeway and west to Madre where she exited for her motel. In the room she took off the blond wig and carefully put it away to preserve the wave.

She thought about the man and his work. Maybe she could do an expose of the life insurance industry. The idea of getting continuing payments as long as the policy was in force amazed her. She was planning her approach when she fell asleep.

Chapter 20

Palmer was at the FBI office early. He was on the elevator and Paul came across the lobby and jumped on just as the doors closed. "Good morning, Paul."

"Good morning to you, Palmer. You're right on time."

When the door opened, Palmer started to get off but Paul said, "That's the public entry. We'll go up two more floors and go direct to my office."

They got off and Paul led into his office. "Sit down and tell me about your case. I've read about your black widow. That isn't part of this, is it?"

"No. I haven't a clue where to start on finding more about the widow. She really covers all her tracks. This involves two other cases that we didn't know were related at first. We had an accidental shooting, reported as a hunting accident, that we didn't pay much attention to. But then someone set a fire and tried to cook the accident victim. The other case started with a vice bust at a hot pillow motel. The girl said she would testify against the owner and two days later someone shot her. The bullet came from the same gun as the hunting accident; our tech happened to remember and put it together. On further study, both cases have a Vegas connection. The hunting victim was running a book and reinsuring in Vegas and the motel was headquarters for Vegas people when they came down here. A lot of overlap in phone numbers."

"That's in interesting combination of cases. I'm afraid most departments wouldn't have been able to connect the dots to see they went together."

"Well, luck helped us do it. I have details in the reports here if you want to go further."

"I do. The city of Vegas and the big casino owners have been trying to keep the mob out but there is a constant attempt to get in. There have been some recent episodes there, with a couple killings that we are trying to get a handle on. There's enough in this that I'd like to pursue it further."

They went over reports and Paul pulled up some information on his computer and then said, "Do you mind if the agent in charge of this investigation sits in?"

"Of course not. Whatever you need to do."

Paul called the agent and as they were waiting, Palmer's cell phone rang. "Sorry. I told them only to call if there was an emergency so I better see." To the phone, he said. "Lieutenant Carson."

"Lieutenant, I thought you ought to know. The widow did another guy last night."

"Oh, shit. Where was it."

"The Pasadena Westin."

"Get Ridley out there. I'm with the FBI on the other cases and I'll be there as soon as I can. Thanks."

"Bad news?" the FBI man asked.

"The widow did another killing last night."

"That is a problem. You'll probably want to continue this later."

"No. I've got a top notch sergeant and I'll trust her to get it going. I'd rather go ahead and tell you as much as I know while I'm here."

The second agent knocked and entered. Paul introduced them. "Parker this is agent Sean Riley. Parker Carson, chief of detectives at Pasadena PD."

"Good to meet you." Carson said. "I'm sure from your name that you have a Chinese background."

"Good to meet you, sir. You may be right, I hear they're taking over the companies of the old sod."

After an hour of going over the case, Sean asked, "Your technician thinks the two bullets were fired from the same gun but isn't quite sure. Is that correct?"

"Yes. They were dum-dum's so were pretty badly deformed."

"We have some more sophisticated ways of studying them. Would you mind loaning them to us?"

"That would be great. We can use any help we can get."

"I do think that it is worth while for us to be involved and I'll have a couple of my team go over these records and see if any of the names or phone numbers mean anything to our investigation. I'd like to take a shot at interviewing the arson victim. I might know enough to get him to consider cooperating. Do you still have the motel manager in jail?"

"Unfortunately no. We set the bail as high as the judge would go but a lawyer from one of the sleezier big firms in LA promptly bailed him. I think we will have to drop the case when it comes up. The DA felt that we might get him with the girl as a witness but with her dead I don't think there's a chance."

"Have you checked into the ownership of the motel?"

"We did but found a holding company that we couldn't crack."

"We will have a shot at that. We might have some connections and sources that you couldn't tap."

"I bet you do. Anything you want to do is fine. I would appreciate it if you would check with either me or Sergeant Ridley if you are going to do something in Pasadena. The chief gets really upset if someone works on our turf and we don't know about it."

"Sure. We'll keep you informed. I know we have a reputation of not paying much attention to local departments but that really isn't our policy. We try to keep them informed and ask them to participate. Some departments are hard to work with and sometimes we get ahead of the reporting but I'll do my best to work with you at all stages of the investigation."

"Thank you. We'll do anything we can. Pasadena with the Tournament of Roses considers itself older and more important than most cities its size and you need an introduction for certain social groups. I can keep you from the briar patch if you get into the local politics."

"I'll remember that. We'll be in touch."

Paul spoke, "I guess you want to be after the widow now."

"Did she do it again?" Sean asked.

"I'm afraid so. They just called me. I'll go see if she slipped this time. So far, she has covered her tracks remarkably well."

"Good luck."

Palmer left and went to the elevator. He said to himself, "Sounds like I'll get some help on the other case. They were very pleasant. I hope that isn't just covering so they can shut us out. At least they can check the Nevada angle. Now I'll go and see what the widow has done this time."

Sergeant Ridley arrived at the Westin Hotel. "You want room 332," the doorman said as she entered. She went up to the third floor. There was a uniformed officer outside a door, so she went to that room.

"Morning, Sergeant."

"Did you get the call, Henley?"

"No, mam. Olsen was the first on scene. I came just after. Looks like the widow did it again."

She went into the room. The body was lying on the floor and a uniformed officer was standing uncomfortably across the room. "Hi, Olsen. Things just like you first saw them?"

"Absolutely. We haven't touched anything."

"I was sure you wouldn't. Either you or Henley can go down to the desk and get a copy of his papers. The other can go back to work. Thanks for taking care of it."

"You're welcome. I'll go back on patrol and tell Henley you want him to do the desk."

"Fine with me." He went out.

Ridley called the department on the radio. "Dispatch. S4. Have the lab and the coroner been notified? How about detective Carnucci?"

"All on the way."

"Good job. Thanks." She started looking at the body. There was a lot of blood in the groin and she could see the bite marks on his penis. There were just a few drops of blood under the sternum where the knife had gone in. She didn't touch him but turned to the closet and the chest of drawers, going over his possessions. There was a knock at the door. "Come."

Henley came in, holding several sheets of paper. "This is what the desk had on him. The lab guys are unloading and I just saw the coroner wagon pulling into the parking."

"Thanks. Would you hang around in the hall for a few with all the coming and going?"

The two lab techs arrived. "Morning, Sarge."

"Good morning. We've got to stop meeting like this."

"Yeah. Damn girl makes it hard for us.'

"Well, you know what to do. I suppose both you and the coroner's investigator will take pictures."

"Yes. They look for a little different emphasis than we do. They'll be up any minute." He took his camera out of the box they brought while the other tech started dusting for prints. "I don't know why we bother. She never seems to make a mistake and leave any."

The coroner's team brought the gurney in and the investigator set up for his pictures. The door opened again and Detective Carnucci came in. "Good morning, Sergeant. What have we today?"

"Same as the first one. Let's get a bag and package his clothes and effects and then we can go talk to people." Then she said to the coroner's man, "When you and our lab guys finish, you can go ahead and take him downtown." To the police tech, "Sid, give me a call on the radio when you're ready to leave and I'll come and lock up."

"OK," he said, not even looking up from the camera.

Ridley and Al packaged the possessions and went out. "Al start knocking on doors and asking hotel guests if they saw anything. You can get a room list at the desk. I'll start with the employees."

Palmer drove out the Pasadena Freeway and up to the Westin Hotel. Parking was underneath the hotel but he pulled up in front in a loading zone and stopped. Usually he was not so flagrant in taking advantage of his police office but he wanted to know what was going on. He went in and asked at the desk, "Where are the police?"

"Room 332. Take the service elevator over here and you'll be very close."

"Thank you."

He took the service elevator up and found a uniformed officer outside the room. "Morning, lieutenant," he said.

"Is anyone inside?"

"The lab crew and the guys from the coroner's office. Sergeant Ridley and Detective Carnucci left a few minutes ago to do interviewing."

"Thanks, Henley." He went into the room. The coroner's investigator was taking pictures. Palmer walked over and looked at the body. There was a little blood from a small wound in the center of the chest. More blood had come from a bitten area on the penis. He was a nice looking man and he looked more pathetic dead than most.

He called Ridley on the radio. "Where are you?"

"Down in the bar. I'll be up in two minutes."

Ridley entered and nodded to him. "How did it go with the FBI?"

"Good, I think. They are interested and are going to restudy the bullets and reinterview the arson victim for starters. They plan to check our phone number lists and names and see if anyone fits into their Vegas investigation. They were very pleasant and cooperative and promised to let us know what they are doing. I hope it goes as well as they say."

"We never know with the feds but I'll give them a chance. The widow is back to her original technique. Haven't found anything so far. She was black haired last night. The lab guys didn't find any prints except those of the victim. So far I haven't found anyone who noticed them in the bar."

Al came back in and said, "Welcome back, Lieutenant."

"Have anything?"

"One couple saw her leaving. She had on a maid's uniform but still had the shiny black wig. They weren't close enough to see her face."

The coroner's investigator came over to the Pasadena police officers. "You guys are going to have to do something before she fills up our morgue."

"She's pretty sharp. We haven't found a damn thing yet."

"Anything else you want or can we take the body?"

Palmer looked at Ridley. "Go ahead," she said. "It doesn't seem to give us any information."

"Who is he?" Palmer asked Ridley.

"Life insurance salesman from Fresno named Powell Cornwell. I notified his wife and I see why he wanted the widow. His wife is a real bitch to talk to."

"Have you interviewed the people in the hotel?"

"A few plus the staff from last night that were available. I've asked Ollie to come over and help Al with the people at the convention. Not that we'll find anything."

"I'm glad to turn some of the other stuff over to the feds. We are getting overextended with that investigation on top of the widow case."

"I wish we could turn the widow over to someone. I'm not getting anywhere with her," Ridley answered. "Did you remember we are supposed to meet with Pomona this afternoon?"

"No, I didn't. We can tell them about the new murder but not much else. You want to ride over with me in the airplane?"

"Sure. I'm willing to live dangerously. Is Al going?"

"I don't see any reason for him to go. He can hold the fort."

"Flores knows about it and I bet she goes. She really is into Detective Finley."

"I don't see why we need her but I guess I'll just do nothing and if she shows that's fine."

"See you at two thirty at the station. I'll continue to check out the employees here and leave the guests with Al."

"I'd better talk to the press before they start accusing us of cover-up. Then I'll get the information the feds want and write up my paper work."

Chapter 21

Both Flores and Detective Finley arrived at Brackett early. "I hoped you would be the first one from your department," Frank said when Flores arrived. They took a table out on the porch. It overlooked the runway and they could watch the planes land and take off. However, the planes were the last thing on their minds.

"I'm glad you were early too."

"I enjoyed talking on the phone night before last. Then you weren't sure you were to come today."

"I'm still not sure. The lieutenant never said one way or the other. So I just assumed I was part of it and came. I wouldn't have taken the responsibility on my own except that I wanted to see you again."

"That's nice. I could hardly wait to see if you were able to be here. What have you been doing?"

"Nothing but routine patrol. I guess you heard that the widow did another killing?"

"Yes, but I don't know anything except what was in the paper."

"I don't either. The detectives didn't ask me to help this time and I haven't heard anything. I don't think they've found anything useful."

"She is one shrewd individual. I don't know if we'll ever catch her. To change the subject: how about dinner tomorrow night?"

"That would be nice. I work the next day so we shouldn't stay too late."

"Work is the curse of the romantic classes to misquote someone. I'll pick you up about six."

"That will be fine. I think we should go Dutch this time. I don't want to use up all your income."

"I'll buy this time as I have a nice, quiet, inexpensive place in mind. I'll take you up on the time after that."

"OK. Where are we going?"

"It'll be a surprise." He squeezed her hand and then let go. "Afraid we are going to get down to business."

Sergeant Acker came out on the porch. "Well, good to see you again, Flores. Are you representing Pasadena alone?"

"No, sir. The others should be along any minute. I didn't talk to either of them today so I don't know their plans. I'm not up to date on the new killing."

Carson had driven with Ridley to El Monte airport. He parked by the hangar and opened the hangar door. He did a preflight, telling Ridley what he was doing. "We drain a little gas from each tank to make sure no water has gotten in. I will turn on the power and lower the flaps so that we can see they are properly attached. Now I'm moving the control surfaces to see that they are free." He checked the oil and looked at the different aerials. He pulled the plane out of the hangar.

He opened the passenger door and showed Ridley how to climb in and fasten the safety harness. He went around and climbed in. He went down the pre-start check list and then started the engine. He held out a headset and when Ridley had it on, said, "This has an intercom and we can talk. It only goes into the radio when I push the switch here on the yoke." He went down the pre-take off check list, reading each item as he checked it. Then he contacted ground control. "Cessna 6457 Tango taxi for take off with Kilo weather."

"57 Tango taxi runway one niner."

At the runway he changed to tower frequency and said, "Cessna 6457 Tango ready for take off. Left turn departure for Brackett."

"57 Tango cleared for take off. Left turn approved."

"57 Tango cleared for take off," he read back and pushed in the throttle. Ridley was fascinated by his apparent competence and care. The plane took to the air smoothly and they turned left at the freeway. He said to Ridley, "We use the full call sign the first time we contact each controller and then can use a shorter one after that."

Soon they contacted Brackett tower, "Cessna 6457 Tango five miles out for landing."

"57 Tango make left traffic for runway 26 left. Cleared to land."

"57 Tango cleared to land on 26 left." Then to Ridley, "You will hear a horn warning of a stall just before we land. That means we are slow enough to land so don't worry."

Acker sat down and watched a Cessna land. "That looks like the one Carson was flying the other day." It taxied off the runway and parked to the side of the restaurant. Carson got out and Acker said, "It is the one. There he is." Then the door on the other side opened and Ridley exited.

"He must have passed his pilot's exam," Finley said. "I'm not sure I would want to be the first passenger after his flight test."

Carson and Ridley came out to the porch. "Congratulations, Palmer," Acker said. "Is it legal to take passengers now?"

"Thanks. Yes, it is. I'm a certified private pilot. What did you think, Ridley? Did I seem to know what I was doing?"

"A good job. Not even a bounce on landing. He learned well. He checks everything ahead."

"That's good to know. Now tell me about the latest on the widow."

"Ridley did most of the work. You tell them about it."

"Same technique as the first one. She bit his penis and when he jerked forward, he hit the stiletto and she opened his heart. No fingerprints, no evidence. The only thing we found out is one couple saw her leave, wearing a long skirted maid's uniform. She must carry that with her and put it on so that people won't be attracted to the short skirt."

"Any reason you can find for this man?"

"He was at a convention at the hotel as usual. I don't think there is any reason she picks a particular one. We aren't getting anywhere with her. How about you?"

"We've had several calls about unsolved rapes from other departments. A couple of rather traumatic ones suggest Washington may have done them. They are doing DNA testing now. He was one bad apple. Too bad she couldn't stick to doing bad guys like him. She would probably get a medal."

"We've been somewhat diverted from the widow," Palmer said. "Did you hear about our arson case and our assassination?"

"Yeah, but not a lot. Want to tell us?"

"I don't think they relate to you but I'll give you a quick run down. The arson victim was saved only because a firefighter saw the beginning of the fire and got him out. He was home recuperating from a hunting accident. We think he was running a book. He was shot with a twenty five caliber marksman pistol and dumdum bullet."

"Makes you wonder what he was hunting, doesn't it?"

"Sure does. But then the lab found the bullet in that case was from the same gun as the shooting on Summit Street. The victim here was a nice girl with a job who turned occasional tricks on the side but everyone found her quiet and pleasant. We think she was killed to prevent her testifying against a motel manager in a hot pillow motel. We just found the murder car—a rental by someone staying at the motel and from Las Vegas. Both cases seem to have Nevada mob connections and we now have the FBI looking into the connection with other mob activities."

"That's interesting. How do you get along with the Feebees?"

"So far they have kept us in the loop and seem to be doing a good job."

"We don't seem to get anywhere on the widow. Do you want to have another meeting or shall we just call if either of us finds something?"

"I think that's adequate. She doesn't leave us much to use in brainstorming. I am getting all the information and will send it to the FBI profiling division and see if they have any ideas. However, I understand that takes quite some time to get an answer."

Acker got up. "We'll keep in touch. It's been nice to share the misery with you."

"Same here. I'll give you a call. We might even prevail on Flores to keep in touch with Finley, just as a favor to the department."

Flores blushed and Finley looked annoyed. Neither answered. Palmer and Ridley went out and got into the little airplane. The other three stayed on the porch until Carson had taxied to the end of the runway and then taken off by the restaurant. "Thanks for coming," Acker said and went out to his car. Flores and Finley walked out together. "I'll keep in touch, just for the good of the department," Finley said with a smile. He walked Flores to her car and gave her a quick kiss as she turned to get into the car. "See you tomorrow."

Palmer asked Ridley, "Would like to steer the plane?"

She could hear well over the intercom and answered, "Is it safe?"

"Sure. Just while we're flying level at altitude. You just try to hold heading and altitude. It isn't too much different than driving, except it's driving in three dimensions. Just take the yoke and try to hold it steady. This instrument is the altimeter and we want to keep it at three thousand feet where it is now." He took his hands off the control and the plane went steadily along. Ridley took the yoke and found that she couldn't keep it as steady as it was by itself. It kept turning a little or climbing and when she tried to stop it, she over-controlled and it went the other way.

"It takes a little practice to get used to the very gradual corrections it needs," Palmer said. "I'll take it now as we need to start descending for El Monte."

Ridley watched how he controlled it with much more appreciation after trying herself. He lined up with the runway at El Monte and when the tower cleared him to land, brought the plane in to a smooth landing. They taxied over to the hanger and put the plane away. As they got into Palmer's car, Ridley said, "That was really interesting. Thank you for letting me try."

"I'd let you do more if I was more experienced myself but this is my first time with a passenger. I think it went well though."

"It certainly did. I wish the case on the widow would go as well."

Chapter 22

The police dispatcher answered the phone, "Pasadena Police."

A hoarse whisper came over the phone, "I know who the black widow is."

"Who is this?"

"Do you want to know who the black widow is."

"Of course. But I want to know who is reporting."

"She is Carmen Sanchez, lives at 1324 West Trails Drive in El Monte."

"May I have your name?"

"No. Did you get the address?"

"1324 West Trails."

"That's correct and that's all I'm saying. Good by."

The dispatcher pushed a button. "Carson," came the reply.

"Lieutenant, this is Della in dispatch. I had a call saying he knows who the black widow is. It was a hoarse whisper, obviously to conceal his voice and he wouldn't tell me anything, just gave the name and address."

"Sounds like a flake but we'll have to check it out. What was the name?"

"Carmen Sanchez at 1324 West Trails Drive, El Monte."

"Thanks a lot. We'll work it. Sergeant Ridley is in the field. Would you radio her to give me a call?"

"Will do."

He put the name in his computer while he waited. She had a driver's license, at that address and had no record or warrants. The phone rang.

"Ridley?"

"Yes, sir. What's up?"

"Where are you?"

"I'm in Rosemead. Just talked to a witness in the Thompson case."

He told her about the call. "It's nearly time to quit but that isn't too far from where you are. Why don't you go by the address on the way back and see what you can find?"

"Sure. I'll call you if I find anything. Otherwise I'll just tell you when I get back."

"That's fine. I'll see if I can find anything on her from here."

Ridley drove to the address. It was in a fairly nice working class neighborhood and was a well kept little duplex. She knocked on the door. A tall, pleasant faced young lady came to the door. "Can I help you?"

"Are you Carmen Sanchez?"

"I am. I just came from work."

"I'm Sergeant Ridley from Pasadena Police. We had an anonymous call, linking you to a crime we're working."

Carmen laughed bitterly. "That will be Hector Garcia, an ex-boy friend. I have a restraining order on him but he keeps trying to find ways around it. Tell me what the crime is and I'll see if I have an alibi. Whatever it is, I wasn't involved."

"He suggests you are the black widow."

"Oh boy, I'm really coming up in the world. If I was, he'd be the first one to go."

Ridley gave her the dates of the three killings.

"On the first date I was in Las Vegas for a company meeting. Stayed at the Sands and I can give you half a dozen co-workers I was with. I don't remember the second." She pulled out a pocket schedule book. "On the third date I worked late, went to dinner and a late movie with Bill Schumann." She turned the pages. "His address and phone number are here."

Ridley wrote them down. "What about Hector's address?"

"I think he is still at 214 Garvey. Phone was 626 497-2316. He works the evening shift as a warehouseman for Walmart at the Temple City store."

"Thank you very much. Sorry to be a bother. I may need some more information but this should do most of it. You've been very cooperative."

"If you find him, give him as much trouble as you can."

Ridley laughed. "I'll put the fear of God into him."

Ridley went back to her car. She reached Carson on the phone. "This is Ridley, lieutenant. I don't think she's involved. She doesn't fit what descriptions we have. She's a very open, nice person who blames the report on an ex-boyfriend who is under a restraining order. He works P.M. shift at Walmart in Temple City and I'll talk to him on the way back. Will you still be there?"

"Sure. I've got lots to do here. I checked on the location of the caller of the report. It was done from a pay phone in the Walmart store there. I'll see you in a bit. Thanks."

Ridley drove over to the Walmart. Going around to the warehouse entrance, she went to the door. An officious middle aged man was at the door. "I'm detective Sergeant Ridley. I want to talk to Hector Garcia."

"We don't allow employees to have company during working time."

"I'm not company. I need information on police business."

"See him at home."

Ridley was really annoyed by his attitude. "OK. I'm going to give you three possible choices: first, get him here; second, get your supervisor here at once; third, go to jail for obstruction." She took her handcuffs out of her purse and swung them around.

He looked mesmerized at the handcuffs for a minute. Then he went to the phone and dialed. "Hector Garcia to the entry. Hector Garcia to the entry," came over the speaker in the warehouse.

Soon a young man with a muscular body and a handsome but weak face appeared.

"Yes, boss?"

"This lady wants to talk to you."

He looked at her carefully. "I'm always happy to help pretty girls. What would you like to do?" He smiled arrogantly at her.

Ridley waved the handcuffs at him. "I'd like to put your smart ass in jail."

This time he looked at Ridley with surprise. "You're a cop?"

"Detective Sergeant Ridley. I don't suppose you are going to try to deny you made the phone report from the pay phone here?"

"What are you talking about?"

"Come on. We know you tried to set up Carmen. I can get you six months in jail for a false police report, even if the judge doesn't think it's a violation of your restraining order and add another year or two."

"I'm sorry I did it. She just makes me so mad. She tries to be so damn superior. She's ruined my life."

"If you think your life is ruined now, try to get your job back after spending a year in jail with a felony conviction."

"I really don't want to go to jail."

"You bet you don't. You don't know half the problems you would have there and afterwards. Maybe we can avoid it if you're honest and shape up. You really know nothing about the widow?"

"No, mam."

"I'm going to let you go for now. Let me give you some advice. This episode will be on your record so if you do anything more to Carmen you are sure to go to jail. I know you've been told to forget her but I mean it. She wants nothing to do with you and you can only get in more trouble. Find someone else and get a life."

Ridley turned to where the foreman stood near the door. "Thanks for your help. Make it a little easier next time if you don't like trouble." She still had the handcuffs in her hand and she carefully slipped them back in her purse, turning so the foreman could see them.

Both men stood speechless as she walked back to the car.

The foreman looked at Hector. "That's one hard-ass bitch."

"I sure don't want anything more to do with her. I bet she would put us in jail."

Back at the station she reported to the Lieutenant. They exchanged information and she ended with, "You know, sometimes it is kinda fun to push your rank around a little. I think both those assholes are going to think twice before they cause any trouble."

"My, my, Ridley. And you come from such a nice family."

They both laughed and left for home.

Chapter 23

Sean Riley called for Lieutenant Carson. "Palmer, we are making progress but not much definite. We would like a favor."

"What can we do?"

"We think that there may be some activity going on in that area tonight or tomorrow. Could you stake out the motel there where the Vegas guys stay from eight tonight until about two in the morning and then from six on tomorrow if nothing has happened?"

"Sure. What should we be looking for?"

"Probably nothing major will happen there but we would like to know the comings and goings at the motel. License numbers of cars, how many people, that sort of thing."

"We'll do it. I judge you don't want us to do anything but just get information."

"That's right. Unless something we don't expect happens, don't get involved. I'll talk to you tomorrow morning and will send out some pictures of people to look for when it's daylight. Not much chance of identification at night."

"OK. I'll have someone out there."

Palmer was debating who to have do this. "Ollie knows the area and isn't working on anything major. I think he's the best bet." He phoned Ollie. "Could you do a stake out from eight to two tonight at the Starlight Motel?'

"Sure. I'll go home early and get some rest. What am I looking for?"

"It's a request from the FBI in their investigation. They want licenses on cars, how many people come and go. Just information, no action unless you see something urgent and unexpected."

"Sound like a nice boring evening."

"I hope it isn't any more than that. Thanks for doing it."

At eight o'clock Ollie was parked up the street from the Starlight Motel. He had his beat up looking old undercover car and had found the best observation point without being too obviously watching. He had brought a thermos of coffee and a sandwich. He settled down in the car and listened to the news as he watched.

A couple cars stopped at the motel. They were not license numbers he recognized but he wrote them all down. A couple came in and the man went to the office. Ollie wrote down the number and a half hour later when they came out and drove off, he noted the time of leaving by the number.

By eleven o'clock he was having trouble staying awake. Nothing was happening and he kept looking around the area to have something to do. Suddenly he saw a movement just at the side of the car. He pushed the door handle and rolled out onto the street just as the passenger side window smashed and he heard the loud pop of a shot. He had taken out his gun as he rolled out of the car and automatically taken off the safety catch. He lay quietly waiting for the shooter to move.

Finally a light flashed on. The flash aimed in the car, then turned off. Ollie didn't move. The light appeared again, coming around the back of the car. Ollie assumed the shooter would be right handed and had the flashlight in his left so he could hold the gun. He shot eight inches to the right of the flashlight. He heard a thud followed by a scream. The flashlight fell to the ground and turned off. He heard another object fall and thought it was probably the gun.

"Is anyone there?" Ollie called. There was a moan and then a hesitant "Damn you."

He crawled toward the spot where the flashlight had landed. Finally his hand hit the light. He grasped it and holding it far out to the side turned it on. A man was lying a few feet in front of him, with blood coming from his right side. Ollie got up with his gun ready. The man didn't move except to breathe and Ollie pulled out his handcuffs and pulling the hands behind him, cuffed him.

"You don't have to do that, I'm hurt bad."

Ollie ignored him and looked for the gun. He went back to his car and took a plastic bag. He pushed the gun into it and sealed it. Then he picked up the mike for the police radio and said, "D-4. Officer involved shooting at Starlight motel. We need the ambulance and back up."

"D-4, are you injured?"

"Only a scratched knee. The bad guy is shot."

"Ambulance and back up on the way. I'm calling the shooting team and Lieutenant Carson."

Ollie heard the sirens and in a minute, a patrol unit was beside him. "You OK?" the patrolman asked.

"Yeah. The ambulance is for this guy." And he pointed to the handcuffed shooter. "He took a shot at me and I had better aim."

The city fire department ambulance pulled up and the paramedics jumped out. They looked at the uniformed officer. "What's the deal?"

"The detective here shot this guy who had shot at him and missed."

The paramedic looked at the shooter. "You got him at the side of the abdomen. It doesn't look too serious but he'll need surgery. Does he need the handcuffs?"

"He's under arrest for attempted murder of a police officer. I'd leave them on until you get to the hospital and they have to examine him more. We need to have a guard for him." The ambulance team loaded him and took off.

Another patrol car arrived, followed by the shift sergeant. The sergeant asked, "Are you alright, Ollie?"

"A little shook up but no real problems. The son of a bitch would have killed me if I hadn't just caught a glimpse of something metal moving along the side of the car. I rolled out on the ground just as he fired. Could you have one of the patrol guys go to the motel and see if anyone is up and saw or heard anything?"

"Good idea. I'll send Henderson." He started over to the patrol officers just as a green car pulled in at the front of the sergeant's black and white. The sergeant turned back to Ollie. "Here's Lieutenant Carson."

"Are you OK, Ollie?"

"Yeah. A few scratches but you should see the other guy."

"What happened?"

"Very quiet evening with a few cars coming to the motel. About eleven I saw something moving along side my car. I opened the door and rolled out, just as the window broke on the passenger's side and he shot. He finally turned on a flashlight and came looking for me. I shot near the light and got him. I found the flashlight, cuffed him, and called the station."

"Did the shot break the window or did he smash it just before shooting?"

"It happened so fast I'm not sure. Incidentally, I have the gun in a plastic bag in my car."

"Forensics will love to get hold of that. Oh, the two guys of the shooting team are here." The shooting team had two roles. One was to get evidence of how and why the policeman shot to protect the department from criticism and to protect or condemn the cop, depending on the correctness of his decision to shoot. The other was to see if the stress of the shooting was affecting the policeman and to decide if he needed psychological help. Each was an experienced officer who had other duties in the department and had volunteered for the shooting team as an additional duty. Each had participated in an officer involved shooting and backed his work by personal experience.

The shooting team asked Ollie to give them the story while they videotaped it. The first man then went to check the car while the other talked to Ollie about how he was feeling. "Are you upset?"

"A little. It was a near miss. If I had dozed off on the stakeout, I'd never have waked up. That bothers me a little."

"How about having to shoot a man? Does that bother you?"

"No. The bastard tried to kill me and it was a good shooting. He deserved it."

The second officer came back. "Story checks. He was lucky as well as skilled. It was a good shooting. Nothing else he could have done. I'll write the report."

The other asked, "Do you want me to take you home?"

"What about my car?"

"I've already called for a wrecker to take it back to the police lot."

Ollie called, "Lieutenant."

Carson came over. "Yes, Ollie."

"They're going to have the car towed. We need to get the gun out before it goes."

"Thanks. You're right. I'll get it myself and then turn it in." He went over to the stake-out car and returned with the gun. "Little fellow in spite of the long barrel."

"In the hands of a good shooter, it's amazingly accurate."

"Want me to take you home, Ollie?"

"I'd appreciate that." He called to the shooting team man who was now checking the fragments of glass from the exploding window, "The lieutenant will give me a ride home."

"OK. Let me know if you have any problems or a delayed stress reaction. I'll be available."

"Thanks. I'll see you again."

Ollie and Carson walked to the car. "I didn't expect this when I asked you to do the stake-out, Ollie."

"I know. Isn't that the way with police work? One never knows even in the most benign situations. Not being ready for the unexpected is how we get officers killed."

"Absolutely. That's the hardest thing to inject into training. You teach how to handle a situation but there's no way to teach all the different things that can happen. We hope to teach flexibility and preparedness rather than specific actions."

"And often the kids just don't believe it can happen to them."

"You're not married, are you, Ollie?"

"Got divorced three years ago."

"Do you need someone to stay with you?"

"No. I'm not upset about this. I'll go right to sleep and then probably dream the shooter is back and I can't get out of the car."

Carson dropped Ollie off and then went home. He picked up the phone and put in Sean Riley's number. "Riley."

"This is Carson in Pasadena. Sorry to wake you but we had an attack on the stake-out officer at the Starlight Motel. Fortunately the officer was alert and shot the attacker. He's now in the hospital."

"Glad you called. That is a surprise. What did he attack with?"

"He had the twenty five caliber competition revolver. Our guys will look at it and then let your forensics people study it too. I think we have the shooter in the Summit case."

"That's great. Let's both spend tomorrow putting together the evidence and then we'll talk again."

"Very good. Go back to sleep."

"Thanks. Same to you."

The first thing in the morning, Carson took the gun to the forensics lab. "Shooter tried to do Ollie on a stake-out last night. Missed and Ollie wounded him. The shooter had this gun, which is probably the one in the Summit killing."

"That's a stroke of luck. I'll see if the ballistics match."

"Check this out as soon as possible and then get it over to the FBI lab. They would like to check it today also."

"I'll make it the top priority. It's a little annoying to have to give it to them so soon but their back up will really help if we get to court on it."

Carson drove out to the Starlight Motel. The manager was at the desk. "Excitement here last night," Carson said.

"I missed it all. I would have thought a gunshot would wake me but it didn't. First thing I knew was when your officer rang the bell."

"Guy's ID shows he was A K Watkins. Was he staying here?"

"No one of that name had a room here."

"Probably would use another name. Can I see the register?"

"Not unless you have a warrant. Your guys stole my old register and never returned it."

"Will you tell me who did stay here last night?"

"Nope. You'll just try to frame me like the last time I tried to give someone some help."

"I'll see you later." Carson walked out. He wasn't too surprised at the manager's attitude. He was still on bail from the procuring charge and had been uncooperative even before that episode. He would talk with Sean. FBI credentials might get the manager's attention. Or he would go to the judge at municipal court and get a warrant.

His next stop was at the hospital. He went up to the surgical ward. There was a uniformed officer outside the room. "Good morning, Lieutenant. The nurses are being difficult about seeing this scumbag."

"I better check with them."

He walked down to the nursing station. An attractive middle-aged woman was the head nurse for the unit. "Good morning, Mrs. Johnson." Carson said. He had worked with her before.

"Good morning, Lieutenant. I suppose you want to see last night's admission. He's still pretty hung over from his anesthesia but will do well. I'm not sure you can get anything but I'll give you about two minutes. That shouldn't hurt him."

"Thanks. I'll be quick and careful."

He walked into the room. "How you doing?"

"Poorly. I didn't know the damn guy was a cop."

"I need to read you your rights before you say anything." He read through the Miranda warning. The patient looked bored. He had heard this before. "You didn't think he was a cop?"

"Some guy had been stalking me and I thought that was him. It was self defense."

"What's your real name?'

"You have my driver's license. I've said all I'm going to."

"OK. Get rested up. I'll talk to you again."

Carson didn't want to overstay the nurse's limit and it didn't seem like the patient was about to say anything more so he had decided not to push it. "Thanks," he said to Mrs. Johnson as he passed the desk on the way out.

"You're welcome. I appreciate you not tiring him out. Many of the cops don't know when to quit."

"I hope they'll learn over time. See you again." She waved a hand at him as he went off down the hall.

Back at the station he told the secretary, "Let me know if either Ollie or Ridley come in."

"Ridley was here. She said she'd be back by lunch time. Want me to put in a call?"

"No. There isn't any rush. Thanks anyway."

He looked over the reports on his desk. There wasn't anything of note. The important reports from last night would be his and Ollie's. So he started writing up his report.

Near the end of the day, Palmer received a call from Sean Riley. "What's new, Palmer?"

"Not much. Our forensic lab thinks they can match the gun to the bullet from the Summit Street murder."

"Our lab agrees with that. They will back you."

"The shooter is in the hospital so we haven't been able to have a line up for the man who felt he could recognize the shooter when he was sitting in the car on Summit but at the time he worked with our police artist and came up with a picture. It's uncanny. I could recognize the guy in the hospital from the picture if I met him on the street."

"That's amazing. I think our people are good at that and often there is a resemblance but I can't remember one that good."

"With that, I don't think we'll have trouble in a line up."

"It seems to me you have a really good case. I'd like to talk with the DA about it. Could you go with me tomorrow to the DA's office?"

"Sure. What time?"

"I'll call and see and get back to you. I'd like to have you bring copies of the reports on the killing, on the gun, and the picture if you can."

"I'll get all that."

"Let's say ten o'clock unless I call you otherwise, at the superior court building in Los Angeles."

"I'll meet you there."

Parker thought to himself after hanging up, "So the FBI is anxious to prosecute this guy. Does that mean they are ready to move on the larger case? I guess I'll find out tomorrow." He told the secretary, "I have to go to the DA tomorrow. I'll go direct from home and hope to be back before lunch. Could you make copies of the reports on the Summit case for me?" He made a list of the files he would need and went over it with her. She had already done most of them but added a few.

"Good luck with the DA, sir."

"Thanks. I'm not sure what is planned. The feds set up the meeting."

"Then you need extra luck. Good night."

"Good night."

Chapter 24

The black widow looked in her mirror. Now that she had the name, maybe she should live up to it. She put away the blond wig and put on the black one. Her skirt tonight was a little longer and not quite so attention attracting. She put in her bright blue contact lenses and picked up her bag. Getting into the car, she drove east to Arcadia.

Soon she was sitting at a table in the bar of the Holiday Inn Hotel in Arcadia, sipping her drink. The bar was busy with an advertising convention. A loud insurance salesman tried to sit down but he was already drunk and she sent him off. An athletic man of middle age approached, "Can I buy you another drink, Miss?"

"Thank you," she replied. He had neatly styled dark brown hair but when he turned to the bar to get the drink, she saw that he had a bald spot like a tonsure on his head. He sat down and introduced himself, "I'm Victor Hansen from Tucson."

"I'm Rachael. I'm down from the Bay area."

"The last time I was here, this hotel was under another name."

"I remember that. What was it, a Doubletree? I don't know why they sold it."

They talked casually for a time, sipping their drinks. Victor was an interesting man and she found him more enjoyable than she had expected.

"Do you work in advertising?" she asked.

"I do, but not in the usual area. I specialize in picture ads of destinations for travel companies, both tour operators and agencies."

"Do you get to go to the destinations to take the pictures? That must be a wonderful perk of the work."

"Occasionally. Most of the pictures are readily available and I don't get to visit as many places as I would like. Sometimes I am able to wangle a trip from one of the companies."

"What destinations do you like best?"

"It's hard to say. There are so many lovely places. I love the Pacific Islands. But I wouldn't give up Italy or France. And Guatemala is such a beautiful place with the old Mayan ruins and the Indians still wearing native dress in the highlands. I could go on and on. I love to travel."

"Do go on. Tell me a little about Italy. That would be my first choice for a visit, I think. I was there once on business but didn't get to do much sight seeing."

"I like the little villages in Tuscany. They have medieval churches and little towers on many of the houses. Set in vineyards, they are all charming."

"How about Rome?"

"A fascinating city. Now they don't allow cars in much of the city center and it makes it much more pleasant to walk. I have a favorite small hotel near the Roman forum. It was a convent for monks and they still live on the top floor. I jog in the mornings and it is close enough so I can jog in the Circus Maximus. It's exciting to be there and think of the past."

He seemed in no hurry and asked, "Would you like another drink?"

"I think not. This seems to be just enough."

Finally he asked, "Would you like to go up to the room?" She nodded her willingness and he paid the bill and escorted her to the elevator. In the room, he offered her a chair. Then he opened the little bar and asked, "Would you like another drink? They do have some bourbon in here."

"I think I've had enough but you have one if you want it."

"I don't need any more but I didn't want to not be hospitable."

He leaned over the chair and kissed her firmly. She returned the kiss and reached up to hold his head to her. He came around in front of the chair and pulled her to a standing position by her hands. Then he kissed her again. She pushed her body to him and he could feel her firm breasts against his chest. He slid his hands under her blouse and along her back. Then he pulled the blouse upward and over her head. He cupped her bare breast in his hand and then knelt and took it in his mouth. She ran her hand along his thigh until it reached his genitals. He moved his lips back to her mouth and then undid the button holding her skirt. It fell to the floor and she was naked. He rubbed her pubic hair gently and then she started unbuttoning his shirt. He took off his shoes sitting on the bed and then stood to take off his pants. She started to kneel in front of him. "No, thanks. I don't much like that way. Let's lie on the bed."

He didn't hurry but spent some time in foreplay. He kissed her face, her breasts, her abdomen. He reached between her legs and gently massaged the clitoris. She began getting excited, in spite of her commitment to her mission. Finally he went over her and pushed his penis between her legs. She loosened the stiletto, readying it for the ear attack while he was trying to insert. However, she was ready enough that his penis just slipped in. It felt very pleasant and suddenly she took her hand away from the knife. He started slowly and gradually picked up speed. She found herself cooperating in the motion. Finally he came and almost immediately she did too.

As she felt the reaction, suddenly her brain opened the blocked area and she remembered all the evenings with Fred. She was overwhelmed. As he moved off her, she said, "Oh, my." He held her gently for a few minutes. She lay with her head on his shoulder. She wasn't used to the rapid breathing and pumping heart that followed the climax. Then she got up and went to the bathroom. She came out, slipped into her clothes, and went to the bed. Victor was lying on his back, with his eyes shut. She kissed his forehead and spoke quietly. Then she walked out.

She sat in her car for a time. She could hardly believe all that she now remembered. This was why she had come back to Pasadena. She had repressed all these memories for many years and now she knew. Fred who she viewed as a father had seduced her. True, he did it slowly with the utmost care not to hurt her or frighten her, taking almost three years to consummate the seduction. But he had done it and that was the secret behind her confusion and upset.

Chapter 25

Palmer was ten minutes early at the Superior Court Building in Los Angeles. When he started to enter the building, a deputy sheriff directed him to a metal detector. He took out his police badge and said, "I'm carrying."

The deputy looked at the badge and said, "I should hope so in this area, Lieutenant. Go this way." He was directed to an aisle around the detector and went to the elevator. The DA's office was at the top of the building, above the court rooms. He went into the office and Sean was waiting and greeted him. "Welcome to Hades." The waiting room was full of people, mostly talking and many coming and going. "We're going to see Lance Miller, the chief trial deputy."

A harassed young lady came out into the waiting room and looked around. "Chief Riley?"

"I'm Riley and this is Lieutenant Carson of Pasadena Police."

"Come this way. Mr. Miller will see you now."

They followed her up a hall, then to another perpendicular corridor, and finally to an office where a large black lady sat guard at a desk. "Chief Riley has an appointment," their guide said to the lady at the desk. She looked at them carefully and pronounced, "You may go in."

"She sounded like St. Peter at the pearly gates," Palmer whispered to Sean as they entered. Sean laughed. A tall heavy set man stood up from behind a desk that matched his size.

"I know Sean. And you're Lieutenant Carson from Pasadena?"

"Yes, sir."

"Sit down over at this conference table." They sat and he said, "Let's get right to business. I'm sure we all have things waiting."

Sean started out. "In a minute I'll let Lieutenant Carson present the case but I want to explain our interest first."

"OK. I understand this is about the Summit murder in Pasadena. Tell me how the feds got involved in this."

"We have a long standing investigation into mob activities in Las Vegas. When Palmer was able to relate this shooting to an arson case in Pasadena and both to gang figures involved in at least bookmaking and with strong ties to Las Vegas, he came to me. We are not yet ready to roll up the investigation. We would like to try the case on its merits and try to avoid the details of motive. I would prefer that the FBI aspects be kept out as much as possible."

"Won't it bother your investigation to have the case in court?"

"Probably. But I think it would be less than if it were held off and the press could start trying to find out why it didn't come to trial. Once tried, I think it would be largely forgotten."

"Well, let's see what Lieutenant Carson has."

"The shooter tried to assassinate a police detective a couple nights ago and was shot but not seriously. We found the gun he was using was the murder weapon on Summit. We have an eye witness who saw him sitting in wait on Summit. Look at the artist's drawing from his description and the actual suspect in the hospital." He passed over two pictures.

"That is amazingly similar."

"We have his fingerprints on the rental papers for the car that was involved in the shooting. He is from Las Vegas and we have him placed at a motel in Pasadena at the time of the first shooting. This is the motel where he attacked the officer later."

Sean added, "We have information that may lead to his involvement in other gang shootings but think this case can go alone."

"Tell me about the arson angle."

After Palmer explained the relationship of the two cases, Miller asked, "What are you going to do about the case against the motel manager?"

Sean answered, "Palmer was going to drop it since his witness is gone but I suggest leaving it alone. The small bail won't bother the mob and I think that the attorney for the motel manager would rather it stay completely off the radar. I don't think they will do anything as long as we don't and it does give us a little leverage if we need it. It also gives an excuse for keeping track of the guy. I'm sure the motel is a center for this mob's activities in Los Angeles. We want to know what goes on but not to scare them. I think the attack on the officer shows the importance of the motel in their functioning."

"If the case goes to trial, what do we do about the motive?"

"We say we can't find any connection of this poor girl to the man. We can't prove it was mistaken identity but maybe. We think he is a big time thug but Pasadena PD doesn't have the evidence for that but they do want to protect their citizens and there is no question that he killed one of them."

"Suppose they set up a series of alibis for him. Proof he was in Vegas at the time?"

"We have him in the area at that time by the fingerprint on the car rental form. My guess is that they will sacrifice him and try to bargain down the time, rather than risk stirring up all their other activities. If they should develop a big case response, we still can put him away on attempted murder of a police officer."

Palmer added, "He admitted that to me and said he had been stalked and thought it was his stalker and it was self defense."

"Well, that certainly is a good fall-back position. And going for that could be done without any involvement of the Bureau. OK. We'll bring him to prompt trial for the murder. Transfer him to the jail ward at County Hospital and I'll send a trial deputy to visit him. That should bring out his lawyer and we'll see where it goes. We can ask for the death penalty for lying in wait. Maybe they would by-pass a trial and accept life."

"That would certainly be a good outcome. Put him off the street and still not require any information about our investigation."

"Unless they already know about that, it should reassure the mob as it wouldn't require any information about his background or other activities. Thank you, gentlemen. We will go ahead on that plan. One of the trial deputies will contact you, Lieutenant, when we have the preliminary hearing. We will need your testimony but I think on the preliminary we can skip having the lab people and other witnesses. We will need the officer who shot him. Then if it looks like trial we will need the department's information and testimony, with the testimony of the lab experts and everybody."

On the elevator down, Sean said to Palmer, "I'm happy with that. I think we can get him put away without showing our hand. Does it satisfy you?"

"I'll talk with the chief but I think we would be happy either with or without a trial. I'll get him transferred to County Hospital Jail Ward first thing tomorrow. We'll be glad to stop paying for his care at the Huntington Hospital."

As they went to the parking lot, Sean said, "Thanks so much for your cooperation. Many departments go ape when we ask them to work with the Bureau."

"Well, you've been very fair and have kept us informed. It's worked well. Now if you can give me some information on the widow, I'll be forever grateful."

"Sorry. I can't do anything for you on that, except wish you luck."

Mack Parke, the trial deputy assigned to the case called Palmer and asked for copies of the forensic reports on the ballistics and on the fingerprints. He told Palmer, "The preliminary hearing will be in two days, on Thursday. It is scheduled for ten thirty. I'd like you to meet me a half hour early to plan strategy. I also want you to bring the officer who actually shot the defendant."

At the court house, Palmer introduced Ollie to Parke and they discussed the case. The preliminary hearing opened with Judge David Engleman presiding. He had a reputation of being firm but fair. Parke opened with his statement, "We will produce evidence that the defendant is guilty of two heinous crimes; murder in the first degree and attempted murder of a police officer."

He called Ollie as the first witness. "Please describe the events of your stake out of the Starlight Motel on the evening in question."

"I was parked across the street, in a position to see cars enter or leave the motel. I had been in position for about three hours without any activity other than a few customers coming to the motel. I was looking around and suddenly caught a flash of light off what appeared to be a gun on the passenger side of my car. I hit the door handle and rolled out of the car into the street just as the window was shot out. I lay still and the shooter came around the car with a small flashlight. I assumed he was right handed and had his gun in the right so the flashlight would be in the left and I shot to the side of the light. There was a scream and the flashlight dropped. I found the flashlight and turned it on the shooter. I saw the defendant sitting on the ground, holding his ribs. I quickly handcuffed him. I then called for back up, an ambulance, and the shooting team. Then I bagged his gun."

"Did you actually see the defendant shoot?"

"No. I couldn't identify anyone until I shone my flashlight on him. At that point he was the only other person around and the gun was where he dropped it."

"Do you think he was planning to kill you?"

"Objection. Calls for speculation."

"Sustained."

"No further questions," Parke said.

The judge asked the defense attorney, "Do you have cross examination?"

"No, your honor. We stipulate that the defendant fired the shot. He had been stalked and thought the officer was the stalker. He merely fired a warning shot to scare him off. We will prove this at trial."

"Very well. Mr. Parke, call your next witness."

"Lieutenant Carson. Please take the stand."

Palmer was sworn and then Parke asked him, "You have conducted an investigation of the shooting of Joy Ronson?"

"I have."

"What did you find?"

"We have a witness who identifies the defendant as sitting outside the house of Ms. Ronson in a black Buick. We have identified the car and found evidence of gun firing from the car. We have the defendant's fingerprints on the car rental papers. Ballistics has shown the bullet killing Ms. Ronson to have come from the gun that the defendant dropped during the attack on Detective Ollie Linton. The defendant is from Las Vegas and we have placed him at the motel at the day of the attack."

"Your honor, I submit that this evidence of the defendant doing the shooting of Ms. Ronson is sufficient to bind him over for trial," Parke requested.

"Objection. The witness testimony and the ballistics are hearsay. I move they be delected." The judge looked toward Mr. Parke.

"Your honor, at trial we will present all these witnesses. However, in the interest of brevity, I have had Lieutenant Carson present the findings. Written copies of the ballistics reports, the fingerprint report, and the witness interview are here for you to peruse. I feel that this is sufficient for a preliminary hearing." He presented the papers to the judge.

Judge Engleman studied the papers. "I agree that the evidence requirements are less strict in preliminary hearings and I am going to bind the defendant over for trial. Is bail requested?"

"Yes, your honor," The defense attorney said.

"There may be other people involved in this and I request the defendant be held for trial without bail. He is from out of state and I think he may be a risk for flight."

"I concur. The defendant will be held without bail. This hearing is dismissed."

They left the courtroom and Mr. Parke thanked the two detectives. "That went better even than I hoped. There will presumably be a trial where you will again have to testify. At that point they will go into more detail and you will be intensively cross examined. All the other witness will have to appear. However, for the moment we have all we could ask and I do thank you both."

"You're welcome," Parker said and Ollie accompanied him back to his car for the ride back to Pasadena.

"Do you want to see him get the death penalty?" Palmer asked.

"I don't care. Life will do. I'm not mad at him as I got off without being shot and he didn't. I got my revenge on him. The one I'd like to get something on is that son of a bitch who runs the motel. He's getting away with something and I'd like to be the one to take him in."

"If we find enough on him to arrest him, I'll remember that and let you do it."

"Thanks. I'll look forward to it and I'll help find something on him."

"I'm glad you're motivated. That helps you find something. So often it doesn't really matter to us what the result is as long as we do the job."

"How about the widow? Has she got you motivated to find her?"

"I am but I haven't any idea where to go on that. Everything seems to lead to a dead end. She's really very good."

"If she keeps at it, she'll make a mistake sometime."

"Yeah, but how many people have to die before that happens?"

"Well, we do what we can. I wish you luck."

Chapter 26

Palmer had just arrived at the police department and was seated at his desk, reading the overnight report when his phone rang.

"Carson."

"Lieutenant, the report just came in. There is another widow job at the Best Western Motel."

"Oh God. I'll take care of it."

"Thank you, sir."

Al stuck his head in the open door. "What's up for today, Carson.?"

"You're just in time. The widow struck again, out at the Best Western on Colorado. Will you go out and start looking around? I have a couple things to take care of and I'll come out. Give me a call when you do the basics."

"That's unusual. All the other times she had been at a hotel where there is a conference going on."

"That's true, though I hadn't thought of it that way. Maybe she couldn't wait for another meeting."

"OK. I'll see what it looks like and let you know."

"Thanks, Al. I'll send the lab techs out and call the coroner."

Al pulled his car into the parking in front of the office and got out. He walked into the office. Before the clerk could offer to help him, he said, "Detective, Pasadena Police. Where is it?"

"Room 214. Second floor to the left of the stairs."

He went up the stairs and looking up the hall saw a uniformed office leaning against a door frame. It was one of the older officers, a corporal now.

"Morning, Al. Got another for you."

"Gee. Thanks. I appreciate your saving it for me."

The cop laughed. "Want me to stay? I don't have anything urgent."

"Yeah. Why don't you hang around until the lab or someone else comes. I'll be inside so it would be helpful to have you here."

"OK. Sorry I didn't bring a book."

"Why don't you go down to the office and get what paperwork there is." He opened the door and went into the room. An undressed body was lying on the bed. It was a fairly lightly pigmented Hispanic man, appearing about five and half feet in height. He had a small paunch. Al walked closer and saw a large wound in the upper abdomen, just below the xiphoid. There was almost no blood. There was a cut on the penis, also without significant bleeding. He looked around the room. A pair of kahki pants lay folded on a chair and a bright green sports shirt was hung over the back of the chair. Shoes and socks were neatly placed in front of the chair.

The uniformed officer walked into the room. "Name is George Sanchez. He said a friend dropped him off and would pick him up later so there isn't a car number. Visa card in the name of Sanchez. Clerk described him: tall, skinny Hispanic. Doesn't sound at all like the body."

"Thanks. I'm going to call the lieutenant." He took out his cell phone and hit a fast dial button. "Al here," the officer heard him say. After a pause as the lieutenant responded, Al continued, "This is a copy cat killing and not a very good one. He was killed somewhere else, with a large knife like a hunting knife, and brought here so that there is almost no blood. A cut on his penis but not a bite. And the victim isn't the one who checked into the room. Clothes neatly folded not like he was hurrying."

Again he waited for the lieutenant's comment.

"No. I don't think you need to come. I'll have the lab guys work it over and see if there are prints and I'll look for anything else. I'd appreciate it if you would start a computer search for George Sanchez. It probably is his real name as they left his credit card record at the desk."

Then to the uniform, "Better go outside and get the lab guys up here when they come."

Al went through the clothes and carefully took out a wallet. He laid it on a table and with tweezers took out a driver's license. George Sanchez with an address and a picture of the victim. He put it all in a plastic bag. Another pocket had a few loose coins but there were no keys. He found the room key on top of the television. There was no suitcase or toilet kit.

The lab tech came in with a large box of equipment, followed by the photographer with his cameras. "So the widow did it again?" he asked.

"Nope," Al said. "This is a copycat and pretty sloppy. Do a good job on the fingerprints because this killer is likely to have left some. Do the belt and shoes too."

Al continued to poke around the room while the lab men did their pictures and print studies. One of them asked, "Can I take the victim's prints?"

"Sure. I don't see anything you can bother doing that."

As the prints were being taken, the coroner's investigators arrived with a gurney. They took more pictures of the body and then asked, "Do you have everything you need? Can we take the body?"

"Sure. Let us know what you find."

"I don't know who will do the autopsy or when. You can call and find out."

After the coroner's crew and the lab techs left, Al told the uniformed officer to go back to patrol. He then bagged the clothes and the sheet the body was on. Taking all his evidence, he locked the door and went down to his car. He left the evidence and then went back to the desk. "Here is the key to the room. I don't think we need anything more but it might be better to leave it until tomorrow to make up and use, just in case."

"Thanks. We aren't very busy so that isn't a problem."

At the station, Al checked in the evidence and then went up to the detective area. He stopped at Lieutenant Palmer's open door. "Definitely not the widow. It was a fairly incompetent job. Did you find anything on Sanchez? I now have his DMV license number if we need it."

"Yeah, I found him easily. A small time thug who has a record for petty theft and disturbing the peace. He was arrested last year for selling drugs but got off because evidence chain didn't hold up. I asked Ollie to stop by. He covers most of the narcotics we see." He handed the record on Sanchez to Al.

Before he finished reading it, Ollie Linton walked up. A small man who was dressed in a quiet but sloppy manner, Ollie realized that no one would notice him particularly. "What's up?" he asked.

"George Sanchez was murdered last night. We wondered if you knew anything about him as he had a previous drug arrest."

"Actually, I know quite a bit. I was in on the arrest. It didn't go to trial because the patrol officer who first saw him put the marijuana in his patrol car and then threw it out with his lunch wrappings. George has been trying to sell again without too much success. He was on the territory of Jesus Ramirez so I'm not surprised that he is deceased."

"You think Ramirez might have retired him?"

"Very likely. I've been watching Ramirez but haven't had enough evidence to take him in. This might get him off the street too. What do you have?"

Al told him about the murder. Ollie thought a minute. "See what the lab gets. We have Ramirez prints on file and if they find any in the room we have a case."

"Thanks, Ollie. I'll keep on it and let you know what shows."

Down in the lab, Al asked the tech, "Did you find any good prints?"

"Several different ones but surprisingly none of the victim. There was a good one on one of the shoes."

"We think the victim was dead before he came to the room. Can you pull up the prints on Jesus Ramirez and compare them with what you found?"

"Sure. Give me a couple minutes."

He worked at his computer and finally said, "The one on the shoe is clearly Ramirez. A couple others around the room look like his but I'll need to work on them a little more but I think we can definitely place him in the room and with the victim's shoes."

"Thanks so much. Now if the widow would leave us a couple prints."

"In your dreams. That one isn't going to slip up."

Al went back up to detectives. "We have Ramirez placed in the room and in contact with the victim's shoes. I'll need to check details but I'd like to get a couple patrol officers and take the guy in."

Carson responded, "Good work. Go ahead and take him if you know where to find him. If not, put out a bulletin. I'm glad it wasn't the widow and we have something to work with."

Chapter 27

Jane parked her car and went to her room. Her mind was flooded with memories of her time with Fred. "How could I have forgotten all this?"

She lay awake most of the night with her thoughts. "Fred stole a part of my childhood. I never had the chance to wonder about boys and to make the tentative experience that most girls have. What would my life have been if that hadn't occurred?"

But then she realized that she had never been forced or exposed to a rape that she couldn't understand. "How could Fred have waited? He spent three years in the process of seducing me. And he did love me in his way. He was the only person who did and he educated me in so many ways. Much of my interest in my work goes back to the curiosity he taught me about different places and different people."

She dozed off and on but was wide awake at five o'clock. She got up, called the airline and made a reservation to New York for that morning. She packed and went to the office as soon as the attendant was up. She settled her bill, getting a return on her deposit.

"Thank you for your care."

"It was a pleasure having you. Do you want a check or cash on your return?"

"I would prefer the cash if it doesn't take all your change."

"We haven't taken last nights deposit to the bank, so there's no problem."

"Thank you very much."

"I hope you'll stay with us again."

"I've no plans but I might be back."

She walked out and put her bag in the car. She went back to the room, checked carefully for anything she might have left, and wiped the tables, the bathroom fixtures, the phone and anything else she may have touched.

She drove the car back to 'Rent-a-Wreck'. Again she was able to get her refund in cash. One of the employees was just taking a car to the airport for someone who had called and he offered her a ride.

"I hope you had a nice visit." He was a pleasant young man but didn't seem too bright.

"Thank you, it was very successful."

"What airline are you using?"

"Alaska, but I'm only going to Seattle."

"I've heard that it is always cloudy and rainy there."

"The climate isn't as good as here, certainly."

He dropped her off and she gave him five dollars and a wave. When the car was out of sight, she pulled her bag across the airport to the United terminal and picked up her boarding pass, presenting her driver's license as Amy.

The flight was uneventful and soon she was back in her apartment. She told herself, "I'm no longer in Pasadena and that is over." Her experience with many trips had enabled her to turn off the happenings once she arrived home to her apartment. She slept well and the next morning was back at work.

"Was your trip successful?"

"Everything OK with the family?" Several coworkers greeted her.

"Got everything settled. I shouldn't have to go back again. Thanks for your interest." Little more was said and she was soon into the swing of work. The time in Pasadena rapidly disappeared from her mind and she thought little of it. However, she did notice a change in her feeling for men and she was soon dating fairly regularly.

After several months of dating various men, she became more and more regular with Jack Reynolds, a young attorney who lived in her apartment building. He was an assistant prosecutor and told her of the strange people he prosecuted and she told him of the strange people she interviewed. It soon became a game of one-upmanship; my contact is stranger than yours. They both enjoyed it and found they had other interests in common. Soon they were going into one apartment or the other for drinks after the theatre. One evening he led her into the bedroom and they went to bed. She found the sex pleasant and not at all threatening. She was over her hang up.

One evening she was giving him oral sex prior to going to bed and suddenly she thought, "If I had the knife, I could use it before he knew it." She laughed at herself.

"What's so funny?" Jack asked.

"I just suddenly thought how strange this would look to someone who didn't know about it. We talk about the strange people we deal with."

"Yeah. I think it was Churchill that said something to effect that the position is ridiculous."

Later he asked, "How about moving in together?"

"I don't think so. I have a lot of trips and strange hours and I'd rather not feel that I had to schedule some of that ahead."

"That wouldn't matter. When you're here you would be here and the same for me."

"Thanks, dear, but I think it will work better for now if we each have our own space and get together when the time is right for both."

"You may be right. I keep some awful hours when I'm in the final of a hard case and I'm not good company. Can we go on as we are?"

"Oh, yes. I love our times together and hope we can continue a long time."

Chapter 28

Victor Hansen walked into the Pasadena Police Department. "I'd like to speak to the officer in charge of the black widow investigation. I may have some information."

"Is it a rumor or have you actually seen her? We've had a lot of false reports."

"I'm really not sure. However, I met a lady a couple nights ago that might fit the descriptions and I think it worth reporting."

"Just a minute, sir." The corporal on the desk picked up the phone.

"Carson."

"Sir, this is Uribe on the desk. We have a man here that offers information on the black widow. He seems like a reasonable person. Do you want to see him?"

"Sure. I haven't anything to lose. Send him up."

"Sir, if you'll take this elevator to the second floor, he'll be in the third office on the right. It'll be Lieutenant Carson."

"Thank you, officer." And he took the elevator up. The door was open and Victor stood in the door. Carson looked up. "Come in. You have some information for me? Sit over there."

Victor was well dressed and quietly competent. He sat and then said, "This is a little embarrassing. I would like my name kept out of it if possible."

"I'll do my best. I can't promise until I get some idea what we're talking about."

"I understand. I'm here for a meeting and staying in the Holiday Inn Hotel. Last night I met an attractive young lady in the bar. We had a drink and she introduced herself as Rachael, no last name. We talked for some time and then went up to my room and undressed. She offered oral sex but I refused. I spent some time in foreplay and then entered her. She seemed surprised but then relaxed and enjoyed it.

"After we finished, she said, 'Oh, my.' in a voice of surprise and then lay on my shoulder a time before getting up to go to the bathroom. As she turned, my arm rubbed across her lower back and I felt some long, narrow metal object taped to her back. She came out of the bathroom, dressed, came over to the bed. She said, 'Thank you.' kissed my forehead, and then whispered, 'Goodbye, Red.' Then she left the room"

"Are you called Red?"

"No. I obviously have black hair. I have no idea what that meant."

"What did she look like?"

"The most outstanding features were her shiny black hair, perfectly coiffured, and the bright blue eyes. Otherwise, the features were attractive but nothing stood out."

"The hair was a wig and I suspect the blue eyes were contact lenses. I think she expected them to overshadow everything else. Could you work with a police artist and try to come up with a picture of her?"

"I'm willing to try."

"Thank you. I think you're right and it was the widow. You're lucky you didn't let her do the oral sex. That is the point at which she prefers to kill."

"Did you see anyone else who might be able to help with her identity?"

"There were people in the bar, but no one I know and I don't think anyone paid much attention to us. I have a meeting this morning but I'll work with the artist right after lunch if that works for you. I'd like to get the evening flight back to Tucson if possible."

"Are you checked out of your hotel room?"

"Yes."

"Give me the number. We'll want to check it."

"Two seventeen."

"I'll see you when you come to work with the artist and if nothing else comes up, I think you should be able to get off to Tucson."

"I'll be back here at lunch time then."

"Thank you. I appreciate your telling us and I see no reason why this should be public at all."

"Thanks for that."

As soon as he left, Carson called the Arcadia Police Department. "Lieutenant Carson, Pasadena Police. Give me the detective division."

When the answer came, he said, "We think the black widow was in one of your hotels last night. We would like to do forensics on room two seventeen of the Holiday Inn if it's OK with you. We will be happy to have one of your men there if you would like."

"That's fine. I'll call the hotel and tell them we have authorized your forensic people to do this. I may have a guy stop by but don't worry about it. Let me know if you find anything."

"Thanks very much. I'll keep you informed."

Carson then put in a call to Sgt. Ridley. "A guy was in this morning who had sex with a woman who sounds like our widow in a hotel in Arcadia last night. I have Arcadia's permission to check it out and I'll call the forensic team as soon as I talk to you. Would you meet them out there? I'll tell you more details later but she was wearing the black wig."

"Anything particular you want me to do?"

"He met her in the bar. Talk to the bar employees and anybody at the hotel that might have seen her. You know the drill."

"Ok. I'll be interested to hear why she didn't do him in."

"We don't know but I'll tell you what I do know. Thanks."

He hung up and then called forensics and asked them to work over the room.

He had prepared a summary of the case to go to the FBI for their profilers to study and see if they could come up with any patterns they could look for. He decided he should add this latest contact to the report and took it from his "out" box and dictated an addendum to go with it to Quantico.

The phone rang. "Carson"

"Ridley, sir. We've been over the room with a fine tooth comb and nothing but a bunch of fingerprints. We did the maid and the largest number are hers. No one seems to have seen anything. Can we get the prints of the guy who rented the room?"

"I think so. He's coming in to make a picture after lunch."

When Victor had finished with the police artist, he stopped by Carson's office. "I'm afraid I didn't do very well. I just couldn't get by the hair."

"That's the purpose of the wig. Could we take your fingerprints? They found a lot in the room and if we could rule out yours and the maids, it would make classification easier."

"Sure."

"Do you have any idea why you lived to tell about the encounter?"

"Not really. I've been thinking a lot. I think she didn't expect me to get into her and would kill me while I was trying. However, I had her ready and I think she was surprised when I did enter her and found it better than she expected. That's the only thing that has made any sense to me but I sure can't understand any of her reactions."

"Well, thanks for all your cooperation. I'll call you if we have any major breakthroughs or if I can think of more questions. Officer Henry will take you to the fingerprint lab and then you're off."

Victor stuck out his hand. "You've been very understanding to work with. Good luck."

Carson took the hand, said "Thank you." and turned him over to Officer Henry.

Carson sat at his desk thinking. "It certainly sounded like Victor had been with the widow. She had the knife with her; why hadn't she killed him? What did 'goodbye Red' mean?" He didn't have any ideas. That of Victor sounded better than anything else he could think of. He wrote a memo on Victor's report and placed it in his file on the widow. He looked at the file a minute and shrugged his shoulders in frustration.

Al stuck his head in the door. "Just a quick report, Lieutenant. I have further dirt on Ramirez. We have him in custody and he says that he just found the body on the street and dropped it off. The whole report is in the pile there and if you approve, the DA is ready to file." He pointed at the pile on the desk.

"Thanks, Al. I'll get it done within the hour. I'm sure everything is OK and we'll go ahead. That will be one case out and I appreciate it a lot."

Chapter 29

When she had non-busy time on patrol, Flores was still on her quest to find the place where the widow stayed. One day on patrol she stopped at the small Comfort Inn on Colorado near Sierra Madre Boulevard. She asked her usual question, "I'm not checking anything at your motel. I'm just trying to find a young lady who we need some information about. Have you had any young women in the past month that stayed for two weeks?"

The very pleasant middle aged lady working the afternoon shift was quite talkative. "Yes, we have had two that meet that description. One is still here."

"What do you know about her?"

"She's a teacher at Pasadena City College and the insurance company is paying for her to stay here. There was an electrical fire in her condo and they are fixing it and repainting. She expects to be back in the condo the first of next week."

"Is she working while she's staying here?"

"Oh yes. She leaves every morning about seven thirty. She says good evening to me when she goes out to dinner and then comes back and grades papers."

"What about the other?"

"She was here almost two weeks. She checked out last Friday. I remember her well because I was on when she came in. She didn't have a credit card. Her identity had been stolen and she was waiting for the cards to be reissued. She made a thousand dollar cash deposit instead."

"That's unusual. Do you know what she did here?"

"Yes, it's most unusual but I've been reading about how common identity theft is these days. Some days she just sat around the pool and read. Others she went out in her car. I don't know what she did. She was a very pleasant person and attractive with light brown hair. I saw her go out in the evening a couple times and she seemed a different person. She wore a wig; I saw her in both black and blonde, and wore very short skirts. She didn't seem to be the same person as she acted the rest of the time."

"Bingo," Flores thought. She asked, "Might I see her registration card?"

"I can't see any harm in that. She's gone and you're with the police. I'll get it."

She was back in a minute. "We should keep the card so I made you a copy. Is that OK?"

"That's just perfect. I'll just check the address. You've been very helpful and pleasant. I do appreciate it and hope to see you again."

"It's been a pleasure to talk with you. Come back anytime. I don't have anybody to talk with most of the time."

Back in her patrol car, Flores looked at the registration. There was an address and also a business card clipped on the original with the same address. The car license plate was listed. She typed the plate number into the computer in the car. It came back registered to Rent-a-Wreck near LAX. She called the phone number on the business card and received an answer, "This number is out of service." She didn't know how to check the address and decided it was time to give her information to someone who knew more about the case.

Parking the patrol car, she went into the station and up to the detective offices. Sergeant Ridley was sitting at a desk. Approaching her, Flores said, "I have some information about the location of the black widow."

"Real information or rumor?"

"It's solid information about where she was staying."

"I think we best let the Lieutenant hear this to." She led Flores to Carson's office. The door was open and she said, "Flores has some information about the widow. I think you should hear it too."

"Do you think it's reliable?"

"I don't know. I brought her direct to you rather than listening to the story."

"OK. What do you know, Flores?"

"Well, sir, I've thought a lot about the case and I decided she must be out of town and needed a place to stay. So I started asking at the motels if there had been any young women staying for a couple weeks. I finally found some today. I hope I haven't done anything wrong."

"You have. It is important for several reasons to contact the investigating officers in such a situation. First because there may be privacy concerns that could get the department sued and any evidence thrown out. Second, one may warn a suspect that there is investigation ongoing and allow her to escape. We had one case with two shift constant surveillance for over a week, trying to find the supplier for a drug dealer. That case was blown when a patrol officer decided to warn the suspect not to sell dope in his area.

"Having said all that, what did you find out?"

"The Days Inn had a renter who met the times. The afternoon receptionist is very talkative. She told me she spent much of her time reading by the pool but became a different person in the evening, going out with different color wigs and VERY short skirts. She registered with a cash deposit, saying she was a victim of identity theft and had cancelled all credit cards and checks. She left last Saturday, paying in cash. I did call the phone number and it is a non-working number."

"In spite of not telling us, that was a good idea that we hadn't thought of and you handled it well. I'm going to make some calls and you can stay and see how the information is handled. Did you run the license number?"

"Yes, sir. It comes back to Rent-a-Wreck near LAX."

He looked up a number and dialed, putting the phone on speaker. "This is Lieutenant Carson at Pasadena PD. I want to talk to someone in detectives."

"Detective division."

"Lieutenant Carson, Pasadena PD. We have a business card with an address in your city and I'd like to know if it is legitimate." He gave the name and address.

"I can tell you to start off that there isn't such a number on that street. One that high would be in neighboring Sunnyvale but the street stops before the border. Give me the company name again and I'll take a look."

While he was gone, Carson typed on his computer. Finally the detective came back. "We have no record of such a company in the city."

"I just pulled up the California Corporation files and there isn't a corporation in the state with that name. Thanks a lot for your help."

Carson dialed again. "Days Inn."

"Lieutenant Carson of the police department. Do you have anyone in room 204?"

"No. It's vacant. Why?"

"We think a suspect was staying there. Don't rent it tonight and my lab people will be over first thing in the morning. Do you need a warrant?"

"Not as long as the room is empty."

"OK. Thanks a lot."

He dialed a shorter number. "Lockyear."

"Bill, it's Palmer. We may have the place the widow was staying. Will your team work over room 204 at the Days Inn first thing in the morning?"

"Of course. Do we need a warrant?"

"No. It's an empty room now."

"I'll let you know what we find."

"Thanks."

Another short number. "Sergeant Blakely."

"Palmer Carson here. I have a special project and need help. Do you think the city would be safe tomorrow if I borrowed Flores for half the day?"

"I think so. If we are too busy, I'll ask the chief to give us a few hours on patrol. I'm sure he could handle Flores' work."

"Thanks much. Good luck with the Chief." He laughed and hung up.

"Flores, I'm going to let you follow up on the car. Go to the agency and get the information on the renter. Get a copy of the driver's license she presented."

"Thank you, sir. Should I go in uniform?"

He thought a minute. "Yes. You aren't used to presenting yourself as an officer when you're in civilian clothes. I think you will be more comfortable in uniform. What are you going to ask them?"

"I'll tell them we think the car was used in a crime and I want to see the renter papers. Then I'll check if the car has been rented again and if it is back on the lot."

"Good. If it is on the lot, see if you can tell if it is worth sending the lab people over. Good luck."

"Yes, sir. Thank you."

"And call Ridley or me if there is any problem or if you find anything remarkable."

The next morning Flores took her patrol car and drove over to LAX. Finding the Rent-a-Wreck lot, she approached the manager. Giving him the car number, she asked to see the papers for the rental for the time that the widow had been at the Days Inn.

189

"Do you have a warrant?"

"No. It isn't necessary if the car isn't currently rented. I can get a warrant but then my boss will come to serve it and he knows how to make such investigations unpleasant and time consuming."

"OK. I'll get you the rental papers."

He came back with the papers. She looked them over and said, "Make me a copy, please. Particularly of the driver's license. Can you blow that up a little?"

He made the copies and handed them to her.

"There isn't any credit card copy. How did she pay?"

"She had her identity stolen and didn't have cards. She offered to give us a deposit for $2000 and we took that. She paid that in cash and got cash in return when she checked the car back in."

"Is the car on the lot now or does some one have it?"

"I'll look." He went to the computer and in a couple minutes said, "It's here now. Do you want to see it?"

"Please."

He called one of the young men working on the cars. "Find this car for this police officer." He handed him the papers on the car.

When they reached the car, she said, "Thank you. You don't need to wait. I'll look at it and find my way out." He noticed how trim she was in her uniform.

"I'll be glad to stay and keep you company." He put his hand on her arm. She removed it.

"I'm able to take care of this myself. You can go back to work," She told him.

"You might need help with something. I don't have anything urgent to do." He rubbed his hand down her back.

She turned sharply to him. "Bug off before I cuff you for harassment." He glared at her a minute and wandered off.

She looked in the car. It had been freshly cleaned, inside and out. All the windowsills and controls had been wiped down. The carpet appeared freshly vacuumed. She looked down in the crack between the carpet and the door. A couple black hairs were there and she carefully picked them up with a pair of tweezers and put them in a plastic envelope. She found nothing else of interest in 15 minutes of looking so she took her papers and plastic envelope. She stopped at the manager's officer.

190

"Thank you very much for your help. I don't think we will need to do anything more to the car. Incidentally, you need to watch that guy. He's likely to get you sued for harassment."

"Thanks for the tip. He's not a very good worker but I didn't know he made passes at ladies on the lot. I'll check it." Flores went out and back to the patrol car.

On the radio, she asked for Sergeant Ridley. "This is Flores, Sergeant. I have copies of all the papers. The car has been freshly cleaned and wiped. I did find a couple hairs at the edge of the carpet and bagged them. I doubt if it is worth looking for prints.

"Good job, Flores. Bring the things in."

"Incidentally, she used the identity theft approach again and got the car with a $2000 cash deposit."

"Amazing how well that works."

"Driver's license number is D4326724. Name is Rachael Compton. Address is the same as on the papers at the motel. We know it's false, so I expect the license is too."

"I'll check it out before you get here."

Flores arrived back at the station and went up to the detective division. Ridley was sitting at her desk. "Yeah, Flores, it is false. Let me see the copy of it." Flores handed it over, together with the rental agreement.

Ridley studied the license for a couple minutes. "It's really a high quality forgery. I wonder where she found someone who can do that quality. Mostly this level are limited to a few good forgers that work for the drug cartels or the gang bosses. It's not easy to get those guys to talk about their work so I don't expect we can find her through that channel."

"I can see why they wouldn't be very helpful. Here are the hairs from the edge of the car carpet. I thought they looked like those from the wig." She handed over a plastic envelope. Ridley looked at it a minute and then handed it back.

"Drop this by the lab. Tell them it's from the widow case and get them to show you how to log it in. You might as well learn that and get to know the lab guys. They can be a lot of help if you are trying for detective and they have worked with you."

"Thank you. It will be nice to learn more about how they work." She took the envelope and went down the corridor to the police lab. It was the first time she had actually been in the lab suite. She looked around with interest.

A young man at a desk said, "Can I help you, officer? Or are you just sightseeing?"

Flores felt embarrassed. Her interest in everything had showed her lack of experience. "I found these hairs in the car the widow used. Sergeant Ridley asked me to log them in here."

"Really? We have the car she used? That's great." He was now interested and more friendly. "I'll take them and take a look right now. You fill in this form and I'll add the number. If there is anything you don't know, ask. It's easier to get it right the first time." He took the envelope and went into the next room. Flores worked on the form and knew everything but the case number. He came back into the room. "I'm Mike, Officer Flores." She was a little taken aback but then realized he had read the name tag on her uniform. "A good job. These are typical of the wigs she wore and certainly will place her in the car. Would you like to see how we do it?"

"Oh, very much if it isn't too much bother."

"No. After finding them, you deserve to know what's done with them." He took her into the other room and said, "Now look in the eyepieces of the microscope here. You see the hairs you brought on the right. One that we found at the site of a murder is on the left. They look identical."

She looked and they did seem the same, though she didn't know enough detail to be sure. "Did you find the car?" he asked.

"I found where she had stayed and they had the car license. We followed it out to Rent a Wreck."

"How did you find where she stayed?"

"I felt she must be out of town and just asked at motels until I found someone who had stayed two weeks."

"Good thinking. We will look forward to working with you when you make detective in another year or so."

"Thank you." Flores glowed with the compliment. Maybe she would be able to make detective. She went back to her patrol car with new enthusiasm for her work.

Chapter 30

Frank picked Maria up at her rooming house at quarter to six. "Traffic wasn't too bad coming this way. It's awful going the other. I had a place in mind for dinner but we wouldn't get there in time. Anywhere here you like?"

"There's a fish place a few blocks out on Colorado. Do you like fish?"

"Yeah. That sounds good."

During dinner they talked like very old friends and he held her hand while they waited for the server. When they finished and went back to his car, he put his arm on her shoulders as he opened the door. She turned and looked up at him and he kissed her on the lips. She threw her arms around him and they held it a long time. "Oh, Frank," She said.

"Yes, dear. Kinda sudden but awfully nice."

"It's the nicest thing I've known."

"Can we go to your place?"

"I have a room mate."

"Let's go to my apartment in San Dimas."

She looked up at him and nodded. They were soon on the freeway and he was hurrying. He looked in the mirror. A car was following him and as he looked, it had red and blue lights flashing on the top. "Oh, shit."

He pulled to the side and the highway patrol car pulled in behind him. "Put your hands out the window." He told Maria.

"Why?"

"We're armed and if the hands are out he'll know we aren't dangerous." They both put their hands out the window. The patrolman came up to Frank.

He looked at the hands and said, "You a cop?"

"Shield is on my belt here." The patrolman looked at it and asked.

"She a cop too?"

"Yes."

"OK. I'll assume you are working. But slow it down and set a good example for the citizens."

"I will. Thank you."

The patrolman walked back to his car and Frank sighed in relief. "Our department gives us three days off without pay if we get a ticket from another jurisdiction."

"Frank, you can't make that twenty mile trip three times tonight after that. Let's go to my place. We can sit in the living room and have some time together anyway."

"I think you're right. As many tickets as I've given over the years, it still makes me a little shaky to be on the other side."

They sat in the living room and he held her close. After several long kisses his penis was so hard it was difficult to ignore. She took a couple Kleenexes from her purse and reached over and unzipped his pants. She took the penis in her hand and in only a few moves, it came. "At least, that should relieve the tension a little," she said.

"Oh, yes, it does indeed. Can I do the same for you?"

She nodded and then stood up. She slipped her panties off and put them in her purse. She then sat down and turned her head up and kissed him. He put his hand between her legs and in a few minutes she gave a groan of pleasure. "Maybe that will help you sleep better."

"Yes, it will." They sat and held each other for a few minutes.

"Tomorrow's a work day. I guess I'd better start back."

"I suppose. Thank you, Frank."

"Next Thursday work? I know your schedule now."

"That will be fine. I'll meet you half way. How about the City of Hope?"

"I don't know anything about it."

"It's a cancer hospital. I had a friend I visited there several times. They have a big parking lot that comes out to the street. There is always parking in that part as it is so far from the hospital. You turn off the freeway at Buena Vista, go under the freeway south and turn left at the light. It's about two blocks and I'll be sitting on the curb there at five thirty."

"I'll pick you up there then. Good night, dear."

"One more kiss." He proceeded to do that and then went out to his car.

Flores found it a little difficult to concentrate on work that week. Her mind kept drifting to Frank. On Thursday she drove out to the City of Hope after work and parked. She had a magazine to read and went out to the curb by the parking six minutes early. Frank was sitting there in his car. She climbed in and told him "To get back to the freeway, you have to turn around and go back the way you came. This road deadends before the 605 freeway."

He leaned over and kissed her before he started the car. She responded and then said, "We start that we'll never get away from here." He laughed and turned the car around. They ate at his favorite little diner in La Verne. They compared the day's work and she admitted, "I've had trouble concentrating on work this week."

"So have I. I've never felt this way about anyone before."

After dinner they went to his little efficiency apartment. Entering, he took her in his arms and kissed her. "Welcome, my dear, to my home. It can be your home too."

They went to bed and after their love making, he said, "Can you stay the night? Will your car be safe?"

"Yes and yes. That parking lot is patrolled and many people leave cars for long times when family is in the hospital."

"We will have to get up early so I can get you to your car and make it back to the department on time. It won't matter to you since you are on four to twelve shift but that makes it harder to get up."

"I don't mind. It will be better than going back now."

He kissed her again. "Have a good night, my dear."

"And the same to you, sweetheart."

In about ten minutes he asked, "Are you still awake?"

"Yes."

"What do you think of looking for an apartment half way between? In Duarte or Monrovia. Would your roommate mind if you moved out?"

"She would be quite pleased. She is really bugged when I'm changing shifts. I think that would be nice. Are you free on Saturday?"

"I am. Shall we look then?"

"Let's do it. I go to work at four but we could have several hours to see what's available."

"It's short acquaintance. Do you feel comfortable considering moving in together?"

"Yes, I do. We mesh so well together."

"Then Saturday is the day we look. Good night, again."

They got up early and took a shower together. They had toast and orange juice and then he drove her back to the City of Hope. "Until Saturday."

"I'll look forward to it." She waved as the car moved away.

Chapter 31

Sean Riley called Palmer. "Sean at the FBI. How are you doing?"

"Well. We haven't found the widow but everything else is going well."

"I looked over the records on her case that you gave me. She seems very sharp and I doubt if anyone ever finds her. However, I have a favor to ask."

"Anything we can do, I'll be glad to."

"Some of the people in Vegas seem to be getting worried about our investigation. They don't really know about it but apparently we have uncovered some sleeping dogs and it is enough to make them nervous. We would like to give them an explanation for the questions that have been asked. Could you give an interview with your local paper and say that you are trying to find the person that hired Watkins and working with other law enforcement agencies? I think that would make them think it was you and the Las Vegas PD and get the heat off us."

"I'm certainly willing to give it a try."

"Thanks. I'll be in touch."

Each morning one of the reporters for the Pasadena Star News stopped by the police station to see if there was any over night action. This morning the desk sergeant said, "Lieutenant Carson wants to talk to you today. Go on upstairs to detectives."

"What's that about?"

"I haven't the vaguest idea. If you go see him like I said, he probably will tell you."

The reporter accepted the implied rebuke and went up to detectives. At Carson's door, he said, "I'm Tommy Hendricks from the Star News. The sergeant said you wanted to see me."

"Yeah. You remember we arrested Watkins for the murder of Joy Ronson?"

"Sure. Something new on that?"

"I thought you might like a little story on it. High officers in the Pasadena Police Department feel that this was a contract killing and would like to find the persons that ordered and paid for the killing. We have been working closely with other law enforcement agencies and feel we are making progress in reaching the persons who ordered the killing."

"Anything more definite?"

"No. But you can say that the department has asked the paper to keep in touch as we hope for arrests in the not too distant future."

"Can I include a little detail on the killing and the present suspect?"

"That would be fine. Off the record, I hope it is a big enough article for the potential suspects to see. I'm hoping to make them a little nervous."

"I'm glad you told me that. We will feature it and make it sound like you have just uncovered important information."

"That's exactly what I need. Thanks for your help."

"Thank you for the tip. It helps fill the paper and gets readers' interest."

"I'll let you know if we do find anything more."

"I'll keep in touch. Take care, lieutenant."

A couple weeks later, Palmer answered the phone at his desk. "Carson."

"This is Lance Miller at the DA's office."

"Good morning. Are we going to have the trial soon?"

"That's what I called about. The trial is off."

"How did that happen? He didn't get away did he?"

"No. Nothing like that. I made a good case for special circumstances by lying in wait and asked for the death penalty. We also had the work of your department, trying to find out who hired him. This stirred the pot and began to worry the people above him. They apparently told him he probably would get the death penalty and talked him into taking a plea and he has pled guilty in exchange for dropping the death penalty. He will be sentenced to life and there won't be any trial or airing of the reasons for his killing Joy."

"I think that makes everybody here happy that we won't have to go through the trial, except maybe Ollie. I suspect that he wants the death penalty for the shooter for having been shot at himself. Are you happy with that result?"

"I am. I think it would have been a difficult trial. The FBI is really happy that the trial won't uncover their investigation. I'm sure Sean will be in touch with you too."

"Thank for letting me know. I'll tell everyone involved in the case."

"You're welcome. Hope to work with you again. You handled it all nicely."

"Thanks. Goodbye."

Chapter 32

Several weeks after Flores work had shown that the widow had left the area, Lieutenant Carson found a report from the profiling division of the FBI on his desk. He read the lengthy report and then reread the summary. The FBI had concluded that the perpetrator was a well educated female between 24 and 36 years of age. She had some knowledge of anatomy but was not a medical professional. She was calm in times of severe pressure and had no fear or concern in dealing with dead bodies.

She was right handed and was fairly strong, though from the minimal descriptions, she did not appear to be particularly large or well muscled. She had access to facilities for making counterfeit identifications and adequate funds to buy expensive wigs and to pay in cash for all her expenses. She had almost certainly been sexually abused as a child.

Carson sat in thought for a time and then read the summary still again. It triggered something in his mind but he couldn't say what. He got up, took his jacket and walked out of the office. "I'll be off call for a couple hours," he said to the secretary.

He drove out to the airport and took the little Cessna up in the air. This cleared his mind like nothing else he knew. He was looking around for other planes with the San Gabriel Mountains clear in the background. Suddenly a picture appeared before him—a fourteen year old girl, sitting calmly when told of her parents' sudden death. It couldn't be. He had followed Jane's career and been proud of her reputation in the news world. Had her stepfather been sexually abusing her?

He landed the plane and almost without thinking taxied it to the hangar. He parked it and turned everything off. He was still thinking of Jane on the drive back to the station.

Once back in his office, he found the number for NBC news in New York. When the phone was answered, he asked for the office of Jane

Norton. Reaching her secretary, he told her, "I'm an old acquaintance from California and I wonder if she is in the office today."

"No. She is out of town."

"Too bad, I'd hoped to see her while I was in town. But from her programs she must travel a lot. Is she gone for long?"

"Only two days on a story in Atlanta. All her trips are short. She does the interview and comes right back."

"Does she travel on vacation too or does she do too much traveling on the job?"

"She hasn't had a vacation since I've been here, over two years. She is a real workaholic."

"I haven't heard that she was out in California. Does she ever come out there?"

"Last year she did an interview in San Francisco but I think that's all. Actually she is in town most of the time so if you let us know when you will be back I'm sure you can catch her. Can I tell her who called?"

"I'll drop her a note and refresh her memory. She will remember me but might not the name. Thanks so much. You've really been most patient."

"You're welcome. Do let us know ahead."

Palmer hung up the phone and sat for a minute, looking into space. "I didn't think it could have been her but she does fit the profile better than anyone I know. She certainly couldn't have done all that in her two day trips." He resolved to put her out of his mind and see who else could fit the profile.

He picked up the phone and dialed. "Ridley. This is Carson. Can you stop by a minute?"

When she entered, he held out the FBI papers to her. "This is the profile from Quantico. It reminded me of someone who used to live in Pasadena but I called her office and she hasn't been to California for a year. See if it gives you any ideas and then make a copy and pass it on to the other detectives who have been involved. It's interesting but isn't specific enough to give us much help when there isn't anyone to even suspect."

"Yeah. I've not turned up anything more and I'm gradually giving more time to other cases."

"We'll keep it open but unless there is something or somebody to work on you'll have to go on to others. Thanks."

"Welcome. I'll let you know if I have any ideas or information." She walked out.

He said to himself, "A bright lady and quite attractive. I wonder if being a detective sergeant turns off the guys. I'm surprised she isn't dating a lot."

Now the FBI report was off his desk, he was going to have to go through the pile of letters and reports. He sighed and took the top one off the pile.

Chapter 33

Jane had been doing a series on new drugs and it was getting boring and she had worked out most of the interesting ones. The invasion of Iraq had created many changes in the news business and several of her colleagues had spent time with the military. In looking for a new challenge, Jane wanted to go to the war zone. She wrote up a program for interviewing women in Iraq and presented it to the decision makers for new programs. She was called in for discussion.

"Jane, this isn't really your area."

"I've done a lot of interviews and I don't see why this is that different. I have used interpreters on a number of occasions before."

"It's too dangerous. We can't afford to lose you."

"I've worked it out. I can hire a native driver and an international security adviser/bodyguard and we won't be going into actual combat zones. I'll stay where the families are so that I can talk to the women. I think their view on the role of Islam in the new government will be fascinating and important."

"What about your present project?"

"I've really worked that about as far as it will go. And I don't have anything new lined up."

"You're very persuasive. I have some reservations but I guess I'll approve further evaluation of it for the higher ups."

"Thank you. I'm sure I can make a good job of it."

"I'm sure you can but I'm not sure that it is the best use of your talents or that it is really safe to do." He got up in dismissal.

Management at the station again talked with Jane and finally decided to let her make the trip. She was elated and that evening told Jack, "I'm going to Iraq in about three weeks and do some interviews with the women there."

"I don't think that is a good idea. It is too risky there."

"Only in certain parts and I don't have to go where the fighting is."

"I still don't feel it is safe and I don't want you to go."

"It'll be a real adventure and also an important step in my career."

"Your career is doing fine. I'm not having you going there."

"You aren't my boss and I'm going."

"I forbid you to go."

"You can't do that. Screw you." She walked out and went back to her own apartment.

Jack made no overtures and she was busy getting ready and didn't bother to try to change his mind before going. She told a friend at work, "He wants to be in control, not an equal relationship. I'm glad I found that out before we decided to get married."

Finally she was ready and the time came. She flew Lufthansa to Frankfort and on to Kuwait. Getting off the plane in Kuwait she felt the heat she had been warned about. She was picked up and taken to her hotel by a representative of the network. She was to meet her team the next morning.

About ten, the desk called her to meet someone in the lobby. She was greeted by her security man, Ian McCloy. He was a six foot two Australian in his forties. A good looking man with sandy hair, which had retracted to leave a high forehead, he exuded confidence. He introduced her to the driver, Mohammed, who spoke no English, and the interpreter, a slight, gentle-appearing Iraqi. Rabaul, the interpreter, bowed and said, "I hope I was told correctly about what you want. I have set up some meetings in villages I know and will try to get you to meet some of the women."

"That is perfect. Thank you so much. I'm going to enjoy working with you. Your English is very good. Where did you learn it?"

"My father was our country's consul in Southampton for two years when I was ten and I went to an English school."

"How soon do you want to leave?" Ian asked.

"Do I need to buy supplies or is everything ready?"

"I think we have everything you will need, except your clothes. I even have a native costume for you if the necessity arises."

"I'll be ready within fifteen minutes."

"Great. I'll be here. I'll send the others to watch the car. Do you need help with your luggage?"

"Not really. I don't have much. But if you walk up with me, you can fill me in on our plans."

They got on the elevator. Ian told her, "We will cross the border and then go south toward a less dangerous part. It is easier to talk to natives where there isn't so much threat from insurgents. Rabaul has set us up to go to a couple villages where he has friends or relatives. That should make it easier for you to get started."

"That sounds fine. Are there places to stay?"

"The first couple villages have something akin to a B & B. Not fancy but they should be adequate. The next one is pretty isolated and we probably won't try to stay overnight."

She opened the room door and they walked in. She hadn't unpacked much and a few things were put into her bag quickly. "Is this appropriate to wear?" She indicated the safari suit that she had on.

"I think that will be fine. You do want to stay well covered in these countries. They would rather you wore a black covering robe but pants are a lot better than skin showing."

She shut her bag and he picked it up. "Ready?"

"Let's get started."

They went back down and out in front of the hotel. A dark green Land Cruiser stood there with Mohammed at the wheel. Rasual opened the doors. "Would you rather ride in front?"

"We can shift around. Why don't we start with you in back with me and you can brief me on the villages and tell me how to approach the women." She turned to Ian, "Is that OK with you?"

"Of course. After our first rest stop maybe you and I can discuss the security arrangements."

"Absolutely. We should do as much planning as possible while we are in the car. And bringing me up to speed with the background and how I should behave."

They climbed in and started off. The network representative had done a good job with Rasual. He understood what she was trying to do and the arrangements sounded very favorable. They discussed what questions she should ask to get her information and how to word them to avoid offense. She found Rasual well-informed, cooperative, and very quick thinking. He seemed an ideal man for the job.

Soon they were at the Iraq-Kuwait border. Ian had papers to allow them to cross into Iraq and after checking out with the Kuwait guards, they checked in with the Iraqi Army control point, where there were US troops backing the local Army group. An American sergeant came out and asked, "Jane Norton?"

"Yes. How did you know?" and she gave him a smile.

"We had warning that you would be passing the check point. Welcome. Let us know if we can help in any way. Also, please tell the American public the true story of what we are doing here."

"I'll do my best. And thanks for your help. I hope we don't need it."

He waved the car on.

Soon they turned off the main road and after a time on a small side road, found the first village. Rasual left them at the town square and went to talk with various people. Finally he returned. "It's all set up. Turn to the right and go a couple of blocks." They stopped in front of a house and he took Jane in and introduced her to a young Iraqi woman. The interview went well, though the woman was embarrassed to talk about personal things in front of Rasual.

As they went back to the car, he said, "Tomorrow we'll be in a village where a lady speaks good English. If we can get her to help you and interpret, your responses will be much better."

They settled into the little guest house and then Jane and Rasual went to meet two more women. The rest house was adequate and they had a dinner of lamb before settling down for the night. Jane asked about transcribing her notes and Rasual said, "The electricity is on tonight for a change. You can plug in the computer and go ahead."

"The computer is on battery but I do need light to use it. And if the electricity is working, I'll save the battery for when we don't have power."

The next morning Jane had a chance to talk to a couple of the village elders and discuss how they felt about women having more rights. There was a considerable divergence of opinion on the subject.

In late morning they drove to the next village on Rasual's plan. He was able to get the English speaking lady to help Jane with the interviews. She was bright and quickly realized what Jane wanted. They were able to work more quickly and do several interviews in a short time. Again they stayed overnight, working with various residents until it became dark. In the morning, Jane asked Kia, the English speaker, if she would go with them to the next village if Mohammed would bring her back before dark. "I'll pay you on an hourly rate."

Work was very difficult to find in this area, particularly for women, so she agreed promptly. In the morning, she met them and they took off for the next stop, which was only a half hour drive. This was a much more isolated village, with no rest house, so they had planned to go on before the end of the day. Her interviews went so well that Jane asked Rasual to see if he could find anyplace that they could stay for the night. When they finally had to stop the interviews, Mohammed took off to take Kia back to her village. Rasual reported, "I found a shed for Mohammed and me but there is only one other room in the village. One house has a room with bed and I finally talked them into renting it. Can you and Ian use one room?"

"We'll have to. It will work out."

After dinner, Jane and Ian went to the room. It had a double bed standing proudly in the middle of the room, with little room for anything else. "I'll take a blanket on the floor." Ian offered.

Jane took off her utility jacket and pants. She had no bra on and Ian looked at her in the fading dusk. "Fine view but I will be professional."

"I learned the first day that in this heat the bra makes a burning band around the chest. I took it off at the first rest stop. It doesn't show with these utilities." She lay down on the bed.

Ian started spreading out a blanket. "Oh hell," Jane said. "If you don't thrash around a lot there is plenty of room for both of us. Get in the bed."

Ian took off his utilities and climbed in. "Are you married?" Jane asked.

"Not any more. The special forces schedule doesn't make one a very good husband. She took our son and moved in with a school teacher while I was deployed in New Guinea."

"Do you keep up with the boy?"

"As best I can. I'm proud of him, even if he isn't a chip off the old block. He is a small, slender, gentle young man of eighteen who studies at the National Institute of Music. Last spring he gave a solo cello concert at the Sydney Opera House, even playing some of his own compositions."

"That's wonderful. Families break up. My mother and stepfather were killed in an auto accident when I was fourteen."

"That must have been hard to lose your mother. Did you know your Dad?"

"No. Mother married when I was one. She was an alcoholic who never cared much for me. She was drunk and angry at my stepfather and pulled into an eighteen wheeler without looking."

"Was your stepfather close to you?"

"Very. He introduced me to sex at thirteen."

"How awful."

"It wasn't too bad. He was very gentle and had spent two years teaching me about sex so that it merely seemed an extension of his teaching. It did spoil my relations with boys as I grew up. Sometime I'll tell you how I purged my soul of the early sex. But not now. Good night."

"Good night. Sleep well."

Jane woke about three in the morning and went to the outdoor bathroom with her flashlight. As she came back, she saw Ian in the light. He was lying flat on his back with his erect penis like a flagpole. On an impulse, she went around the bed and took the penis in her mouth. He came almost immediately. He reached down and felt her soft skin. "Jesus. I thought it was a dream."

"Maybe it is."

He started stroking her and soon he was hard again. He inserted himself gently into her and she responded until they both came. She lay with her head on his shoulder. "I guess we can tell Rasual that one room works OK," Jane said. They drifted off to sleep.

Jane woke early and woke Ian by rubbing him and they had sex again.

After breakfast, they started off to the next village. As they came in Rasual said, "I think this one has a rest house but I don't know how much room there is."

"One room works fine for both of us," Jane replied.

Rasual looked at her a moment with a raised eyebrow but said nothing more.

Jane stopped her interviews early the next night and spent some time on her computer, putting all the material on a CD. "Maybe we can get this sent off tomorrow so I won't lose too much if we lost my notes or the computer."

"The mail in Iraq isn't reliable at all. Maybe we will meet some American military who could take it to Kuwait." Ian suggested.

After another pleasant night in their shared room, they got an early start and drove over to the main road again. "We will go several hours and then turn off into another rural area." Rasual said. Shortly after hitting the main road, they passed an American convoy heading for Kuwait. They pulled to the side, out of the way and parked. A jeep pulled up beside them and a young lieutenant got out. "Are you Jane Norton?"

"Yes. The word seems to be out that I'm here."

"We got a note to look for you. Is everything going OK?"

"Doing fine. I've had some very successful interviews. I have them on a disc. Do you suppose you could get it to the network representative in Kuwait City?"

"Absolutely. I'll have a day or more there while they reload the convoy and fill the tankers. I'll make sure it gets to him."

She handed over the CD. "Thank you very much."

"My pleasure. The best of luck to you." He pulled in behind the end of the convoy and Mohammed pulled their truck back on the road. They stopped for lunch at a small village. As they started to get back in the SUV, three men appeared out of nowhere, two carrying rifles. One pointed his gun at the two Iraqis while the other aimed at Ian. The third started to bind Ian's arms. With a sudden lunge, Ian grabbed the rifle from the man aiming at him and hit the other man with it. The rifle caromed off and the two men jumped to control Ian. One has trying to hold his arms while the other was choking him. Jane took out the stiletto. Putting her arm around the neck of the choker, the other hand drove the stiletto into his chest at the lower border of the rib cage. She swung the knife back and forth and then pulled it out. The man dropped to the ground with a scream.

This attracted the attention of the third man and when he turned to help his comrades, Mohammed jerked the gun away and it slid across the pavement. The man jumped on Mohammed and tried to bring him to the ground. Rasual stood with open mouth, like a deer frozen in headlights. As the man pushed his head back with strain pulling at Mohammed, Jane ran the stiletto across his neck. The rush of blood from the carotid arteries made a gurgling sound as his breath escaped from the opened throat. He was dead within seconds. As Mohammed pulled himself back erect, there was a sharp crack. They turned to Ian who had just snapped the neck of the third combatant.

"We make a good team," Ian commented. "You have a knack with that knife, Jane."

"They didn't even look at me. I guess they thought all women are harmless and ineffectual."

"A big mistake on their part."

"Should we report to the police or someone?"

"No one will do anything. We'll tell the American troops about it when we see some, just so we'll be on record as self defense."

They got back in the truck and started off. That night's stop had a small rest house and the people were friendly and helpful. Jane was able to interview the village elder and also a couple of the women.

The next day was a longer drive. They passed another American convoy and exchanged information and pleasantries with the convoy leaders. They reported the attack and the Captain in charge told them, "This area hasn't had too many problems but there are a few of that type almost anywhere. They get captives and either get ransoms or sell them to the religious fanatics who behead them on video. I'm glad you were able to fight them off."

"Is this road fairly safe?" Ian asked.

"Not as bad as many. We haven't had a bombing in this area for almost a month."

"I guess you are never really sure in this country," Jane commented.

"That's right. Keep your eyes open and good luck."

Both sides drove off.

A few miles later, Mohammed suddenly pulled the truck to the right to avoid a break in the pavement. Jane was thrown to the side, then she heard a tremendous roar followed by a terrible pain in her legs for a moment and then nothing.

The tail of the convoy heard the roar and saw the column of smoke. The guard humvees came back and found a huge hole with a burning, almost destroyed van at the edge. The fire was finally put out but the occupants were so torn apart and then burned that no one was identifiable. Body parts were placed in body bags and taken with them for transfer to the Army identification laboratory in Kuwait.

Some of the parts were so damaged that they couldn't be matched to the rest of the bodies. DNA studies were done and the bodies matched up.

Two were identified as typical of the Iraqi pattern. Ian's DNA was on file with the Australian military and could be identified. The remaining one, the only female, was considered to be Jane Norton. The DNA pattern was sent to the United States to the central storage files. Jane Norton had no specimen on file but she did match the DNA on file in unsolved cases. It was decided to notify the filing police department but then close it out as deceased.

Chapter 34

Captain Carson sat at his desk. The phone rang, "Captain, I think this call is for you, though he said Lieutenant," his secretary said.

"Captain Carson."

"Oh, congratulations. We have you down as Lieutenant. This is Tim Atwater at the DNA registry. We have a match for a case you sent us some six years ago."

"Do you have the number there?"

"Yes. It's on the record of the sample you sent." And he read off the number.

Carson couldn't have given the number but he recognized it when he heard it. It was the material from the Black Widow case.

"That's amazing. Do you know where it came from?"

"It's a rather odd story. The person was one of four who were killed by a roadside bomb in Iraq. The bodies were badly burned so the army lab took DNA to confirm the identities. This was the only female in the group, so it must have belonged to the newscaster Jane Norton. I don't know what your case was but that is a definite match. Since she is deceased we have closed out the file."

"That fits as she was a native of our town. I thank you very much."

"You're welcome. I'll send you a copy of the materials in the mail."

"I appreciate your help." He hung up.

So Jane Norton was the black widow. His hunch had been right but had been shot down by the network. She was dead, so what should he do with this information?

He placed a call to NBC TV in New York and asked for personnel records.

"Records."

"This is police captain Carson. Let me speak to the manager of the department."

"This is Linda Treves."

"Captain Carson of the Pasadena Police Department in California. Jane Norton was from our city and we are trying to find out when she was last here for a memorial. Could you look up her records from 1999 and tell me if she made any trips to Southern California?"

"I can't see any harm in that now that she is gone. Let my try one thing on the computer. If this doesn't work, I'll call you back as it will take some time."

"Sorry. It doesn't come up. I'll call you when I find the papers."

"My number is 626 796-5455. I appreciate your help—"

"I will get back to you."

An hour and a half later his phone rang again. "This is Linda at NBC. I have the reports of her trips for business. Lots of one day trips—Atlanta, Cincinnati, Chicago but nothing to California."

"I'm particularly interested in May."

"There's a two week break there. Special leave for urgent family business. There isn't even a contact phone or address listed. She was back to work on time."

"Thank you so much. That must be the time we're looking for. You've been a great help."

"Glad to be of service. Goodbye, Captain."

"Goodbye."

Porter leaned back in his desk. He needed to be out of here. He told his secretary he would be off call and went to his car. He drove to the airport. Now an experienced pilot, he pulled out the little Cessna Cardinal he owned with two other pilots. He flew toward the mountains and then turned east. Passing Brackett airport in LaVerne, he banked around and started back to El Monte. Suddenly it struck him—Fred, Red. It hadn't been Red she had whispered in the room but Fred. Fred must have sexually abused her and the widow's actions were her revenge on Pasadena. He made the approach and landed, hardly thinking what he was doing.

The next morning Porter went into the Chief's office. "Do you have a few minutes for a matter of extreme secrecy and importance?"

"You excite my curiosity, Porter. I will keep my mouth shut. Go ahead."

"Sir, I have the identity of the black widow."

"That is news. How did that come about.?"

"It's Jane Norton, the TV news reporter. She was killed in Iraq and they took her DNA for identification as the bodies were badly burned. Put in the registry, it matched the sample we had sent in. I checked with NBC and she was on a leave for a matter of family urgency that two weeks and no one had her address."

"That's a strange kind of serial killer to do that many and then never again."

"I think her stepfather, Fred, sexually abused her and her killings here purged her and she didn't need to suffer from it longer. If you remember, we actually had a potential victim come in and report that he had sex with her and she seemed most surprised. She told him 'Thank you.' and he reported she said 'Goodbye, red.' as she left. It must have been 'Goodbye, Fred.'"

"I guess that makes sense. What do you think we should do with the information?"

"There isn't anything we can do to her. She is now quite a heroine and to show that she was a killer would put down a lot of girls who are taking inspiration from her. I would put a note in the file that the DNA proved someone dead had been the widow and the case was thus closed and file it."

"I agree. It would be a real circus if the media started on this."

Parker wordlessly passed a paper to the Chief. He read it. "Thought I might agree with you by the looks of this." He took his pen and signed the paper. He handed it back to Parker. "File it yourself. We don't want those file clerks to start wondering about it. Anyone else you think should know?"

"Yes, sir. I'll file it after hours. Yes, I'd like to tell Lieutenant Ridley. She really put a lot of herself into this case. She is extremely discreet and I'm sure we can trust her with it."

"OK. You've worked with her for years and should know. Thanks for bringing me something interesting. This has been a terrible week: nothing but complaints and paperwork."

The next evening Porter went over to Ridley's apartment. She offered a drink and when they were seated, he said, "There are two subjects I want to seriously discuss with you. The first is known only to the Chief and me and should go no further. We know the identity of the black widow."

Ridley sat up straight. "Really! How did that come about?"

He told her the story and when he mentioned Fred she broke in, "It wasn't Red she was saying goodbye to, it was Fred."

"Yeah. It took me a couple hours to figure that out. I have placed a note in the record, signed by the Chief and me, saying that we have evidence that the perpetrator is now dead and the case is closed. I personally filed the record away this evening after all the file clerks had gone home."

"Truly amazing. Jane Norton, the TV personality, a serial killer."

"I knew her a little. She came to autopsies at the mortuary as a kid. I had to break the news to her that her mother and stepfather were killed in a traffic accident. I've never seen a more controlled person. The FBI profile reminded me of her but I thought it couldn't be. I even went so far as to call NBC and try to find out if she had been out here but they told me no."

"Are you going to tell Flores-Finley?"

"Nope."

"She invested a lot in the case and helped us."

"I know but if I tell her, she's going to tell Frank. He is her husband and also was on the task force on the widow. Then he won't be able to stand not telling his boss, Acker, who also worked on it. And on it goes. No one but the Chief, you, and I will know."

"I see the point. This is going to take some thought and getting used to. What was the other thing?"

"Let's go to bed and talk about that."

When they were sitting in the bed with their drinks, Palmer said, "You are very discreet. That's one of the reasons I told you about the widow. We've been together for about a year now and I don't think anyone at the department has had a suspicion."

"A year and two weeks to be precise."

"Anyway it has been so successful that I think we might go a little more public."

"What do you have in mind?"

"Will you marry me, Ridley?"

"Well, Captain, sir, I—My God, you're serious."

"Yes, I am."

"It would make me very happy to marry you, dear."

She put her head on his shoulder and he put his arm around her. They sat a few minutes like this. She looked up at him, "Do you suppose the Chief would give me away?"